Also edited by Michael J. Rosen

THE COMPANY OF DOGS:
21 Stories by Contemporary Masters

COLLECTING HIMSELF:
James Thurber on Writing and Writers, Humor and Himself

HOME:
A Celebration of the Home
to Benefit the Homeless

The Company of Cats

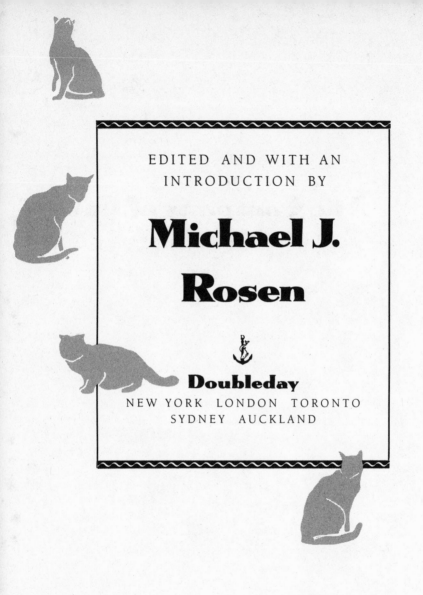

EDITED AND WITH AN
INTRODUCTION BY

Michael J. Rosen

Doubleday

NEW YORK LONDON TORONTO
SYDNEY AUCKLAND

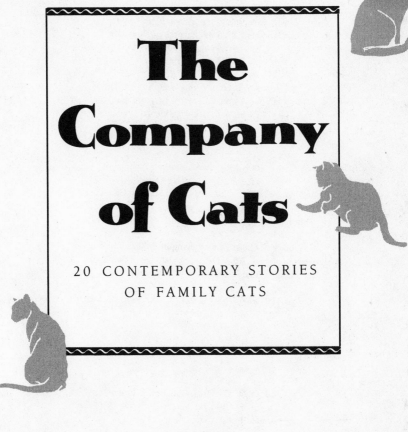

The Company of Cats

20 CONTEMPORARY STORIES OF FAMILY CATS

PUBLISHED BY DOUBLEDAY

a division of Bantam Doubleday Dell Publishing Group, Inc.
666 Fifth Avenue, New York, New York 10103

DOUBLEDAY and the portrayal of an anchor
with a dolphin are trademarks of Doubleday,
a division of Bantam Doubleday Dell
Publishing Group, Inc.

Permissions to be found on page 261

Book design by Marysarah Quinn

"Cat" and "Black Cat" from "Les Fleurs du Mal" by Charles Baudelaire.
Translated by Richard Howard. Copyright © 1982 by Richard Howard.
Reprinted by permission of David R. Godine, Publisher.

Library of Congress Cataloging-in-Publication Data
The Company of cats : 20 contemporary stories of family cats / edited
and with an introduction by Michael J. Rosen.
p.   cm.
1. Cats—Fiction.   2. Short stories, American.   I. Rosen,
Michael J., 1954–
PS648.C38C6   1992
813'.010836—dc20   91-25002
CIP

ISBN 0-385-42077-3
Copyright © 1992 by Michael J. Rosen
All Rights Reserved
Printed in the United States of America

Profits from this anthology will be donated to animal welfare agencies. The efforts of the contributors will directly aid individuals providing emergency and ongoing care for cats in neighborhoods throughout the country. This includes rescue and intervention services, spaying and neutering clinics, adoption education for new providers, and other means of assuring humane treatment and care of these companion animals.

It is to each contributor, caretaker, and compassionate reader that this collection is dedicated.

Contents

Contents

Loving the Distance Between Us: An Introduction

Let me admit that the title, as well as the need, for this book issued naturally from its predecessor, *The Company of Dogs*. Much later, while productively fogged in with submissions, I began hearing from friends and contributors that the title embodied an oxymoron and created a strange companionship of words. If "company" appropriately governed those stories containing a family dog, didn't this collection warrant a complementary title to characterize our familial arrangements with cats? For instance, should the title have included the concept of independence—something like *The Solitude of Cats?* However, dogs and dog people have no exclusive franchise on "company" or "companionship"; by applying these words to our time with cats, we can describe a richer definition both for those terms and for another extension of our capacious hearts.

The privilege of reading hundreds of short stories with cats at their center exposed the level and range of our involvement with these solitary creatures. This association rarely extends to training or collaboration, sometimes involves brief or tacit communication (beyond mealtime), and usually incorporates touching and cohabitation; yet quite often the cat's consent or even acknowledgment is neither required nor requested. Company can be nothing more than a human projection, something we cast on those around us beneficently as light, insouciantly as shadow.

These fictional accounts argue that a more deferential and demure accompaniment (the root word is still "company") is not an apparent contradiction; it is, rather, our recognition of and our invitation to a remarkable relationship with cats. It is the inarticulate *and* comforting, unmistakable *and* ineluctable, fickle *and* dependable, predictable *and* unpredictable nature of the cat that appeals to our love—love that we often chart, come to think of it (and these stories do), with these same contradictory coordinates.

Stories themselves are human projections, a kind of company we offer one another through sharing concerns made shapely by a mastered language. That would make this anthology the sharing of stories about sharing, the company of company. Although each story is *about* human conditions more than cats', it is the cat in each human life that reveals the significance of both the story's and the character's experience.

The "highest task of a bond between two people," wrote the poet Rainer Maria Rilke, is "that each should stand guard over the solitude of the other." I'd like to adopt this definition—a combining of company and solitude—for our idiosyncratic affiliation with cats. Rilke elaborates: "All companionship can consist only in the strengthening of two neighboring solitudes, whereas everything that one is wont to call giving oneself is by nature harmful to companionship: for when a person abandons himself, he is no longer anything, and when two people both give themselves up in order to come close to each other, there is no longer any ground beneath them and their being together is a continual falling." But, he says, once two people acknowledge the "infinite distances [that] continue to exist" between them, "a wonderful living side by side can grow up, if they succeed in loving the distance between them which makes it possible for each to see the other whole and against a wide sky!"

While I can't propose that Rilke's words were cast for our relationship with cats (though he did possess an exceptional responsiveness to animals), this body of stories is that ground beneath us, aspiring to Rilke's claim, rising to that ideal even when it falls short. This collection asks if it is possible that the cats we invite into our lives strengthen and protect our individual selves sometimes better than our fellow humans. Is the affection a cat offers us, as well as the intact disengagement it maintains, a salutary distance for love? This anthology's answer, at the very least, is that a cat invited into a story creates possibilities for a writer and for a reader that might not otherwise exist—heartening realizations that may have, in a society stiffened with competition for sympathies, become endangered, if not extinct.

CHOOSING BETWEEN CATS AND DOGS

Considering the differences between stories with cats and stories with dogs fuels more than the debate between proponents of each species' virtues. The character of these differing relationships lays bare a deeper understanding of companionship and of the whole fictionalizing enterprise.

Permit me, then, to omit expressions like "most often" and "frequently," to ignore the significant exceptions that I have welcomed, and to use the oversimplified declarative in order to emphasize the suggestive powers of each characterizing notion. (Moreover, I am confining these remarks to that subcategory of animal stories where the companion animal is a significant part of a family's life, invited only for the work of company.)

The most pronounced distinction between dog stories and cat stories involves the level of interaction between the animals and the people. Maeve Brennan charmingly portrays this in her story "In and

Out of Never-Never Land." Upon Mary Ann's return, the old Labrador retriever Bluebell "panted, her tail hammered on the floor and her eyes roved wildly around the room, reclaiming everything she saw, but most of all reclaiming Mary Ann. 'I choose you,' Bluebell's eyes said to Mary Ann, 'you, you,' and her gaze turned fervently to the kitchen, where her dinner waited." Mary Ann's cats "showed a faint, lazy interest in all this commotion. The biggest of them, the bright orange, sat up and then stood up and stretched, and lay down again, wrapping himself up in his own coat. 'I am ignoring you,' each cat said, opening its eyes just enough to show a gleam of light, and then, closing its eyes again, each cat said, as always, 'I choose myself.' "

Our stories acknowledge that by nature the cat is a solitary hunter, while the dog is a member of a pack. While dogs require company, cats can enjoy, tolerate, or decline it. Stories with dogs concern families, corroborations, communities, and collective reconciliations; stories with cats concern independence, individual solitudes (even when others are present), separations, and insights into personal and family identities. Stories with dogs concern long-term responsibilities, ongoing negotiations, and the consequences of our actions; stories with cats concern the challenge of the fortuitous, the possibilities of trust, the limitations of protection. Stories with dogs are more about human dependence; stories with cats, about human independence. (Again, I speak from a deductive average.)

So many stories with cats involve single, mobile, elderly, private, or isolated individuals whose lives a cat can share in ways a dog could not. Cats seem unfortunately "suited" for irresponsibility and indifference, haphazard care, a prolonged absence of caretakers; their "neglectability" is often the very reason people cite for having cats. In some cases, stories show us how this attitude depicts cats as expendable (there's a sign *Free Kittens* nearly everywhere to prove it), useless, and seemingly able and even eager to have independence. This, of course, discredits our mistaken trust in a cat's ability to revert from a domestic state to a wild one, which has contributed inestimably to the number of unwanted litters, stray populations, and road-killed or euthanized cats that plague our alleys, shelters, and consciences.

A most conspicuous trait of stories with cats is consequently the introduction of the cat: One day a cat is happened upon, abandoned, handed off, found. A story with a cat is a story of unexpected accommodation. (Rarely is the cat selected and invited by agreeing parties.) Likewise, a cat's death is usually sudden and without much human planning.

In contrast, dogs in fiction are usually well ensconced in a family or situation from the story's first sentence. With some regularity, these narratives include a dog's departure—determining what to do with an elderly dog or a dog suddenly inappropriate for a changed situation. A dog's death is most often a deliberate human (but not always humane) act.

Cat stories seem like entrances; dog stories, like exits. In each case, it is a human who attends the gate.

This idea affects plot in various ways. Cats introduce a schism into a family relationship or into an individual's thinking, in which someone or some part advocates the cat while another contests it; the difficulty lies in justifying the cat's presence, justifying one's love for this animal. This is hardly the case for dogs. Characters in stories with dogs usually end up justifying their dog's behaviors, the dog's demands, the ordeal of having the dog; but why the dog is loved and significant just isn't challenged.

One logical reason for this is that dogs make their affections clear enough, while cats require a bit more interpretation—detractors would call it self-indulgence on behalf of the fawning human. I don't mean to suggest that the cat has a diminished range of emotion; the cat's physiology is partly responsible. Unlike the dog, the cat lacks the facial musculature necessary to arrange its features into expressions to which we can attach or presume meaning.

Confronted with such a stoic face, it is no wonder writers wax continually about a cat's eyes, the locus that seems to hold all the responses we cannot otherwise translate from its face. Transcending simple differences in vision, the cat's view is often portentous. Its mix of aloofness and watchfulness can represent scrutiny, calculation, or even judgment, as in Edward Albee's "A Delicate Balance," where Claire tells the story of her cat's defection: ". . . one day I realized she no longer liked me." Attempts to persuade the cat so frustrate Claire that ultimately she has the cat put to sleep. "She and I had lived together and been, well, you know, friends, and . . . there was no *reason*. And I hated her for that. I hated her, well, I suppose because I was being accused of something, of . . . failing."

Primarily, the cat is a character of being; the dog, a character of doing. The cat in every story is Bartleby, Melville's passive scrivener who arrives ingenuously into the humans' lives, demands little, presumes nothing, ekes out a mostly self-reliant routine, while the caretaking humans are at great pains—in lieu of any other confirmations and rewards of gratitude—to entertain, coax, comfort, and appease. If we could translate the cat's reply to our many offers and requests, its likely response would be Bartleby's reiterated statement, "I would prefer not to." Nevertheless, we continue our efforts—drastic, dramatic, antic, doting—presuming to be the cat's protector and benevolent Fate, while surely the cat is responsible for such fateful alterations in the fabric of our stories and our days.

Who is in control, what and how much can be controlled—these are the issues a cat precipitates in fiction. This follows from the cat's own nature. The cat is self-employed. It has no regular work hours. Mostly, it sleeps on the job. Besides vivisection, where physical restraint is required to submit the cat to our service, we have only mutually obliging intersections with a cat. Stories, like a Venn diagram, show that within a universe, "U," there are two subsets, "H"[uman] and "F"[eline], and a slender, common convexity, shaded by affection, which they share.

Beyond this, the cat has "performed" but a single job ever since humans began to store grain in silos: exterminating, a crucial task— economically and epidemiologically—throughout history. Domestication has hardly shaped the cat's skills. We merely sanction the specific arena for said duty to be executed.

The rest of their decidedly few waking hours, our cats, for all their attention-getting, child-distracting, patient-calming, elegance-lending efforts, toil at the kind of work we humans are hoping for in the hereafter. And this is just: for the cats among us, heaven *should be* on earth.

So in exchange for creature comforts, all a cat can do to earn its keep is mouse, amuse, and accept our anthropocentric emotions. And here, in this self-appointed servitude, lies the cat's enviable charm. Cats are at their God-given tasks (survival, really) with little more than blessed abidance from us. We have glorified their nature by calling it work. Or company. And it is good.

A MEASURE OF OUR DAYS

I have reached the age when most of the professionals in my life are my contemporaries; the people who work on my house, my body, my car, or my finances are peers.

My veterinarian, whom everyone addresses as Bobby, is probably ten years older than I am. He's been married twice, has had children with both spouses, and conducts his practice in a neighborhood close to where I grew up. His office is a small, one-story house about the size of the one my parents built when we were young children. He shares the space with two groomers who seem infinitely amused by the steady parade of bedraggled, flea-besieged animals. Beyond ministering to his veterinary clients, Bobby is receptionist, bookkeeper, and friend of the family—many families, I suspect.

The last time I had Bobby inspect a hot spot on my retriever, it was five o'clock and the groomers' clients were picking up their dipped and clipped cats and dogs. Emerging from the holding crates, the dogs resembled cartoon characters revving up to flee: bodies fixed in one place while legs skedaddle on the linoleum at breakneck speed. No actual distance could be covered, but time was certainly *recovered*—those suspended hours spent here while their humans' day advanced. The cats were surely as relieved to be taken from this place of water, scissors, and sprays, but their faces bore their imperturbable look. (Is one of the groomer's tasks to renew, like a permanent, that poised countenance?)

Amid the commotion of these reunions, a woman, my own age I supposed, and a lean and prepossessing girl walked through the crowded waiting room and into a closed examining room. Once the loudest pair of dogs and humans had left, Bobby asked if I knew the two people who had just entered. When I admitted I didn't, he told me they were his first wife and daughter.

"You have a daughter in college?" I guessed, subtracting eighteen from my own age and arriving at an early but not implausible parenthood.

"A senior. In high school," he replied. "Our seventeen-year-old cat is in there, the one we got when we were first married. She's had a couple of bad strokes. Today's the day I have to put her down. They're saying their good-byes."

With that, Bobby left me and my young dog and our embarrassingly clean bill of health. What was to follow was sadly familiar: Bobby has euthanized several suffering and elderly animals in my extended family. But the idea that he might be called upon to perform such a duty for his own companion animal, for his family, for himself—this had never before appeared in the two-way mirror between doctor and client. Still, I had no impediment to imagining that imminent moment: the three of them gathered around the cat, their good-byes reduced to lingering hands . . . and then, instead of an impartial, consoling third party, the kindly doctor, Bobby would perform this most perfunctory of veterinary procedures for a family brought together from their workable estrangement by a failing cat.

The contagion of that experience—the pervasive, unbounded

compassion that caused my own tears as Bobby left us in the waiting room—was not only the sadness at the death of a long-time companion animal. Nor could I evade this grief by insisting on the mercy and expediency we offer the death of our companion animals, yet barely offer ourselves. No, the irrevocable thought that I couldn't dismiss as I drove my dog home was how that singular feline life bound its humans' lives—Bobby, his first wife, and his daughter—with its companionship, a volume labeled "1973–1990," a volume of family history.

The lives of our cats and dogs so often share intervals of human duration, coinciding with the start or finish of some familial landmark—a birth, a move, a death, a change—and extending for the ten or fifteen years that compass such spans as education, careers, childhood and childrearing, occupancies, employments. Even a long-lived animal must establish a beginning and ending date in a human's typically longer life.

If this volume I continued to imagine were a photo album, the cat would be captured in most of the scenes, often no more than an innocent bystander nearly cropped out by the frame, verifying that each occasion took place. For Bobby's particular cat, that volume contained the evolution of one marriage, the childhood and adolescence of one girl, the whole of a veterinary education, a decade of a growing practice, most of the 1970s and 1980s—those are but the increments I can hazard from my impersonal vantage. How much more could the three family members inscribe between those dates of the cat's adoption and its death? How easily I conjured such albums in my own extended family.

A STORY OF RESTORATION

The life of the family cat is essentially contented routine. Barring unforeseen tragedy, aside from their first months as a kitten and minor modifications of aging, a cat's accommodation of our hectic lives is a peaceable constant. (See Roz Chast's cartoon "The Seven Ages of Cat," page xx.) This very fixity acts as a kind of retention—like the snapshots just mentioned—holding us at least in one place.

Cats can endow our memories because they do not make the overwhelming demands and remonstrations of so much else that competes for our daily attention. As Ursula LeGuin writes of a cat in "Shrödinger's Cat": "He hasn't that frenetic quality most creatures acquired—all they did was ZAP and gone. They lacked presence. I suppose birds always tended to be that way. . . . Worms shot like subway trains through the dirt of gardens, among the writhing roots of roses. You could scarcely lay a hand on children, by then: too fast to catch, too hot to hold. They grew up before your eyes." A slower pace, a determined consistency, uncomplicated communication, fewer requisites of expectation, recognizable routines—all these help retain and reinforce a relationship with a cat.

The power of this bond is only too obvious when the bond is severed. Life after a companion animal, at least as recounted here, endures a terrible ambivalence, a consolation plagued by trivialization or obsession; few stories record a middle ground. Even when a fiction excerpts only the long and contented life of a cat, the author can still discover a opportunistic motive for its inclusion: the cat interjects the confounding issues of custody, the finite reach of human care, the urgency of compassion, all within the manageable confines of the short story. Transferred to a human/feline relationship, these difficult issues are not simply "tested" (as in some literary vivisection), but investigated for their own intrinsic consequences.

In Carl Van Vechten's exhaustive compilation on the cat, *The Tiger in the House,* he suggests that our observations of the cat may disclose more than ethological and psychological commonalities—they may offer inspiration. Speaking of a cat's behaviors and instincts, he writes, "But who can say that these rhythms are not superior moral laws and if the beasts do not progress it is because they sprang perfect into the world and do not need to, while man gropes, searches, changes, destroys, and reconstructs without being able to find anything stable in intelligence, any end to his desire, any harmony to his form? It is well to remember, O Christian reader, that it was man that God ejected from Paradise and not the animals."

If the cat, just one of the animals, remains in Paradise (which in pragmatic terms must be Nature), then welcoming a cat into our lives and stories must reveal an access to that paradisiacal life and provide direct terms for understanding the world—surely *that* is a healthy survival skill. James Serpell, a philosopher who has written extensively on our treatment of animals, theorizes that "one possible reason why children find it so easy to relate to animals is simply because they are not yet fully indoctrinated with all the paraphernalia of culture, and are therefore more animal-like themselves. They can identify freely with the feelings and needs of animals, whereas the motives and desires of human adults may be quite beyond the realms of their own personal experience."

Can we carry this further and assert that humans of all ages enjoy this reasonable, this more identifiable nature of their companion animals? Can stories about animals permit this possibly romantic but nonetheless true understanding of the nature of living? This is what I argued in *The Company of Dogs,* claiming that our relationship to animals exists in the pastoral mode. "A pastoral maintains the romantic concept of a limited, controlled oasis of simple ways and means. . . . The author writes of the world on a lucid, smaller scale, and a reader accedes to this. The laws of humans, of nature, and of God are all present in less confused and complex manners. In so many contemporary stories, a central dog [cat] renews this pastoral contract."

Zoologist and author Desmond Morris proposes that a cat offers a "relationship that lacks the complexities, betrayals, and contradictions of human relationships. . . . [For] those with severe mental scars . . . a bond with a cat can provide rewards so great that it may even give them back their faith in human relations . . ." If faith is one element cats bring to our lives and our stories, then perhaps we can tread lightly along the lines of a Christian interpretation: the cat as a figure of restoration; a figure of unmitigated devotion, of heartening fealty; a figure who may even be sacrificed in fiction—through accident, neglect, or spite—in order that the humans may awaken to a deeper compassion.

Consider Pamela Painter's "I Get Smart," which begins this anthology. There, the act of restoration—of a marriage? of a fulfilled self?—begins with the mere task of renaming the family cats, and, from that point, inspired and boundless, reinvents the names—and, indeed, the nature—of the other key elements in the speaker's life.

Severe or mild, questions of self-worth, self-sufficiency, and what we might call "rootedness" often possess the characters in contemporary stories with cats. They are not, as a group, miserable people, but the stories told of them arise from a point of need, a precipitation of conflict. The unchanging cat provides a manageable occasion for possible change.

THE HUMAN NATURE OF THE BEAST

In an early essay Robert Bly argues that current literature is impoverished by the lack of those deeper qualities of Nature. He quotes the psychoanalyst Georg Groddeck, who in 1907 wrote what could alternately be considered literary criticism, advocacy for animal welfare, and inspiration for the human potential movement: "Only a person with really sluggish blood could put up with the average interior state of the human being without yawning, and to make art out of it is impossible, at least not in the way Shakespeare or Beethoven go about it. . . . The only poet who could make anything out of it is a man who sees in human beings a part of the universe, for whom human nature is interesting not because it is human, but because it is nature."

A story about a human's life with a cat can establish a context in which we glimpse the Nature in human nature. Our stories confirm the idea that an animal's language frees us from the burden of our own, its responses cast off the ambivalences of our own emotions, its silence affords us an occasion to concentrate. Their inability to contradict, or even condone, allows us the chance to venture, to inquire, and even to listen to ourselves. All these conditions permit an occasion where the distinction between inspection and introspection is dissolved. Baudelaire established this metaphor in his poem "Cat": "As if he owned the place, a cat / meanders through my mind. . . . I hear ecstatic news— / it seems a telling language has / no need of words at all."

Certainly with both cats and dogs, the most telling language we have is tactile, the pair-bond reinforcement, the tacit acceptances that touch maintains.

With the dog, this realliance with Nature is furthered by active participation, unselfconscious yielding to doggish mannerisms, and concomitantly, investing the dog with approximations of human behaviors. Self-abandon, innocence, allegiance, and a treaty of expectations suspend the distinctions between species so we can reveal—as we revel in—a partnership that is *kindred.*

The introduction of a cat affords much less participation; our reconnection with Nature, just as profound, derives from permitting ourselves occasions for keener observation, for attention to marvels of ingenuity, patience, idiosyncrasy, unfettered play, uncompromised zeal. We can be startled into seeing our own status in the phyla of life when the cat suddenly evinces a behavior we're inclined to call "almost human," or conversely, when it unexpectedly manifests something altogether savage from its human-instated domesticity. The cat's acquiescence, rather than allegiance, can suggest itself as an underlying example of our own miscalculated position on earth.

In *A Cat Is Watching,* Roger Caras concludes that we have been watching the cat watch us for four thousand years. We have been observing the observer, as if the cat were a mirror that revealed a part of ourselves (this natural side) that we cannot see ourselves, cannot show one another. Rilke speaks of this, too, in his poem "Black Cat": "She seems to hide all looks that have ever fallen / into her, so that, like an audience, / she can look them over . . ." Then, "she turns her face to yours; / and with a shock, you see yourself, tiny, / inside the golden amber of her eyeballs / suspended, like a prehistoric fly." The cat's gaze fixes us in our momentary histories, frames us in all our individual moods, so that we see ourselves, however fleetingly, in a continuum of history, of Nature. A cat halts us in our oblivious rush toward the unknowable future.

Though these stills and freezes occur in a majority of the stories collected here, Wright Morris depicts one such moment explicitly in "The Cat's Meow": "Morgan tirelessly wants to know what earthly good such a cat is, and Charlotte tirelessly reminds him what a cat is good for is a cat's business. There are moments, however, somewhat infrequent, in no conceivable way to be relied on, when Pussy-baby will pause, as if petrified, as he crosses a room or enters the kitchen, holding a posture only seen in the low reliefs of creatures and birds on Egyptian temples. A captured moment of time! It might last a full minute, neither Morgan nor Charlotte breathing, then the merest twitch of his stub tail would indicate the time destroyer, life itself, once again circulating in his tiny veins, starting up his motor so that he could pick up from where he had stopped. Charlotte and Morgan are agreed that these moments almost justify his endless exasperations, and that if cats were as rare as diamonds people would pay more money for them. What good is it for Morgan to remind her that they are not?"

THE CAT AS CAT

Though cats possess a range of personalities and individual behaviors, cats are physiognomically similar: They are about the same size, with longer or shorter, variously colored and patterned coats, and a few manipulations of tail size, eye color, and ear conformation. Such crude generality is meant to imply that cats, specifically in fiction, most likely portray the character *Cat,* the species personified. (Surely this accounts for the enormous appeal of cat products and collectibles

—an overriding recognition of similarities rather than differences. Choices for dog-related items remain more breed-specific; dogs in fiction are, likewise, individual dogs in specific predicaments.)

The cat arrives, then, with personality, with the persona of the creature Cat, and, additionally, I'll argue, with the personification of Nature itself, if we allow as background Bill McKibben's arresting idea that Nature has been, until recently, precisely those places that have not been made by humans. With the far-reaching consequences of industrialization, we have taken Nature into human custody. "We have changed the atmosphere, and thus we are changing the weather. By changing the weather, we make every spot on earth man-made and artificial. We have deprived nature of its independence, and that is fatal to its meaning. Nature's independence is its meaning; without it there is nothing but us." The cat's familiar independence is more than a trait of the species; it is, in this light, an example of something outside humankind, beyond our engineering hand. Couldn't a story's account of relationship with a cat summon some of these larger, even global, issues of dominion? Couldn't the cat be a figure of metonymy, a part that stands for the whole—a whole, which, in this case, is the ultimate idea of wholeness, the Nature from which we have wrenched ourselves?

ONE CREATURE

In his memoir of his wife, Colette, Maurice Goudeket writes: "It is not enough to say that she loved animals. Before every manifestation of life, animal or vegetable, she felt a respect which resembled religious fervor. . . . One evening . . . We were at the cinema, watching one of those shorts which show germinations accomplished in a moment, unfolding of petals which look like a struggle, a dramatic dehiscence. Colette was beside herself. Gripping my arm, her voice hoarse and her lips trembling, she kept on saying with the intensity of a pythoness: 'There is only one creature! D'you hear, Maurice, there is only *one* creature.' "

We find ourselves, part of a single creation, sharing this earthly habitat with every other part of creation. Perhaps nothing better exemplifies the concept of sharing than the cat. Hardly a symbiosis or parasitism, hardly a situation of predator-or-prey, humans and cats overlap territories and take comfort in the provisions each offers for the common good. In practical terms, humans have offered protection, warmth, food, and veterinary care, asked for recognition and affection, and conceded the cat its instinctual life. The cat has offered itself utterly, conceded us our doors, walls, litter box, and off-limit zones, and accepted us as giant, two-footed cats, alternately mothers and kittens.

But is it really a trick we are playing? Has instinct made cats oblivious to such a domesticated reality, or has instinct suggested that this dissembling and domestic displacement is an advantageous compatibility in the long run (in which the cat has certainly outdistanced us)? Again, Colette muses in the voice of her dog Poucette: "All your animals lie to you, you ponderous Two-Footed Ones! When you lift your walking-stick for the pale greyhound to jump over, do you imagine she's using the whole force of her powerful thighs, when she shoots over it like a spurt of flame? When you throw the ball for the cat, he jumps short on purpose and lets it roll under the armchair. . . . It's partly caution and partly wisdom and sometimes fear that make them all lie to you."

A DIFFERENCE THAT CLAIMS US HUMAN

My close friends noted another oxymoronic character in this anthology—the editor. Because of an allergy that landed me in the emergency room one Thanksgiving, the most sustained physical contact I've since had with a cat occurred during my joint photo session with Nina, Tony Mendoza's cat. My appreciation of the cat has been, necessarily, second-hand: observation, reading, shared conversations (all companionship shares a single parlance), and a college background in animal behavior.

Almost twenty years ago, as a nineteen-year-old pre-med student, I understood more about the anatomy of *Felis catus* than I did about a live cat. Years have managed to dismiss all that data and detail never brought to supposed fruition as a doctor—"repressed" may be the better word, the psychological equivalent to whatever physiological mechanism inured me to the reek of formaldehyde during those three-hour dissection labs. Now it is Howard Nemerov's adaption of a T. S. Eliot line that applies to this period: "We missed the experience, but we had the meaning."

My commitment to this collection has come from my passion for the contemporary short story and my compassion for the animals that share our lives—our companion animals and their less lucky litter mates: the 27 million cats and dogs killed each year, intentionally or unintentionally; the eight of every ten cats that are never adopted from shelters. The statistics go on, just as the situation does, encouraged by carelessness, nurtured by callousness. How much more indignation is necessary—on the part of animal welfare advocates or any of us with a sense of conscience—to convince everyone that solutions to this matrix of problems are within reach? The predicament of pet overpopulation does not await a miracle cure, require exorbitant financing, or absorb all our volunteer hours.

This ironic idea of a person allergic to cats editing a collection about companionship with cats reflects a significant quality of human nature and of the nature of fiction: empathy. By definition, empathy is our ability to feel without having experienced; to hear or witness or read of another's experience and to derive—projected from remembered and imagined emotions—a related personal experience.

This empathic capacity rests at the core of artistic communication: Readers must be able to take each story to heart, coming up not only with sympathy for a writer's or character's plight, but with feelings from and for their own. Empathy derived from each author's convincing craft allows us all—including people with allergies to cats and people with no exceptional interest in the species—to care about the creature concerns of this collection. Doesn't this potential distinguish us from the other animals? We can empathize with their condition; we can sense (not simply witness) their suffering. And with this greater understanding, our greater responsibility must follow.

This anthology opens not by avoiding contradictory notions in our alliance with cats but by welcoming them as a permanently curious part of our covenant. It opens by suggesting that this companionable tolerance is a healthy, protective art in the survival of the species —perhaps even a fundamental, ancient kind of bargain. Yuko Tsushima offers a figure for this in her story "The Silent Traders," which recalls a cultural moment in Japanese history when mountain men and villagers traded a year's worth of various goods without negotiation or meeting. "The trading was over in a flash, before either man had time to catch sight of the other or hear his voice. I think everyone wishes privately that bargains could be made like that." In the Japanese village of her story, people continually release their unwanted cats into the nearby woods; sometimes, the cats return to another part of the village to be fed by other people. This cyclical exchange is "a bargain for survival. People trying to survive . . . can take some comfort in living beside a wood. We toss various things in there and tell ourselves that we haven't thrown them away, we've set them free in another world, and then we picture the unknown woodland to ourselves and shudder with fear or sigh fondly. Meanwhile the creatures multiplying there gaze stealthily at the human world outside. . . ."

Let us begin here, then, at the border of our solitudes, at this interface of companionship, with the possibility of love. Here, too, is the bargain—these stories—we authors have left for you, our readers. Having never met, we have nonetheless exchanged something on this common ground of humans and cats. What an honor to say that our offering is to be reciprocal: Your sharing in this book has generated funds for animals in need of human care. In all likelihood, none of us will meet these recipients either, these cats who accept our gifts unaware. On behalf of each party—author and animal—I extend a collective gratitude, a plea for further prosperity.

Michael J. Rosen

I love cats because I love my home, and little by little they become its visible soul. A kind of active silence emanates from these furry beasts who appear deaf to order, to appeals, to reproaches, and who move in a completely royal authority through the network of our acts, retaining only those that intrigue or comfort them.

Jean Cocteau

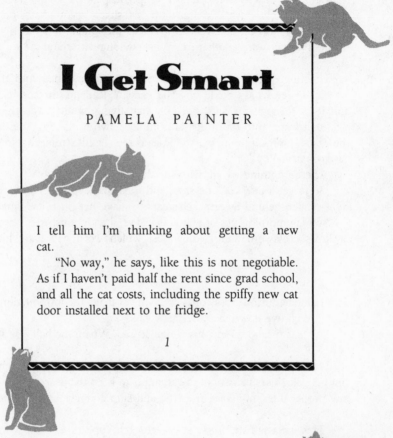

I Get Smart

PAMELA PAINTER

I tell him I'm thinking about getting a new cat.

"No way," he says, like this is not negotiable. As if I haven't paid half the rent since grad school, and all the cat costs, including the spiffy new cat door installed next to the fridge.

1

I say I've been to the Animal Rescue League and they have seventeen adorable kittens—all colors. "You get to pick the color," I say.

"Hold it," he says. He lines up his sharp accountant's pencil across the top of his crossword, cracks the knuckles of his right hand. "I do not want another cat. What's wrong with the three we've got?"

The three we've got hear our voices rising and pad into the kitchen to see what's going on. The Persian, Jeanette, threads back and forth through my legs, her long hair flying, while gray-striped Fitzhugh leaps onto the fridge and blinks down at us. Sweetpeach, the calico, jumps into my lap and kneads my chenille stomach. Not a cat goes near Roy.

"There's nothing wrong with the three we've got," I say.

"So forget a new cat," he says, and turns back to his crossword.

I scratch behind Sweetpeach's ears to make her purr, and finish my Sunday morning pot of real coffee. I've already finished a Xerox of Roy's crossword and I know just which word will hang him up.

Next Sunday during crosswords and coffee I make the introductions. I say, "Well, we now have three new cats."

Roy gets macho, points his pencil at me. "Where the hell—I told you—"

I tell him calm down, don't get all riled up before you meet them, but his voice rises in spite of my attempts to keep the peace. So as in any proper duet, my voice rises too and sure enough the cats come by.

"This is Savannah," I say as Sweetpeach appears, her tail whipping the air, weighing my distress.

Roy snorts and I try to remember if he ever called the cats by name.

"And that is Joe-Namath." I point to Fitzhugh eyeing us from the top of the fridge where he is poised in a three-point stance. "He never acted like a Fitzhugh," I say. "Parents should change their kids' names every few years for just that reason. Or give them nicknames."

"It's the other way around," Roy says. "Kids named Moonbeam, Taj Mahal, and Free are now calling themselves Susie, Pat, and Jim."

"You see," I say.

"No," he says. "I don't." His eyes refuse to focus on me or the cats. He lets his coffee get cold.

Jeanette springs onto the counter and highsteps over the stove to the window, where she watches the action at our veggie neighbor's high-tech catproof bird-feeder. I tell Roy he'll be sure to remember her name. "You're always saying, 'what a pill.' So that's Pillow."

"Don't do this," he says.

"So we have not one but three new cats," I say, burying my nose in Savannah's spotted fur. She's as limp as her new name and warm. Her cat's eyes seem to remember hot African grasslands and prey ten times larger than she is.

"We have three cats—period," Roy says. He has a way of making syntax dull.

"Three new cats," I say.

"Bull!" Roy's pencil bounces high like a cat toy.

Joe-Namath jumps from the fridge onto the table and skids into Roy's crossword, pouncing on his pencil. Roy tackles him and heaves him into the dining room, where he turns and spits. Pillow, the birdwatcher, cantilevers one ear around to hear if she should abandon her post.

No doubt thinking he's had the final say, Roy scoops his pencil from the floor and goes back to his crossword. Three words earlier he went wrong, but he won't know this until I tell him. If I tell him. I shiver Savannah off my lap and leave to shower.

During the next two weeks, Roy gets mad every time I call the cats by their new names. But he is more mad that Savannah, Joe-Namath, and Pillow take to their names so quickly. It's all in the tone of voice, I tell him.

I get happy with my new cats.

After a couple of months I get smart. Come Sunday breakfast it isn't Roy filling in the crossword; it's a new man—better with words and cats—named Ralph.

Getting a Cat

PHILLIP LOPATE

1

After so many years of living alone, I broke down
and got a cat. I really didn't want a cat. Once I was
in Jungian therapy and the therapist said to me,
"You should get a cat." He was a very decent man,
I gained a lot from him, I listened respectfully to
everything he said, except when he gave me prac-

5

tical advice like this. "You should try it. You'll learn interesting things about yourself. . . ." And then he slid away into his mysterious smile. One might almost say, a Cheshire cat smile.

You can't imagine how many people have been offering me their superfluous kittens over the years. Why was everyone so eager to give me a cat? I saw them all smiling, rubbing their hands: "Ah, he'll get a cat, very good, it's a good sign, means he's settling down."

By what Darwinian logic was I supposed to graduate from one to the other? Maybe I was to start with a cat, then go to a sheep dog, next a pony, then a monkey, then an ape, then finally a Wife. It was far more likely that, if I got a cat, I would stop there. What annoyed me was this smug assumption that because I lived alone, I was barren; I needed to start making "commitments" to other living creatures, to open my heart to them and take on responsibility. As far as I can piece it together, the idea seems to be that we should commit ourselves to something in this black hole of a universe. We should make an effort to join the Association of fellow creatures. Now, "commitment" comes into popular discourse when belief in love starts to slide. They're not so sure anymore, the experts, the theologians, that there is such a thing as love. So they tell you you should build up to it—practice. Throw your arms around a tree. Myself, I still believe in love, what do I need commitment for? So this was one reason for my not getting a cat. Plus my apartment is too small—there are no doors between the rooms—and I sometimes have to travel on the spur of the moment. Most important, I didn't feel I needed a cat.

Very well, you might ask, how did it happen that I got a cat?

It was partly a misunderstanding. I was in the country one weekend, where one is always more prone to sentimental longings and feelings of incompleteness. That's why I stay out of the country as much as possible. But I was visiting a friend; and there was an old man also staying at the house, a respected old writer, a lovely man whom I'll call Claude. This old man has beautiful silky white hair. He moves with graceful modesty, slight of build and wearing threadbare sweaters with holes in them, not because he can't afford any better but because he has already stopped caring about making an impression. He lives alone and seems wonderfully self-sufficient, except for his cats. He and I were standing inside the threshold of his bare country room and bending over a box where the mother cat was sleeping with her four kittens. The children were all sleeping head to foot, with their tails in each other's mouths so that together they looked like one big cat.

They made, I had to admit, a cute effect. I was trying to get a suitably fond expression onto my face and he was explaining about their delivery.

"There was a lot of hard labor involved. Usually she likes me to be around—some cats don't. There has to be a box ready. She knew just what to do. She ate the umbilical cord, and the afterbirth, which is supposed to be good for them. Then she licked off the first kitten and was ready for the next. Each kitten comes in a different sack . . . they're not like humans that way."

"Hm," I said, impressed with his knowledge of nature. Each kitten had a different coloration: one gray, one black, one cinnamon orange, and one whitish. A Mendelian demonstration. I liked the gray cat, because he was so straightforward, your basic alley cat. I was also drawn to the milky-orange one but distrusted her because she was *too* pretty.

Claude's hand, which was large and sensitive, pale veined with brown spots—I shook it every chance I got—descended to stroke each of the cats along its furry back.

"What are you going to do with all the kittens?" I asked idly.

"I'll give away as many as people want, and let her keep one to raise; and the rest will have to be taken to the vet to be killed. That's the difficult part," he said. The fold above his eye twitched as he talked, and he turned his face for a moment deliberately toward me, with a politeness and candor that showed he was not afraid to look me in the eye. "But she isn't willing to do it," he said, "and so I have to. I don't need more than one cat, you see."

I was so taken with this, with his acceptance of the world as it was, that I wanted to have one of his cats. I spoke up like a fool who raises his hand at an auction just to participate, to release the tension, and offered to take a kitten. He looked at me with a kind, piercing gaze, and asked if I was positive I wanted one. I said I was absolutely sure, trembling at what his look of examination might have told him about me. For a while he pretended I hadn't made the offer at all, in order to let me gracefully off the hook. But I kept forcing myself toward a firm statement that I wanted one of his kittens—the gray one probably. Although the cinnamon-orange one was pretty too. And suddenly I became horribly torn between these two animals, as between two ideals.

If I took the gray alley cat, I would be opting for everything that was decent peasant stock, dependable, ordinary and hardworking in myself. The idea pleased me. But I would be turning my back on beauty. I stood over the box, wondering if I should be ruled by a flash of prettiness, mystery, the gamine, the treacherous, as I had been so often in my life, or if, by embarking on this new, "more mature" stage of commitment, I would do better to choose sturdier virtues for companionship. In the end I picked the gray, partly because I was feeling guilty for having wanted to go back on my promise to him, after noticing a new, more fetching piece of fur.

Two or three days later, back in the city, grimly contented, cool-headed, myself again, I realized I had made a terrible mistake. I didn't want a cat! I wanted to be this old man. I wanted to grow up more quickly and be done with my idiotic youth and literary ambitions and sexual drives that bossed me around, and—I wanted to be Claude, gentle, pure. I must have fallen in love with his white beard and his spotted hands; and under his spell, in their charmed propinquity, whatever he had warmed with his glance that moment I probably would have coveted. Fortunately it was only a cat; it might have been worse.

I had to find a way to tell him I was backing out of the deal. For a long while I did nothing. I sat on my hands. Finally I wrote a card to him saying that I hadn't forgotten, that I hoped he was keeping the gray kitty for me—but maybe it was the orange one I really wanted, I couldn't make up my mind. It was a scatterbrained, sloppy note, and I hoped it would convey the impression of an irresponsible young man who cannot be counted on for anything he says. You may be amazed at this subterfuge, but it was the closest I could get to telling the truth.

In any case he did not get the hint. Like Death coming to call, Claude telephoned me once he was back in New York, and said that it was time for me to stop by and collect my kitty.

With a heavy heart, I rode down in the taxi next to the black metal carrying box that friends had lent me, my Black Maria. I had already provisioned my apartment with the supplies that Claude, in a moment of doubting me, had called to remind me to have ready as soon as the cat should enter its new home. I climbed the stairs to Claude's loft, wondering how the old man managed them every day. He opened the door to me with a peculiarly impish smile.

I wanted to get this over with as quickly as possible. "Hello, kitty," I said, bending down to pet the gray kitten.

"No, that's not your cat. I gave that to someone else. Here's your cat," he said. "There she is—she was under the bed! She's a very timid creature. Not like her brother Waldo, the gray. *There* she is! *There* she is." He held her in his arms, and poignantly gave her over to me.

I need not say how grateful I was that it was the orange one. She was warm in my hands, and gorgeously, obscenely pretty. Old Claude must be some student of the human heart.

The rest was odds and ends, formalities of transfer. She had already had her first distemper shot but I was to take her again in four months. I would be better off not giving her too much milk at first. She liked Purina tuna most of all the brands he'd tried. She was a good jumper—a first-class jumper; but as she had been up to now in the shadow of her brother Waldo, she seemed retiring. That would probably change. He had noticed it sometimes happened with girls, when they had brothers, that the boy kittens would be very active and dominate them. A good thing was to get an empty crushed pack of Winstons, which she liked to play with. Did I smoke? he asked. No, I said. "Well, then get your smoking friends to save them for you. She also likes to play with a little toy ball, and I'll give that to you." He located the ball, and his last empty cigarette pack, and gave me a box of dry cat food and would have piled on several cans of tuna if I had not stopped him and said I had plenty at home. "Very well," he said, simply and with loss. "I guess that's it."

We were caught in such an emotional moment that I wanted to throw myself into his arms and comfort him, or be comforted myself. Instead, I shook his hand, which was always a good idea.

"Good-bye, *****," he said, calling her something like Priscilla, or Betsy. I didn't want to hear; I wanted her named existence to begin with me. "You're going off to your new home," he said. "Have a good time."

"Won't she be lonely for her brother and her mother?" I asked.

"Yes . . . but that's life," he replied, smiling at both the threadbareness of the phrase and the truth of it.

He walked me to the door and stood at the top of the stairs with me. "If you have any questions, ask people who have cats for advice. They'll be more than happy to give it to you, and most of it will be wrong—but that's all right, they'll all have dozens of tips. And of course you can call me anytime you want if you're having problems with her. I know very little but I can hold your hand."

2

And so I settled down to my comfortable married life. After she had overcome her first shyness, the girl began to demonstrate her affectionate nature. She would take my finger in her mouth and lick it, and move on to the next finger, and the next. Her little pink tongue, rough as a washcloth, would sand away at my skin until it became sore. Then I would push her away, and pick up my book.

But a little while later, I would try to entice her back. "Come here, Milena," I would say. She would look uncertainly, mistrustfully up at me. I would wave my hand in the air, a gesture that hypnotized her each time, and wiggle my fingers until she jumped at them. Then I'd *catch* her and clutch her to me and squeeze her. She didn't like to be squeezed, or at first even petted; she would immediately turn around and start licking the hand that tried to stroke her.

In the evening she would curl up on my lap and close her eyes and make that motor-running, steady-breathing sound. I didn't have the heart to move, with her on my lap, purring like that. Moreover, she held her paw on my wrist, as if to detain me. How could I reach for a pencil?

On first arriving, she had investigated every corner of my apartment, going around the perimeters of the living room into the bedroom, the kitchenette, and finally into the bathroom, where she took note of her cat box. I was wondering when she would begin to use the box. The first day passed, and the pebbles were unruffled. Then another day came and went, without commission, and I thought she might be so nervous from the move that she was constipated. On the third day I sat down on the couch; something was wrong. My nostrils opened. Right next to me on the sofa was the most disgusting pile of shit. I nearly retched. I cleaned it off distastefully and dropped a piece of it in the cat box, so that she would know that was the proper place for it. Then I lowered her into this same cat box and she hopped out of it as quickly as from an electric shock. This was too much. Claude had assured me that she was toilet trained! I sprayed the sofa with Lysol disinfectant. She kept returning to the spot like the criminal she was, and sniffing the upholstery, trying to puzzle out the two different smells, and backing away, bewildered.

That afternoon I called Claude, to get the exact name of the cat litter he'd been using. I told him what she had done. He said, "Oh, dear, that must be disagreeable; I'm so sorry to hear it . . .." Never mind, I thought, just tell me the name of your cat litter. It turned out to be another brand; so, hoping this would make the difference, I went from supermarket to supermarket until I had found the preferred gravel. I lugged twenty pounds of it home with me and poured a deep, cloud-releasing stratum in her box.

That night I couldn't sleep. I was so revulsed by the image of finding that bundle on the couch, I felt as if my house, my sanctuary had been ruined. Why had I gotten a cat? That night my dreams were full of unpleasant surprises.

In the morning I awoke to the smell of a stack of her shit on the white brocade armchair. This could go on for weeks. My work was suffering, I couldn't concentrate, I couldn't do a thing until I had broken in that cat and shown her who was master. I bet she knows that's her box, I thought, but she just prefers taking a crap on a nice comfy armchair or a sofa surrounded by pillows. Wouldn't we all? She must think I'm a total sucker.

I sponged the chair, again sprayed with Lysol, deposited a piece of her droppings in the cat box. Then I grabbed her by the neck, not so gently, and dropped her into the gravel. She jumped out like a shot. I caught her and put her in again. She hopped out, whining. I threw her in again. Romance of education: she was the wild child, Helen Keller, I was the stubborn tutor. I was willing to treat it like a game: you jump out, I'll throw you back. She bounded, I caught her. My arm was stuck out like a fence to grab her as soon as she escaped. Each time she grew a little slower in leaving the box, a little more pensive and frustrated. Staring at me with her big, victimized pussy-cat eyes. "That look is wasted on me," I told her. She fell in the gravel, defeated. She seemed to chew over the situation for a half minute. Then she sat up in the posture of evacuating, and lowered her bottom ever so gradually. She got off (it was a little pee) and carefully kicked some pebbles over the spot. Hurray!

After that we had no more surprise "bundles." Life fell back to normal, or let us say, my new normal, which seemed to consist of my spending days running to the store for cat food and litter, and buying a vacuum cleaner to swoop up the cat's hairs so that my allergic friends could visit me, or locating the right scratching post before it was too late. Milena had found the underguts of a chair and was taking clumps of stuffing out of it for sport. In fact she was doing nightmarish things to all the furniture. Since I live in a furnished apartment, I was terrified of what would happen if my landlady came snooping around. My landlady is not fond of signs of life in any form. I had been afraid to ask her permission in the first place, and had sneaked in the cat on the *fait accompli* principle. If I had asked her, I knew, she would have said no; this way she would either have to accept it or start costly eviction proceedings.

One afternoon, as I was walking up the stoop of my house, where my landlady lives also, unfortunately, directly beneath me, she told me that "there was someone knocking" at my door. I thought this was odd; but then I noticed the scowling, misanthropic expression on her pudgy face and the two tufts of dirty-blondish hair sticking angrily out of her ears (God, she looked like a bulldog!), and via this animal association I realized that she was referring in her elliptical way to my cat. She followed this "knocking" statement with: "No cats, Mr. Lopate. We can't have cats here. They smell up the place and destroy the rugs and we can't have cats here, you understand?"

I said nothing, and proceeded past her into my apartment and closed the door, trembling with anger. I was ready to fight her to the bitter end. I turned to Milena, all innocent of the threat against her. "Don't worry," I said. "I won't let her throw you out. We'll move first." So our destinies were tied. "But you must," I said, "you must control your destructiveness. We live in this woman's house, don't you see; this is her furniture! If you go tearing large holes in everything it will cost me a fortune. Look, I bought you a scratching pad; can't you bring yourself to use it?"

In the meantime, something had to be done. I consulted friends. Some advocated declawing, others were aghast at the idea, with a foaming passion that made you suspect they were talking about something else. Anyhow, someone said, a kitten her age was too young for the operation. When I learned that it was indeed an "operation," that she would have to go to the hospital for it, I postponed the project indefinitely. Instead, I clipped her toenails and coaxed her to try the new scratching post (I had replaced the cardboard stand with a fabric one). The man in the pet shop said, "If you put some catnip around the base she'll be sure to like it." I bought a container of fresh catnip—anything for my baby girl. I spread the leaves up and down the scratching post. She did love the smell; she licked at the catnip and slept on the fabric base when she needed a rest from her more exhausting vandalisms.

3

After that, a strange, sullen period began for us. At times I thought I loved her, at other times I would be completely indifferent to her. I would kick her off the bed when she tried to sleep with me, because I wanted to be alone and not worry about rolling onto her. But always when I had almost forgotten she was there, she would crouch into my vision.

She had the annoying habit of trying to stop me when I dialed the phone, as if jealous of my speaking to anyone else. She would smudge the dialing circle with her paw, forcing me to dial the same number several times. We often got in each other's way. She and I competed for the bright red armchair—the one I considered my "writing chair." Milena always seemed to be occupying it just as I was getting ready to lower myself. Sometimes I would come home after work and find her sleeping on that chair, a lazy housewife. She would blink her eyes as I turned on the light.

When I totally ignored her, she began knocking down my knick-knacks. She would tear through the house. She seemed to be taking over the living space and squeezing me into a small, meaningless corner. I resented having to smell her all over my apartment. At my typing desk, in the kitchenette, there was that warm, cloying, offensively close odor from her shed hairs. And I got cross at her for not raking under her shits. Cats were supposed to be "fastidious creatures" and do that instinctively. It seemed a violation of the contract.

I was looking for violations, I suppose. In the back of my mind I kept thinking that I could send her away. It was hard for me to grasp the idea that I was going to have to care for her always. Until one of us died.

Claude called from time to time, "to hold my hand," as he put it. He was very sweet. I was delighted to have the chance to talk more often with him, even though our conversations were rather specialized. Once he suggested that I spread baking powder through the cat litter to cut the smell. Not a lot on the top surface—she wouldn't use it if you did—but a little throughout the mixture.

All this lore of cats! It was too much to take in; and it was only the beginning. As Claude had predicted, everyone had instructions for me.

Now, there were four things I could never stand to hear people going on about: one was their dreams, two was their coincidences, three was their favorite restaurants and meals, and four was their pets. And I never did like going over to a friend's house and in the middle of an intense conversation watching the friend's eyes turn senile with fondness as he interrupted to draw my attention to the cute position his cat had gotten herself into.

Now that I had this cat, every visitor started off with fifteen minutes of reaction to her. Women friends, particularly, made much of Milena. One commented that it was rare to find an orange female. Another said the cat was so elegant that she herself felt "underdressed" around her. Kay, my old flame, remarked: "Your cat is so gentle. I can't get over how delicate—how attuned she is! Oh, she's exquisite."

I felt abashed for not having perceived this special "attunedness" in Milena. From my point of view she was doing a kitten's job adequately, she was holding down the role, earning her can a day, but not setting any records. They all seemed to want to find something unique about Milena, whereas I, on the contrary, liked her precisely because she was just a cat. True, she had an appealingly pathetic stare: those black pupils with two concentric circles of olive around them. But I resisted the flattering appraisals, which seemed to me as farfetched as newborn-baby compliments. I had no idea how fond and proud I had grown of her until I came up against a nonbeliever.

My friend Emily remarked, without having seen her: "She's not as nice as my cat, is she?" and assured herself no, as if it were self-evident. I was furious. Not that my cat is so great, but why should hers be better? Emily was my model of the delusional cat owner. She had theories about how her cat knew her moods better than anyone, stayed away from her when that was the right thing to do, comforted her when she was down, intuitively kept her claws in—a miracle of a domestic cat that didn't need to be declawed, spayed or altered or anything else cats usually need to be, because it was so considerate and discreet. Her cat was a Colette novel. Often, people hurt Emily with their rudeness or selfish insensitivity, but her cat—never. Her cat sets the standard, I thought sardonically, that all of us, her friends, must chase after and miss. When Emily shuts the door on her last visitor of the night, she curls up with her kitty cat, the understanding one.

This would never happen to me, I vowed. First of all, I have no fantasies that Milena understands me. How could she, when our interests, our hobbies, our yearnings, are so different?

I don't pretend to guess her secrets. I watch her.

There she is, chasing a fly.

Now she knocks a spoon off the table, a Magic Marker from the desk, and starts kicking it about. Everything is a toy to her. She drags her booty through a square hole she has scratched in the white brocade armchair. I don't know how to stop her from gouging the seat covers. This one tearhole particularly has a use in her play. What does it mean to her? Someone said to me, "Kittens have such imaginations. They think they're in the jungle!" Is that it? Are you thrashing through the Amazon brush chasing enemies? Milena, you have your toy, you have that rubber ball with chimes inside. But to you, all the world is your plaything.

Milena can do all kinds of tricks. She can tear a paper towel into shreds and strew it over the apartment. She can stand on her hind legs and turn on the lamp. It's the truth.

When I go into the bathroom she likes to come in with me. Even when I shut the door she manages to squeeze inside. She crawls into her cat box and inspects the gravel surface, then sifts through to see if the droppings are still there. They're her property, her valuables in the safe-deposit box. You're like a rich old dowager, Milena, with your orange-and-white mink coat and your jewels.

Then I come out of the bathroom with my robe on and she starts squeaking. She wants to eat! Take your time, you'll get it. She's so eager that she doesn't let me scoop out all her canned food. She gets in the way so that I can't even put the rest on her plate—a clump of it drops on her head. You see that? If you'd only let me . . .

Now the cat is quiet. She has gotten what she wants to eat, her tuna. She sits in a pool of sun. The days are getting shorter and shorter. Winter is coming, Milena, I explain to her.

Cats

ROBLEY WILSON, JR.

When Kate woke up in the night and felt the warmth of one of the cats against her legs, she could tell which cat it was by reaching out to touch its fur. Cass was sleek, soft as mink or sheared beaver—coats she had touched once when she had gone with Alice Rand to the Lord & Taylor

18

salon—and he was fine-boned, delicate as the yellowed cat skeleton she remembered from her high school biology classroom of nearly thirty years ago. Tibb, who was younger, was also coarser, and his skeleton was both bigger-boned and more compact—a tougher version of cat-ness than Cass—and it was Tibb who was more likely to want to be playful. Where Cass would nuzzle Kate's hand and shift into a new sleep position, Tibb, often as not, would go over on his back and embrace her wrist with the needles of his claws. Sometimes when the two cats were on the bed, one on either side of her, she would lie in the dark and stroke both of them, marveling at the peculiar sensuality of her life.

Lately, after a long time of keeping to herself, she had begun to get involved with a man. His name was Barry, and she had met him at the county clerk's office in June, when she was renewing her driver's license. He stood just behind her in the short line leading to the counter. When she pushed her old license toward the clerk, the man spoke.

"Same birthday," he said.

For a moment she hadn't realized he was talking to her, and then —because no second voice responded—she turned, looked at him.

"We have the same date of birth," he said. "June fifteenth."

"Yes," she said. She smiled at him—a nervous smile, she imagined, for what sort of answer to his flat statement did the man expect? Isn't it a small world. What a funny coincidence. Did he truly think there was something portentous here? "But probably not the same year."

"Nineteen forty-seven," he said.

She shook her head. "No, not quite."

He looked expectant.

She laughed. "You don't really expect me to tell you that I'm older than you, do you?"

Now he was sheepish. "Of course not," he said.

Then it was her turn to be photographed—she wished they could have reused the old picture; it actually looked like her—and she sat on a wooden bench nearby until the new license came out of the laminating machine. The man—tall, trim mustache, exactly thirty-seven years old—sat next to her on the bench.

"I hate to see what it's going to look like," she said. "The picture."

He cocked his head to look at her. "I shouldn't think you'd have to worry about that," he said.

When he asked her to have lunch, she decided to accept. He flattered her, he seemed unthreatening, and if he turned out to be married—well, this was only lunch.

In the restaurant, they sat at a table by a window, where they were surrounded by hanging planters and overlooked the river, so slow-moving at this time of year that it held the shade of the nearest bridge in a perfect inverted arch.

He extended his hand across the table. "Barry Miner," he said.

She took the hand for a moment—it was warm, dry—and released it.

"Kate Eastman."

She was nervous then, and that meant she talked too much. She said far more about herself than she had done, or had the opportunity to do, in the two years since her divorce. She confessed that she was older than he was, by five years, and that she had two grown sons. She told him—brightly, as if it were something she was by now entirely comfortable with—how fortunate she was to have married a man decent enough to stay with her until the boys were sent through college. She told him she had just started working as a paralegal in the office of one of her former husband's friends.

Through all of this he listened intently, never taking his eyes from her face, and finally she tried to encourage *him* to talk. "What is it you do?" she said.

"I'm a psychotherapist. In that clinic across from the courthouse."

"Oh, heavens. I'd better watch what I say." And she wondered what she had already let out that might have marked her in his eyes as a "case."

In the weeks that followed, she became more comfortable with Barry, less compulsive. She learned all over again—such a long time since she had forgotten!—that her own silences could draw a man out, that she did not need to interrogate him. He told her that his mother had recently died of cancer—something he revealed almost apologetically, almost as if the woman had done it because it was popular.

"We all worry about it," Kate said, defending her. "It's a terrible, fearful thing, and women have to deal with it."

He had gone silent then—rebuked, perhaps—and she felt vaguely guilty. That was the first night she went to his apartment, the first time she let him persuade her into bed. Afterward she was flustered by what she had done and woke him long before dawn to tell him that she had to leave, that she couldn't be out all night.

"But you live alone," he said.

"Not exactly," she said. And she told him about Cass and Tibb while she put on her clothes to go home to them.

At first he seemed amused by her fondness for the cats. She realized she had let herself in for a good bit of teasing from him, as if she were an eccentric, tolerable despite her odd behavior.

"Do you talk to them?" he asked her once.

"Certainly," she said. She was in bed with him, the second time— later on she would be chagrined to notice that she could remember each time they went to bed by some curious talk that had passed between them—and he was on one elbow, searching her face for God-knew-what knowledge he thought she was keeping to herself. "Shouldn't I?"

"You don't catch yourself sometimes and feel a little foolish?"

"What for?"

"For talking to animals?"

She pondered, not certain how he expected her to respond. "I'd feel foolish if they answered back," she said. "Is this a real discussion, or are you just filling in the time until you get excited again?"

He laughed then, and hugged her. "I'll have to meet them myself," he said. "The cats."

"They'll think you take the world too seriously."

"I suppose. At least I take you seriously."

"I wonder why. I almost feel as if you're picking me apart."

"I don't know what it is," he said. "I guess it seems to me that women like you live your lives on the edge of your emotions."

"Women like me?"

"Older, living without men." He reached out to touch the wisp of hair that had fallen alongside her right temple. "You're at risk somehow."

"But men without women . . . ?"

"Not the same. Men are more inner-directed."

"You have such piercing blue eyes," Kate said. "I'm glad I'm not one of your clients."

But she was thinking about what he had said, and whether she thought it was true or not. What came immediately to mind was her husband—her ex-husband—and how when he worked on the car, sometimes a bolt would be rusted and immovable, or something would break or get scratched while he was trying to remove it. She remembered how he would come into the kitchen, his hands black with grease and orange with rust, and sit at the kitchen table, putting his head in his dirty hands and sobbing quietly. How she would stroke his hair, try to console him. How finally he would stop crying, and lift his face to her, and she would smile because the grease and rust had made splotchy patterns on his cheeks.

"So am I," he said.

"So are you what?"

"Glad you're not one of my patients."

I should hope so, she thought; all that fuss over talking to pets.

· · ·

22

Less than a week later she invited him to her house to spend the weekend. She imagined things were getting "meaningful," that when a woman began to make a habit of a man, "something should come of it"—a statement she dimly recalled hearing from her mother.

"I think he has me at a real disadvantage," she said once in the midst of a conversation with Alice Rand. "I haven't been courted in twenty-five years. I don't remember what's expected of me, let alone what's expected of him."

"There aren't any expectations anymore" was Alice's response— Alice, who had chosen "career" in place of marriage and thought all men were children; who had finished law school and now, nearly fifty years old, was a partner in the firm. "Maybe you should just enjoy your disadvantage," she said.

Still, Kate had expectations she could not define—Barry was so intense with her, so relentlessly attentive. She appreciated the attentiveness. She waited for it to "come to something."

Saturday after dinner he said, "I don't think it's healthy for you to live in this solitary way. It isn't normal."

"How much time does a therapist spend with 'normal' people?" she said.

"You know what I mean." He sighed in what she imagined to be a professional exasperation. "You should have more contact with the world. Maybe you should entertain, play bridge, give a party once in a while."

"I'm a terrible bridge player. I have no card sense."

"Monopoly, then. Trivial Pursuit."

"And I hate giving parties—running around pouring salt on the carpet where the burgundy got spilled, rubbing Vaseline into the piano to get rid of the rings from wet glasses." She poured more coffee. "The cats are sociable enough, and a lot easier to deal with."

He sat back in the chair and looked at her. "Easier than me, I suppose," he said.

"I don't know," she said. How ought she to respond to that wistful expression on his face? "I truly don't."

"Why don't you find out?" he said.

"How?"

"Live with me."

She set the coffeepot back on the stove. Alice was right: Mother would never have expected that; and she gave the proposition—it certainly wasn't yet a proposal—her careful consideration. Would she give up the solitude? Probably. Could she be married again, to someone like Barry? She thought so; she had imagined it often enough. Would she move in with him? She didn't know. She was distracted all evening, and slept badly all night.

At the breakfast table on Sunday, Barry rattled the comics while she cooked bacon and eggs. Domestic bliss. Sunday had always been the one day of the week when she felt most like a woman, when she could wear a frilly robe without feeling overdressed.

Barry cleared his throat. "What was all that racket at three in the morning?" he said.

"It was my fault," she said.

"No, it was those damned cats—on and off the bed, scratching the box springs, meowing in my ear. What was the matter with them?"

"It took me a while to figure out. I kept thinking they wanted to be let out, but every time I got one of them near a door, he bolted back inside. After I'd gotten out of bed three times—" She stopped, the spatula poised above the frying pan. "How do you like the yolks? Runny? Hard? In between?"

"Between."

"After three times I finally got the message. The cat dish was totally empty, not a grain of Cat Chow to be seen. It's the first time they've ever confronted an empty food dish, and it put them in a tizzy."

"I'll bet," he said.

"Once I'd filled the dish—and the water bowl was low, too—they quieted down."

"What time was all this, actually?"

"I think it began around quarter of three, and I didn't solve the problem until four-fifteen or so. Some mother, aren't I?"

He shook his head. Sadly, she thought.

She turned the eggs and brought two plates down from the cupboard. "I've been thinking about what you said. About moving in with you."

"And?"

"And I've been thinking about some of your favorite words. 'Healthy' is one of them, and 'normal.' " She arranged three strips of bacon on each plate. "But they always seem to be applied to things *I* do. How about you?"

"Am I healthy and normal?"

"I mean, how normal is it to be thirty-seven years old and never married?"

He seemed not to have been offended by the question. Instead, the next time he visited her, he was even more serious toward her. He stood at the living-room window, looking out over her three acres with their cedars and plums and spruce, and talked, solemnly and at great length, about women and his life. He was an only child. His father had died when he was three, he had been raised by his mother and his mother's elder sister, and he had never really known male comradeship—a "male role model." He hadn't owned a dog, or turtles or gerbils or a pony—any of the masculine trappings of conventional boyhood. His aunt had a canary, which sang in a brass cage. He remembered his first day of kindergarten: he hadn't even gone into the school building at the boys' entrance, but instead went in with the girls, holding hands with Betty Jean, the daughter of his mother's best friend, who lived next door. Still, he told Kate, he believed he was well adjusted. Did she really believe he ought to have married? Wasn't that what men expected of women, and didn't women despise the expectation?

Kate had no answer to that. Hers was an opposite experience, she told him: three brothers; a he-man father—duck hunter, fisherman, camper—still robust in his early seventies; the attentions of uncles and boy cousins and, in school, plenty of boyfriends. She had married a man her father approved of, had given birth to two boys, had been surrounded all her married life by males—husband, sons, a succession of male dogs, the two cats. Perhaps she'd been out of line with the marriage comment, but Barry could see, couldn't he, how different her life had been.

"You don't have to apologize," he said.

"I'm not," she said. Good Lord, did he think she was?

A week passed. Kate wondered how long she would put off deciding whether or not to live with him, but she convinced herself that she only wanted to give him time to understand her. For one thing, it seemed important that he accept the cats.

"Sometimes when I get up in the morning, only one of them will be at the porch door," she said to Barry. "If it's Cass, I'll give him his breakfast and then let him out again. 'Go find your brother,' I'll say. And sure enough, in five or ten minutes Tibb appears. And vice-versa."

"If Tibb comes home alone, you send him after Cass?"

"Yes."

He sipped her bitter coffee. "I thought they weren't brothers," he said.

"They aren't, really. But they think they are. It can't do any harm if I let them go on thinking so, can it?" She smiled at him. "As a psychologist, what's your opinion?"

"I think it's all coincidence, of course. The other cat just happens to come back shortly after the first has gotten fed. I think it's all right to be silly over animals, so long as you know you're being silly."

"How can it be silly if it pleases me and doesn't hurt anyone else?"

"I said it's okay, if you know you're doing it."

"But you see," she said, "it isn't coincidence. If it only happened once in a while—that would be coincidence. It happens regularly."

He sighed. "If you say so," he said.

"Do you think I'm crazy?" she said. "Or only neurotic?"

Gradually, Barry began to be impatient. She caught him watching her, one eyebrow raised, as if he expected her to blurt out what he wanted to hear. He sat on the edge of the bed after they made love, his hands folded, his head bent in thought. He made her terribly nervous; she wondered if he wanted her to feel guilty. Guilt he could probably cope with.

"I don't mean to press," he said one day. They were having drinks together, in a bar near the courthouse. "But I wish you'd give me an answer. You know how I feel about you."

She thought she did.

"I realize how much you like living on the outskirts," he said. "But think about the conveniences of living in town. Shopping. Closer to your work. The gas you'll save."

"I think about Cass and Tibb."

He looked away, revolved a sweating tumbler between his hands.

"I know you think I'm foolish," she said. "But I couldn't give them up, and I couldn't ask them to be house cats, never able to go outdoors—to hunt, to have all that freedom."

"They could go outside," he said.

"In all the town traffic," she said. "I'd be worried sick. I'd—" She stopped herself, having at that instant an image of one or the other of the cats—they looked so much alike that in the distance of the image she couldn't tell which it was—stiff and dead in a gutter, gold eyes staring, empty. "What might happen," she said. "I can't even think about it."

"And I suppose that means you can't think about living with me." His eyes were averted; his mouth was petulant.

Indirection, she thought. We reach a place without knowing we were headed toward it.

"I'm sorry," she said. "I suppose it does."

· · ·

He stopped calling her—which was a kindness, Kate thought. At least it was not sex he wanted from her, or not sex only, and for a while she luxuriated in having reclaimed her bed. She imagined the cats were pleased: they were less restless beside her. And she slept better as well—though one morning she woke out of a nightmare in which Cass appeared in the bedroom with a small rabbit squirming in his jaws. Awake, she couldn't decide whether the rabbit was a gift or a warning.

That evening when she fed both cats and let them out, the disturbance of the dream was forgotten. She talked with them as she held the door, saying to Tibb, "Now you be careful," and to Cass, "You take care of Brother, won't you?"

Later she stood at the kitchen window, putting together a salad for her own supper. The cats were moving down the long driveway—Cass in the lead, purposeful, rarely looking back; Tibb following, stopping, then trotting to catch up. Watching them go, she felt a welling-up of emotion she hadn't known since the days when her sons went off to school together.

That's love, she told herself. *There's nothing foolish about love.*

Peril

MOLLY GILES

Joan kneels on the dirt in her old blue jeans, a
package of carrot seeds clutched to her heart. No
one can see her, which is good, because if they
could see her they would decide she was crazy.
She may be crazy. She may need to see Dr. Lippman tomorrow. The tremor and flush she is feeling

out here, alone in her garden on a Sunday afternoon, may be the first signs of a nervous breakdown. No one should fear putting seeds in the ground. Seeds are just seeds. Joan opens her eyes, stares at the illustration on the packet: five slim golden carrots, like a spread of sunburned fingers. Then she studies the minuscule, beige-colored specks in her palm, and bows her head again. Please, she prays. Please. Her mind blanks. She never knows what to pray for. Please let them live, she thinks. Don't let me kill them.

She draws a furrow through the raked earth with her trowel, then another and another. Frowning, she begins to sprinkle the seeds. They crowd and drift, as she knew they would, already lost, as she knew they'd be. The drawstring on her sweatshirt dangles before her as she works, and sweat greases her forehead and chin. She can hear traffic behind the hedge that separates the yard from the street. Now and then her son's motorcycle coughs into life from inside the garage; the telephone rings in the distance for her daughter. When the back door bangs open she can hear John, at the piano; it must be halftime in the football game he's been watching all day. John is playing something new; he starts and stops, then starts again. Joan empties the packet, waiting for him to find the melody. Then she pats the earth flat, leans back, and sighs. A car screeches to a halt in the street. A man screams, "Watch out!" and an orange kitten leaps the hedge to land beside her.

"Keep your goddamn cat inside your goddamn yard," the man yells.

"It's not my cat," Joan yells back.

But the man guns his motor and takes off down the hill.

The kitten crouches by Joan's knees. She puts a hand over it, feeling for broken bones. The kitten starts to purr. She tips its chin back to see its face. Small amber eyes meet hers with a rush of ready trust; the purr thickens. Maybe it belongs to the people across the street, she thinks. She does not know the people across the street. She and John have lived on Lansdale Avenue for almost five years, but know very few neighbors. She stands, the cat tucked under her chin, walks to the gate, checks the street for traffic, and crosses. The man across the street is unloading firewood from the back of a pickup truck.

"Excuse me," Joan says, walking up to him, "but I think I've found your kitten." She tries to disengage the little cat, but its claws have dug in and caught in her sweat shirt.

"I don't know who that cat belongs to," the man says, not looking up. "It's been following me around all day."

"Oh," Joan says. She stands by the man as he continues working. She looks up and down the street. Lansdale Avenue bisects the village. At the foot of the street there is a small shopping center with a liquor store, a bicycle shop, and a laundromat; then comes a block or two of bungalows and summer houses, then the street rises to the Cape Cod–style houses of Squirrel Ridge, where she and John live. Above Squirrel Ridge are the huge new redwood and glass houses of Lansdale Heights at the top of the hill. "I guess I should go from door to door," Joan says. The man doesn't answer. She strokes the cat and walks back across the street.

"You're not going to like this," she says as she walks into the living room.

John looks up from the piano bench. He has the television on but the sound turned off, and the football players seem to be crashing into each other in time to his chord changes. He stops playing and frowns. "Don't feed it," he says.

Joan walks past John and goes down the hall. Her daughter Jillian is sitting on the floor of the hall, talking on the telephone. "Guess what I found," Joan says. She kneels and places the cat on Jillian's lap. Jillian lifts an eyebrow—a sophisticated gesture, Joan thinks, for an eleven-year-old—and pats the cat once on the top of its head. "I can't believe he said that," she says into the telephone.

Joan picks the cat up again and takes it into the kitchen. Her son

Jeffery is leaning against the sink drinking milk from a milk carton and eating peanut butter out of the jar with his finger.

"Did you wash your hands?" Joan says severely. "That grease you use on your motorcycle is extremely poisonous."

"Aaagh," gags Jeffery, clutching his stomach and reeling back.

"It is," Joan insists. "You know it too." She sets the cat on the kitchen floor and smiles as it starts to sniff at Jeffery's boots. "What do you think?"

"Looks a lot like a cat."

"It is."

"Looks a lot like an ordinary cat. I thought you said our next cat was going to be something fancy, Mom, like a Persian."

This is true. Joan has been going into pet stores lately. "Just looking," she sings out, when the salespeople come to help her. She looks at everything—the bright fish in their dark glass tanks, the tropical birds, the mice—but she has been particularly drawn to a large gray Persian kitten that has been kept caged in one shop in the village. The kitten has looked so hot and cross and bedraggled, and Joan has hated to see it dozing in its own soiled litter box. She has thought about buying that kitten, just to save it. "Persians," she tells Jeffery now, "are two hundred dollars apiece. And this isn't our 'next cat.' It belongs to someone. You can tell."

"Sure you can," Jeffery says. He grins, bends down, and offers a finger capped with peanut butter. The kitten comes and licks with quick, dainty, ravenous flicks.

"Don't let it lick any motor oil," Joan warns.

"God, Mom. You worry too much." Jeffery shakes his head, wipes his hands on his jeans, and turns to go back into the garage. As he opens the back door the dog and the other three cats come bounding inside. Joan is ready to swoop down and rescue the kitten, but she sees there is no need. The kitten crouches and hisses and the other four animals freeze in shock. Then the old cats spit, their ears flat, and the dog starts to bark. "No Brandy, no Fluffy, no Polly, no MacHeath," Joan chants. The kitten growls staunchly below her.

"This is Peanut Butter," Joan says, introducing the kitten. "Peanut Butter is going to stay with us a while." She gives the dog a piece of cheese and puts him outside. She gives Fluffy, Polly, and MacHeath a plate of dry kibble, pushing it close to their flat, hissing faces. She carries the kitten to another corner of the kitchen and puts him before a saucer of milk. "We are not going to fight," she announces. "We are going to behave like ladies and gentlemen." The cats eat, their eyes on each other. While the kitten is drinking its milk, Joan lifts its tail and sees what she expected: two small beige balls, neat as acorns. A male. When he is through with the milk she gives him cold meat loaf, breaking it into bits with her fingers. Then she puts him outside on the sun deck. "You'll be safe here," she tells him. She checks on him several times during the evening. Once she sees him playing with a leaf, bouncing across the deck like a blown leaf himself. Just before she goes to bed she slips another saucer of milk out the door. When John says, "Where'd you put that damn cat?" she says, in all honesty, "Don't worry. It's out."

But Jeffery lets it in early the next morning and at six Joan hears John yell, "That does it," from the kitchen. She rolls over to John's side and hugs his cool pillow. John starts to stomp and curse from the kitchen. He seems to get angrier and angrier every day. When she asks him what's wrong, he says, Nothing. I'm happy. I love you, he says. That's what he tells her. Joan wonders what he tells Dr. Lippman. She closes her eyes and pretends to be asleep when John stomps back into the bedroom. He sets her coffee cup down so hard she can hear it spill on the nightstand. "Get rid of that thing today," he says. "I mean it. Your other cats are bad enough. I hate cats," he says. "I have always hated cats. If you don't get rid of it today I'm taking it to the pound tonight."

"I work today," Joan reminds him. She is a teacher's aide at Jillian's school and she is scheduled for yard duty and library hours. "I'll put some ads around," she promises.

John interrupts her. "I'm tired of living in a zoo," he shouts. His face is very pale and there are shadows under his eyes. Joan sits up and sips her coffee. She is becoming angry herself and she hopes John will leave soon. But he stops in the doorway. "It's my new song," he says. "I'm stuck on the bridge."

"Your song?" Joan lets out her breath and puts down her cup. John is always bad-tempered until he gets his songs just right.

"Come in and listen," he says. "Maybe you'll know what I'm doing wrong."

He walks toward the living room and Joan quickly disentangles herself from the bedclothes and follows. She curls in the armchair beside the piano, her bare feet tucked under her long flannel gown. She will listen as carefully as she can. It has been a long time since John has asked for her opinion.

"It's called 'Blues for Vivaldi,' " John says. He laughs. Joan starts to laugh too but the first chords astonish her so much she is left with her mouth open. They are dissonant, loose, almost ugly chords, and the melody John picks out is shrill and as monotonous as wings beating or crickets scrapping inside a cage. She listens to the song and hears anger, panic, a great fight to get free. She stares at John. He looks the same. His mouth has the slack expression it always gets when he concentrates, his tie is loosened, his hair, just beginning to gray, falls over his forehead in familiar waves. "This is the part I can't get," John says, and plays some notes over. "I don't have the end right yet either," he adds.

"It's the best thing you've ever composed," Joan says when he's finished.

"You always say that."

"It's the most powerful thing you've ever composed," Joan amends. "There's something about it . . ."

"The bridge," John nods. He retightens his tie, picks up his briefcase, and stands. Joan trails him to the front door, reluctant to let him leave.

"That song," she says. "What's it about?"

"Oh," John says. "You know. Time running out."

"Time running out?"

"Like now," John says. He taps his watch, kisses her good-bye, and leaves. Jeffery follows him out the door, fastening the strap of his motorcycle helmet.

"Drive carefully, both of you," Joan calls out. She goes into the kitchen, opens the jar of vitamin pills, and sets the jar in front of Jillian, who is reading her horoscope and picking raisins out of her toast. Then she goes to the back door and peers out for the kitten. He is asleep on a deck chair. She pulls some cards from her recipe box and turns them to the back, so the "Here's What's Cookin'" on the front can't be seen. In big letters she prints: "Found. Male Tiger Kitten. Very Cute." She puts her phone number and address on the card and underlines "Very Cute." She stops on her way to Jillian's school to post one card to a new redwood fence on Lansdale Heights, she tacks another to a telephone pole on Squirrel Ridge, and the third she leaves on the laundromat bulletin board. Jillian waits inside the car, applying lip gloss with her little finger, eyebrows raised as she looks in the mirror.

At the lunch recess Joan walks around the schoolyard, stooping to tie shoelaces, help with stuck thermos caps. Her job is to make sure the lower-level children pick up their lunch rubbish, play safely, and share the sports equipment; she is also supposed to break up fistfights and keep an eye out for older teenagers who might be trying to sell marijuana or pills. So far she has not had to do this, but she is glad nonetheless when Cliff Iverson, who is six feet three, walks up and joins her. "You've been getting some sun," Cliff announces, staring closely down into her face.

"Gardening," Joan admits. She smiles. She likes Cliff Iverson. His wife, Sandy, has cancer, and Cliff has had to nurse her. Cliff teaches Social Studies, and lends her books and records he thinks she might enjoy. "I'm putting in a winter garden this year," Joan says. "Carrots. And things."

"You garden too?" Cliff says. His voice is loud and amazed and Joan looks at him quickly, wondering if he is making fun of her. She can't always tell with Cliff. He shakes back his hair, which is long and gray and not too clean. "You're quite some woman, Joan Bartlett. You make your own bread. You bake the best apple pies. You've got the little hoodlums here eating out of your hand. You're kind to strangers. You take in stray animals."

"We have a new one now," Joan says. She laughs as Cliff slaps his forehead. She can see his eyes peering out at her from under his fingers. He seems to be staring at her bosom. She half turns aside and calls, needlessly, "Be careful," as two fourth-grade girls skip past. "A little stray tiger cat," she says. "John says I can't keep it."

"Does John tell you what to do?" Cliff asks. He is still staring at her bosom.

"No," Joan says. "Of course not."

"Do you tell him what to do?"

"No." She smiles, confused. "Neither one of us tells the other," she says.

"Obviously you don't talk at all then," Cliff says.

Joan can think of nothing to say to this, but somehow she doesn't have to, for one of the skipping girls drops to her knees and screams. Joan hurries to help her, aware of Cliff's eyes still on her, on her hips this time. She finds herself bending more gracefully than she might otherwise as she helps the girl up and examines the wound, which is shallow but bloody and which will require prompt washing to avoid infection.

The kitten is waiting for her that afternoon at the back door. Joan says his name—Peanut Butter—and picks him up. She kisses the top of his head, his chin, the soft seam where his ears join his neck, his neck itself. His fur smells like outdoors and his purr is loud with health. She wishes he could stay a kitten, young and strong, forever. She thinks of Sandy Iverson, Cliff's wife, who just last summer won the women's singles at the tennis club. Now Sandy weighs less than a hundred pounds and has to wear a wig. These things happen so suddenly. No one can prepare for them. She remembers Cliff's eyes on her, frowns, and sets the cat down. Oh what does he want? she thinks irritably. Why does he look so unkempt and malnourished?

She thinks of Cliff sitting by Sandy's bed, feeding her soup, wiping her chin; that is the picture of him she wishes to keep.

She is glad when John comes home. He comes home late on Mondays after his appointment with Dr. Lippman. He pours himself a beer and turns on the football game. "I'm so hungry," he says, "I could eat a cat." Joan brings him two meat-loaf sandwiches on home-made bread and stays to take a sip from the beer he offers as he watches the game. He puts his arm around her, pats her hip, and lets her go. Jillian, who has been picking all the bits of onion and green pepper out of her sandwich, looks up and smiles slightly. Jeffery, stretched out on the floor, smiles too. Joan reminds them to chew slowly and not yell at touchdowns with their mouths full. Then she goes to the back door and puts out more milk and tuna for the kitten.

When everyone has been fed, she takes her book and sits at the polished dining room table, all alone. The book is one Cliff Iverson lent her. Cliff called it a "cult book," an underground classic. Joan finds it pornographic. Several times she puts it down but then she picks it up again. She makes herself read on. It is important, she tells herself, to learn new things. She is still reading when she goes to bed that night, and she wakes up at three in the morning with a head-ache. It seems to her that John is awake too, he lies so still beside her. She moves close and presses against his back, but it is impossible to tell; he does not make a sound. Somewhere down in the village a siren sounds and Joan presses closer, glad that her own children are safe in their beds. "Don't," John says, or she thinks he says; the word is so indistinct he might have said nothing. But she thinks he said, "Don't." She withdraws her arm and rolls on her back on her side of the bed. "I wish Jeffery would sell that motorcycle," she says out loud. She falls back asleep and does not wake up until John drops the kitten on the end of the bed.

"It was sleeping on my car," he says. His voice is aggrieved but not really angry. "There are little paw prints all over the hood."

"Oh dear," Joan says. The cat nuzzles her armpit.

"You can keep it," John says, "if you'll let me take Fluffy and

MacHeath to the pound instead; Fluffy threw up on the kitchen floor and MacHeath got into the garbage again." He kisses her, a nice, strong, coffee-flavored, married-morning kiss. Everything's all right, Joan thinks. "I've got to go," John says again.

Joan feeds the animals, picks the garbage off the kitchen floor, washes the kitchen floor, gets dressed, goes to the cleaners. At the supermarket she buys cream and liver and flea powder; she hesitates at the produce section (are her pies really "the best"?) and buys a bag of green apples. She does not stop to look in the pet store. As she lets herself into the front door she hears the phone ring. An angry woman's voice says, "Do you still have that cat?"

"Why yes," Joan says, setting down the groceries. "It's here."

"I came by this morning but you were out," the woman snaps. There is a long pause. "So I guess I'll have to get in the car and drive down again. Right?"

"Down?"

"You stuck your card right on my fence," the woman says. "The new redwood fence I built especially to keep that cat from running off. The one that cost almost a thousand dollars. That one."

"Oh," Joan says. She remembers the fence on Lansdale Heights. "Well. I'll have him ready for you."

The woman hangs up. Joan goes around the house, calling the kitten. He's asleep in the laundry basket. She picks him up and carries him into the front yard to wait. The sun feels good on her back as she walks back and forth and the purr of the cat against her chest feels warm and good too. "I'll miss you," she says. "But you come from a good home, and it's time to go back. I've enjoyed our time together. I'm glad I got to know you." She can't think of anything more to say; she feels as awkward talking to the kitten as she sometimes does talking to John or the children. She starts to hum but stops when she realizes the tune—sad and shrill—comes from John's last song. She walks back and forth in silence and is almost relieved when she hears a car door slam.

The woman fumbling with the gate is about Joan's age, but she is prettier than Joan; she has stylishly frizzed hair and wears a lavender silk shirt. A small blond boy in a private school uniform is with her. "There's your Tom-Tom," the woman says to the boy. Joan holds the kitten out with a smile; the boy grabs it and begins to ruffle its stomach. "He can climb right over that fence," the woman says to Joan. "So what am I supposed to do? Stay home every weekend? My son already spends every weekend with his father in the city. That leaves me and the cat." Joan nods. Her eyes are drawn to the woman's shoes. They are lavender jogging shoes. They look like silk too. "I'll have to lock him in when I leave," the woman says. "But then he'll stink up the house." She twists a hand through the gold chains hung at her neck. "Happy?" she says to her son. They turn to go.

Joan tries to catch the kitten's eyes to say good-bye but he is poised and purring on the boy's shoulder. "He's a wonderful little cat," Joan says. The boy looks past her and the woman waves in dismissal. It is not until they have driven off that Joan realizes neither one of them said thank you to her. I fed that cat for two days, she thinks. I saved its life. Without me that cat would have gone to the pound or been killed by dogs or been run over. I gave it food and milk and shelter for two whole days.

It is absurd to feel hurt by someone else's rudeness. Joan tells herself this. It does not work. She feels hurt. She hugs her arms and says, "You're welcome," in a bitter voice, then laughs. Anyone watching would think she was crazy. She feels a little crazy. She has crazy thoughts. She thinks that John is going to leave her, Cliff Iverson is going to seduce her, Jillian is going to reject her, and Jeffery is going to replace her, and she thinks all these things are going to happen soon, before she is ready, if anyone can be ready, ever, for disaster. Because disaster, Joan thinks, as she walks to the hose and turns it on, is always out there, waiting to fall down on somebody's head. She drags the hose toward the carrot bed. Either John or Jeffery has taken the nozzle off for one of their own projects, and she has to spray the water on the carrots through her bent thumb. The distribution is uneven. Water sprinkles on her good brown shoes and runs down her arm. Some of the seeds are going to be drowned by this, she thinks. Some are going to bloat and pop. Others will be washed away, and others yet will be left to die, high and dry. It's a miracle, she thinks, that anything survives at all in this world. She looks all around her. No one can see. She bows her head. She prays.

Lost Cat

ALICE ADAMS

Her cat is lost. Maggie calls and calls, standing there at the edge of the woods, in misting, just beginning rain. In Inverness, California, Maggie's parents' weekend house.

But the cat is gone, is nowhere. Not answering, invisible for an hour.

41

And generally sensible Maggie feels that she cannot continue in her life without this cat. Without red-gold Diana, regal Diana, of the long plumy tail and wide, mad yellow eyes. This is the breaking point, the true turning downward of her life, Maggie thinks. It is what she always dimly, darkly knew would happen: Diana gone. No more beautiful cat, whom she never deserved, who was only a visitor in Maggie's life.

Still calling, "Kitty, kitty, Diana"—at the same time Maggie knows that what she is feeling is ludicrous: preposterous to care so much for a cat that you think you will die without her. But Diana is me, Maggie next (and even more crazily) thinks. If Diana is gone, I am gone.

And such thoughts from a woman in the very field of mental health! Maggie is a psychiatric social worker, has had years of therapy; she is steeped in theoretic knowledge of the mind. She spends her days helping others to be a little more sane (or trying to help them), or at least to cope in some way with their given lives.

Behind her the huge house looms, gray-shingled, mullion-windowed. All tidy now and tightly packed for her leaving, as it has been for the past hour. Her clothes and books in their bags, her parents' kitchen immaculate. A big sane house. In that moment, though, the moment of calling out to Diana through the rain, everything that once seemed all right now looks crazy, including the house. Crazy that she, Maggie, an independent (in most ways) young woman, long out on her own, should still seek a lonely weekend refuge in the family stronghold—and should spend at least two hours, as she just now has, in tidying, tightening up the house, as though to leave no trace of her own light passage there. As though she, like Diana, were some light-footed visitor. Temporary. A shadow of a person.

"Diana, Diana, kitty . . ." she calls, sure that no one and especially not Diana, the wily cat, can hear her.

In the meantime the mist has become true rain, gentle rain but very firm, persistent. Maggie's face is wet, and her long hair, her Shetland sweater, her skirt. It's getting dark. Harder and harder to find a willful cat who could have simply strayed off into the woods. Been attacked. Badly hurt. Or simply lost. Gone, for good.

On the other hand, a more sensible, practical Maggie thinks, cats generally come home. If she goes back into the house, maybe makes a cup of tea, Diana will very, very likely emerge, from wherever. She will stroll out nonchalantly, not even especially friendly, not imagining that either scoldings or excessive greetings are in order.

Diana is fifteen now, not remarkably old for a cat, but fairly old; could she have chosen now to go off into the woods to die? In the darkening thickets, tangled bent gray cypresses and tall heavy firs, in the rain?

An outrageous cat, more outrageous even than most cats are. She is sometimes passionately affectionate; she will press her fine-boned body against Maggie's leg, or her shoulder, with purrings and rubbings. But at other times, which are wholly of Diana's choosing, she can be haughty, even cross; she has a large vocabulary of negative sounds, as well as her loud, round purr.

But where—oh, where is she now?

Maggie's chest hurts, and her breath comes hard, and at the same time she is humiliated, deeply shamed by what strikes her as deranged: such an extreme, an "inappropriate" reaction to the loss of a cat, whom she surely must have known would someday die.

Turning from the woods (where Diana is?), Maggie heads slowly back across the tousled pale winter lawn to the house, the enormous house, every inch of which she has searched: under beds, back into closets, under sofas and chairs, behind shelves and more shelves of books.

In the kitchen, her mother's kitchen (now entirely her mother's, so clean, all traces of Maggie removed), with tranced, slow motions Maggie puts on some water for tea as she wonders. Why is it that by this time of her life she does not have a place of her own, other than her very small North Beach rooms, in San Francisco? Because I can't afford to buy anything, or to rent something larger, another familiar, more reasonable voice responds. Because in a quite deliberate way I chose an underpaid field, social work. And have chosen (more or less) not to marry, only to like men somewhat similarly engaged— recently Jonathan, a sculptor. Never lawyers or doctors or men in stock or real estate, *never.*

Pouring tea into her own blue pottery cup, Maggie then sips, and she tries, tries very, very hard, to think in a rational way.

One solution would be to spend the night out here, in Inverness; obviously, the longer she is here, the more time there will be during which Diana could somehow show up. Maggie could redo her bed and get up very early, get back to the city by eight, when she has an appointment with Hue Wan Griggs and his mother, who are always meticulously prompt—coming all the way to the clinic from their Tenderloin (condemned) hotel.

However, at that vision of herself, raw-eyed with sleeplessness and still quite possibly without Diana, Maggie's mood plunges once more downward, blackly, into hopelessness, and she has what is really her most deranged thought so far. She thinks, If Diana does not come back, if I never find her, it means that Jonathan will leave, go back to Boston, and that the next time I have a mammogram they will find something bad, some shadow on the film that means I will die.

Loss of Jonathan and getting cancer are Maggie's most familiar fears, and at worst they seem (if unconsciously) related, try as she will to separate them rationally.

Jonathan: a sculptor who works in a restaurant that he despises, for a living. He too lives in North Beach, in an even smaller, cheaper place than Maggie's. Living together would save them money, they know that; however, they also agree that for them having the two places is much better. Both privacy and a certain freshness are preserved. They can take turns playing host at dinner, enjoying small ceremonies. Or on the nights that they do not spend together (Jonathan often likes to work at night) they will meet for breakfast, fresh hard Italian rolls and morning love.

That is how in good times Maggie and Jonathan "relate" to each other. (The jargon of Maggie's profession, mixed with worse from pop psychology, is ironically used by them both, part of a well-developed private language.) In bad times Jonathan hates San Francisco, along with his job in the silly, pretentious restaurant; and sometimes Maggie feels herself included in his discontent.

Cancer: Maggie's history is "unfortunate." Her mother and two aunts had fairly early mastectomies. However, all three women are still alive and seemingly well: successful surgery. Conscientious (frightened) Maggie has yearly mammograms, and she worries. Especially when Jonathan rails against the city, when he says that he is sure he could find a better job in Boston, or even in New York—then, imagining his departure, Maggie imagines too that in her grief she will also find a lump. And her full awareness of the total irrationality of this view is not much help.

And now—Diana.

Her tea, though, has imparted some hope to Maggie, along with its comforting warmth. Or, having gazed for some moments at the wilds of her own unreason, she feels more reasonable?

In any case, she stands up resolutely, and stretches a little before taking her teacup and saucer over to the sink, neatly washing and drying and putting them away. *Of course* Diana will show up sooner or later, Maggie now thinks. If not tonight, tomorrow. At worst, she, Maggie, could call in sick (a thing she has never once done); Hue Wan and his mother, and her five or six other appointments could get through the day without her. Couldn't they?

Going outside to try calling Diana again, and again, she thinks that now, for sure, Diana will emerge through the trees, with her slightly loose-jointed walk, her mad yellow blinking eyes, in the dark.

At the upward slope of the house a wide path leads to the crest of the hill, from which one can see the ocean—on clear days, the brilliant Pacific. Almost nothing would be visible up there now, in the gathering, thickening dark; still, Maggie has an odd impulse to take that path, to hike up across gullies and fallen trees and rocks to the top of the ridge, to look out at the black space where the sea must be.

However, even for Maggie in her current state of unreason, this seems too extreme a step, and she finds herself thinking instead about Hue Wan Griggs, whom she might or might not see tomorrow. Hue is part Vietnamese, part black, very dark and small for his age, with wide, amazingly beautiful, luminous, heavy-lashed eyes. And diagnosed as autistic—no contact, just hitting, bumping into things, staring off. But last week he smiled, he actually smiled in what Maggie believed was her direction. And now she feels a pang of loss at the thought that she could miss another such smile.

But no Diana. In the light, steady rain and the increasing cold, Maggie stands and calls, and calls, and no cat comes. And all her plans and half-decisions seem then to dissolve in that rain. Whether she stays overnight or goes back to the city is wholly unimportant, for nothing will work, she now thinks. Her superstitious wooing of Diana or perhaps of fate itself was to no avail. Of course not.

Sodden-hearted, she turns again toward the house, without a plan. Irrelevantly and painfully she is remembering a weekend that she and Jonathan (and Diana, of course they brought her along) spent at this house last summer, a time that she later came to think of as perfect. Or as close to perfect as imperfect humans can arrive at. (And cats: Diana, a non-hunter, chased mice and squirrels, and lost, but seemed to enjoy the chase.) Perfect soft bright weather for hikes and picnic feasts. Amazingly brilliant views of the sea, and of further piney ridges, cliffs of rocks. Amazing love.

Looking up at the huge square gray house before her, Maggie now sees it as inhabited by shades. By Jonathan, and by her parents. By beautiful, gone Diana.

Reluctantly she opens the front door. She goes into the living room, and there, an orange-gold mound in the middle of the sofa, there is Diana: Diana entirely engrossed in grooming her tail, licking, burrowing for a probably imaginary flea. Not even looking up.

And of course there is no way to find out, ever, where she has been, and much less why: why she should hide for what is now almost three hours, why hide when she must have heard Maggie call, and call, from wherever she was, in however deep a sleep.

An hour or so later, Maggie is driving her small car back across the Golden Gate Bridge, in the murky yellow lights (the supposed suicide-deterrents). Her overnight bag and the small sack of leftover food and her books are on the backseat, and Diana, as always, is sleeping on Maggie's lap; she is simply there, asleep and lightly purring, shedding golden hairs on Maggie's dark, still-damp skirt.

And Maggie can no longer even invest the return of her cat with magic meanings: Jonathan might still decide to throw it all up and move back to Boston, or New York; a mammogram could still hold bad news for Maggie. None of her wildest, her most despairing thoughts are assuaged for good. Tonight when she gets home she will call Jonathan, who may or may not feel like coming over to see her. And tomorrow morning at eight she will meet with small, doe-eyed Hue Wan Griggs, who may or may not smile.

Residents and Transients

BOBBIE ANN MASON

Since my husband went away to work in Louisville, I have, to my surprise, taken a lover. Stephen went ahead to start his new job and find us a suitable house. I'm to follow later. He works for one of those companies that require frequent transfers, and I agreed to that arrangement in the beginning, but now I do not want to go to Louisville. I do not want to go anywhere.

Larry is our dentist. When I saw him in the post office earlier in the summer, I didn't recognize him at first, without his smock and drills. But then we exchanged words—"Hot enough for you?" or something like that—and afterward I started to notice his blue Ford Ranger XII passing on the road beyond the fields. We are about the same age, and he grew up in this area, just as I did, but I was away for eight years, pursuing higher learning. I came back to Kentucky three years ago because my parents were in poor health. Now they have moved to Florida, but I have stayed here, wondering why I ever went away.

Soon after I returned, I met Stephen, and we were married within a year. He is one of those Yankees who are moving into this region with increasing frequency, a fact which disturbs the native residents. I would not have called Stephen a Yankee. I'm very much an outsider myself, though I've tried to fit in since I've been back. I only say this because I overhear the skeptical and desperate remarks, as though the town were being invaded. The schoolchildren are saying "you guys" now and smoking dope. I can image a classroom of bashful country hicks, listening to some new kid blithely talking in a Northern brogue about his year in Europe. Such influences are making people jittery. Most people around here would rather die than leave town, but there are a few here who think Churchill Downs in Louisville would be the grandest place in the world to be. They are dreamers, I could tell them.

"I can't imagine living on a *street* again," I said to my husband. I complained for weeks about living with *houses* within view. I need cornfields. When my parents left for Florida, Stephen and I moved into their old farmhouse, to take care of it for them. I love its stateliness, the way it rises up from the fields like a patch of mutant jimsonweeds. I'm fond of the old white wood siding, the sagging outbuildings. But the house will be sold this winter, after the corn is picked, and by then I will have to go to Louisville. I promised my parents I would handle the household auction because I knew my mother could not bear to be involved. She told me many times about a widow who had sold off her belongings and afterward stayed alone in the empty house until she had to be dragged away. Within a year, she died of cancer. Mother said to me, "Heartbreak brings on cancer." She went away to Florida, leaving everything the way it was, as though she had only gone shopping.

The cats came with the farm. When Stephen and I appeared, the cats gradually moved from the barn to the house. They seem to be my responsibility, like some sins I have committed, like illegitimate children. The cats are Pete, Donald, Roger, Mike, Judy, Brenda, Ellen, and Patsy. Reciting their names for Larry, my lover of three weeks, I feel foolish. Larry had asked, "Can you remember all their names?"

"What kind of question is that?" I ask, reminded of my husband's new job. Stephen travels to cities throughout the South, demonstrating word-processing machines, fancy typewriters that cost thousands of dollars and can remember what you type. It doesn't take a brain like that to remember eight cats.

"No two are alike," I say to Larry helplessly.

We are in the canning kitchen, an airy back porch which I use for the cats. It has a sink where I wash their bowls and cabinets where I keep their food. The canning kitchen was my mother's pride. There, she processed her green beans twenty minutes in a pressure canner, and her tomato juice fifteen minutes in a water bath. Now my mother lives in a mobile home. In her letters she tells me all the prices of the foods she buys.

From the canning kitchen, Larry and I have a good view of the cornfields. A cross-breeze makes this the coolest and most pleasant place to be. The house is in the center of the cornfields, and a dirt lane leads out to the road, about half a mile away. The cats wander down the fence rows, patroling the borders. I feed them Friskies and vacuum their pillows. I ignore the rabbits they bring me. Larry strokes a cat with one hand and my hair with the other. He says he has never known anyone like me. He calls me Mary Sue instead of Mary. No one has called me Mary Sue since I was a kid.

Larry started coming out to the house soon after I had a six-month checkup. I can't remember what signals passed between us, but it was suddenly appropriate that he drop by. When I saw his truck out on the road that day, I knew it would turn up my lane. The truck has a chrome streak on it that makes it look like a rocket, and on the doors it has flames painted.

"I brought you some ice cream," he said.

"I didn't know dentists made house calls. What kind of ice cream is it?"

"I thought you'd like choc-o-mint."

"You're right."

"I know you have a sweet tooth."

"You're just trying to give me cavities, so you can charge me thirty dollars a tooth."

I opened the screen door to get dishes. One cat went in and another went out. The changing of the guard. Larry and I sat on the porch and ate ice cream and watched crows in the corn. The corn had shot up after a recent rain.

"You shouldn't go to Louisville," said Larry. "This part of Kentucky is the prettiest. I wouldn't trade it for anything."

"I never used to think that. Boy, I couldn't wait to get out!" The ice cream was thrillingly cold. I wondered if Larry envied me. Compared to him, I was a world traveler. I had lived in a commune in Aspen, backpacked through the Rockies, and worked on the National Limited as one of the first female porters. When Larry was in high school, he was known as a hell-raiser, so the whole town was amazed when he became a dentist, married, and settled down. Now he was divorced.

Larry and I sat on the porch for an interminable time on that sultry day, each waiting for some external sign—a sudden shift in the weather, a sound, an event of some kind—to bring our bodies together. Finally, it was something I said about my new filling. He leaped up to look in my mouth.

"You should have let me take X rays," he said.

"I told you I don't believe in all that radiation."

"The amount is teensy," said Larry, holding my jaw. A mouth is a word processor, I thought suddenly, as I tried to speak.

"Besides," he said, "I always use the lead apron to catch any fragmentation."

"What are you talking about?" I cried, jerking loose. I imagined splintering X rays zinging around the room. Larry patted me on the knee.

"I should put on some music," I said. He followed me inside.

Stephen is on the phone. It is 3 P.M. and I am eating supper—pork and beans, cottage cheese, and dill pickles. My routines are cockeyed since he left.

"I found us a house!" he says excitedly. His voice is so familiar I can almost see him, and I realize that I miss him. "I want you to come up here this weekend and take a look at it," he says.

"Do I have to?" My mouth is full of pork and beans.

"I can't buy it unless you see it first."

"I don't care what it looks like."

"Sure you do. But you'll like it. It's a three-bedroom brick with a two-car garage, finished basement, dining alcove, patio—"

"Does it have a canning kitchen?" I want to know.

Stephen laughs. "No, but it has a rec room."

I quake at the thought of a rec room. I tell Stephen, "I know this is crazy, but I think we'll have to set up a kennel in back for the cats, to keep them out of traffic."

I tell Stephen about the New Jersey veterinarian I saw on a talk show who keeps an African lioness, an ocelot, and three margays in his yard in the suburbs. They all have the run of his house. "Cats aren't that hard to get along with," the vet said.

"Aren't you carrying this a little far?" Stephen asks, sounding worried. He doesn't suspect how far I might be carrying things. I have managed to swallow the last trace of the food, as if it were guilt.

"What do *you* think?" I ask abruptly.

"I don't know what to think," he says.

I fall silent. I am holding Ellen, the cat who had a vaginal infection not long ago. The vet X-rayed her and found she was pregnant. She lost the kittens, because of the X-ray, but the miscarriage was incomplete, and she developed a rare infection called pyometra and had to be spayed. I wrote every detail of this to my parents, thinking they would care, but they did not mention it in their letters. Their minds are on the condominium they are planning to buy when this farm is sold. Now Stephen is talking about our investments and telling me things to do at the bank. When we buy a house, we will have to get a complicated mortgage.

"The thing about owning real estate outright," he says, "is that one's assets aren't liquid."

"Daddy always taught me to avoid debt."

"That's not the way it works anymore."

"He's going to pay cash for his condo."

"That's ridiculous."

Not long ago, Stephen and I sat before an investment counselor, who told us, without cracking a smile, "You want to select an investment posture that will maximize your potential." I had him confused with a marriage counselor, some kind of weird sex therapist. Now I think of water streaming in the dentist's bowl. When I was a child, the water in a dentist's bowl ran continuously. Larry's bowl has a shut-off button to save water. Stephen is talking about flexibility and fluid assets. It occurs to me that wordprocessing, all one word, is also a runny sound. How many billion words a day could one of Stephen's machines process without forgetting? How many pecks of pickled peppers can Peter Piper pick? You don't *pick* pickled peppers, I want to say to Stephen defiantly, as if he has asked this question. Peppers can't be pickled till *after* they're picked, I want to say, as if I have a point to make.

. . .

Larry is here almost daily. He comes over after he finishes overhaul-
ing mouths for the day. I tease him about this peculiarity of his
profession. Sometimes I pretend to be afraid of him. I won't let him
near my mouth. I clamp my teeth shut and grin widely, fighting off
imaginary drills. Larry is gap-toothed. He should have had braces, I
say. Too late now, he says. Cats march up and down the bed purring
while we are in it. Larry does not seem to notice. I'm accustomed to
the cats. Cats, I'm aware, like to be involved in anything that's going
on. Pete has a hobby of chasing butterflies. When he loses sight of
one, he searches the air, wailing pathetically, as though abandoned.
Brenda plays with paper clips. She likes the way she can hook a
paper clip so simply with one claw. She attacks spiders in the same
way. Their legs draw up and she drops them.

I see Larry watching the cats, but he rarely comments on them.
Today he notices Brenda's odd eyes. One is blue and one is yellow. I
show him her paper clip trick. We are in the canning kitchen and the
daylight is fading.

"Do you want another drink?" asks Larry.

"No."

"You're getting one anyway."

We are drinking Bloody Marys, made with my mother's canned
tomato juice. There are rows of jars in the basement. She would be
mortified to know what I am doing, in her house, with her tomato
juice.

Larry brings me a drink and a soggy grilled cheese sandwich.

"You'd think a dentist would make something dainty and precise," I say. "Jello molds, maybe, the way you make false teeth."

We laugh. He thinks I am being funny.

The other day he took me up in a single-engine Cessna. We
circled west Kentucky, looking at the land, and when we flew over
the farm I felt I was in a creaky hay wagon, skimming just above the
fields. I thought of the Dylan Thomas poem with the dream about the
birds flying along with the stacks of hay. I could see eighty acres of

corn and pasture, neat green squares. I am nearly thirty years old. I have two men, eight cats, no cavities. One day I was counting the cats and I absentmindedly counted myself.

Larry and I are playing Monopoly in the parlor, which is full of doilies and trinkets on whatnots. Every day I notice something that I must save for my mother. I'm sure Larry wishes we were at his house, a modern brick home in a good section of town, five doors down from a U.S. congressman. Larry gets up from the card table and mixes another Bloody Mary for me. I've been buying hotels left and right, against the advice of my investment counselor. I own all the utilities. I shuffle my paper money and it feels like dried corn shucks. I wonder if there is a new board game involving money market funds.

"When my grandmother was alive, my father used to bury her savings in the yard, in order to avoid inheritance taxes," I say as Larry hands me the drink.

He laughs. He always laughs, whatever I say. His lips are like parentheses, enclosing compliments.

"In the last ten years of her life she saved ten thousand dollars from her social security checks."

"That's incredible." He looks doubtful, as though I have made up a story to amuse him. "Maybe there's still money buried in your yard."

"Maybe. My grandmother was very frugal. She wouldn't let go of *anything.*"

"Some people are like that."

Larry wears a cloudy expression of love. Everything about me that I find dreary he finds intriguing. He moves his silvery token (a flat-iron) around the board so carefully, like a child learning to cross the street. Outside, a cat is yowling. I do not recognize it as one of mine. There is nothing so mournful as the yowling of a homeless cat. When a stray appears, the cats sit around, fascinated, while it eats, and then later, just when it starts to feel secure, they gang up on it and chase it away.

"This place is full of junk that no one could throw away," I say distractedly. I have just been sent to jail. I'm thinking of the boxes in the attic, the rusted tools in the barn. In a cabinet in the canning kitchen I found some Bag Balm, antiseptic salve to soften cows' udders. Once I used teat extenders to feed a sick kitten. The cows are gone, but I feel their presence like ghosts. "I've been reading up on cats," I say suddenly. The vodka is making me plunge into something I know I cannot explain. "I don't want you to think I'm this crazy cat freak with a mattress full of money."

"Of course I don't." Larry lands on Virginia Avenue and proceeds to negotiate a complicated transaction.

"In the wild, there are two kinds of cat populations," I tell him when he finishes his move. "Residents and transients. Some stay put, in their fixed home ranges, and others are on the move. They don't have real homes. Everybody always thought that the ones who establish the territories are the most successful—like the capitalists who get ahold of Park Place." (I'm eyeing my opportunities on the board.) "They are the strongest, while the transients are the bums, the losers."

"Is that right? I didn't know that." Larry looks genuinely surprised. I think he is surprised at how far the subject itself extends. He is such a specialist. Teeth.

I continue bravely. "The thing is—this is what the scientists are wondering about now—it may be that the transients are the superior ones after all, with the greatest curiosity and most intelligence. They can't decide."

"That's interesting." The Bloody Marys are making Larry seem very satisfied. He is the most relaxed man I've ever known. "None of that is true of domestic cats," Larry is saying. "They're all screwed up."

"I bet somewhere there are some who are footloose and fancy free," I say, not believing it. I buy two hotels on Park Place and almost go broke. I think of living in Louisville. Stephen said the house he wants to buy is not far from Iroquois Park. I'm reminded of Indians. When certain Indians got tired of living in a place—when they used up the soil, or the garbage pile got too high—they moved on to the next place.

It is a hot summer night, and Larry and I are driving back from Paducah. We went out to eat and then we saw a movie. We are rather careless about being seen together in public. Before we left the house, I brushed my teeth twice and used dental floss. On the way, Larry told me of a patient who was a hemophiliac and couldn't floss. Working on his teeth was very risky.

We ate at a place where you choose your food from pictures on a wall, then wait at a numbered table for the food to appear. On another wall was a framed arrangement of farm tools against red felt. Other objects—saw handles, scythes, pulleys—were mounted on wood like fish trophies. I could hardly eat for looking at the tools. I was wondering what my father's old tit-cups and dehorning shears would look like on the wall of a restaurant. Larry was unusually quiet during the meal. His reticence exaggerated his customary gentleness. He even ate french fries cautiously.

On the way home, the air is rushing through the truck. My elbow is propped in the window, feeling the cooling air like water. I think of the pickup truck as a train, swishing through the night.

Larry says then, "Do you want me to stop coming out to see you?"

"What makes you ask that?"

"I don't have to be an Einstein to tell that you're bored with me."

"I don't know. I still don't want to go to Louisville, though."

"I don't want you to go. I wish you would just stay here and we would be together."

"I wish it could be that way," I say, trembling slightly. "I wish that was right."

We round a curve. The night is black. The yellow line in the road is faded. In the other lane I suddenly see a rabbit move. It is hopping in place, the way runners will run in place. Its forelegs are frantically working, but its rear end has been smashed and it cannot get out of the road.

By the time we reach home I have become hysterical. Larry has his arms around me, trying to soothe me, but I cannot speak intelligibly and I push him away. In my mind, the rabbit is a tape loop that crowds out everything else.

Inside the house, the phone rings and Larry answers. I can tell from his expression that it is Stephen calling. It was crazy to let Larry answer the phone. I was not thinking. I will have to swear on a stack of cats that nothing is going on. When Larry hands me the phone I am incoherent. Stephen is saying something nonchalant, with a sly question in his voice. Sitting on the floor, I'm rubbing my feet vigorously. "Listen," I say in a tone of great urgency. "I'm coming to Louisville—to see that house. There's this guy here who'll give me a ride in his truck—"

Stephen is annoyed with me. He seems not to have heard what I said, for he is launching into a speech about my anxiety.

"Those attachments to a place are so provincial," he says.

"People live all their lives in one place," I argue frantically. "What's wrong with that?"

"You've got to be flexible," he says breezily. "That kind of romantic emotion is just like flag-waving. It leads to nationalism, fascism— you name it; the very worst kinds of instincts. Listen, Mary, you've got to be more open to the way things are."

Stephen is processing words. He makes me think of liquidity, investment postures. I see him floppy as a Raggedy Andy, loose as a goose. I see what I am shredding in my hand as I listen. It is Monopoly money.

After I hang up, I rush outside. Larry is discreetly staying behind. Standing in the porch light, I listen to katydids announce the harvest. It is the kind of night, mellow and languid, when you can hear corn growing. I see a cat's flaming eyes coming up the lane to the house. One eye is green and one is red, like a traffic light. It is Brenda, my odd-eyed cat. Her blue eye shines red and her yellow eye shines green. In a moment I realize that I am waiting for the light to change.

Chicago
and the Cat

SUSAN FROMBERG
SCHAEFFER

Sometime during the night, the huge wooden clockwork in back of the sky ticked, moved once, and now the weather changed. The heat was gone and the humidity with it. A crisp wind blew in the hopsacking curtains his girlfriend Marie had made for him. He refused to call her his *significant other*.

The phrase was ludicrous, and he never knew how significant she was, or how other. In conversation she remained, therefore, his girl-friend, although the phrase seemed, among his friends, antique, as did his habit, in spite of his training, of attributing human purpose and intent to events in the mechanistic world. The world might well be a tapestry knotted together by intersecting forces and vectors, but when he was not in the laboratory, he preferred to see everything as if it were animate and full of purpose, so that each unpredictable thing might, at any moment, decide to alter its nature, and perhaps in so doing, change the significance of the entire design.

The wind blew the navy blue curtains into the room so that, for an instant, they floated up toward the ceiling like the last long, thready clouds of the night, and then dropped down, every thread in the fabric visible. There was a sharpness to the air that smelled like apples, and the wind rustled dryly in the oak leaves, a sound that reminded him of his mother's taffeta slip as she dressed for a wedding one night, in the winter, long ago, in New York. Summer was gone. Autumn had come for it, plunged its sharp teeth through its sluggish, long throat and carried it off. He looked with regret at Marie, who sat on the blue couch, pressed against the armrest, in the same position she'd been in for hours, weeping without sound, occasionally lifting her hand holding a handkerchief to her nose, then lowering her arm and letting it rest once more across her stomach. She was wearing jeans and a peach-colored brassiere, and over it she wore her white chenille bathrobe. He must have interrupted her, she must have been doing something, getting ready for something, when she asked him, "Do you still love me?" and he said, he said it immediately, because he had been asking himself the same question for months, for almost a year, "We never meant this to last forever." She put down her mascara and began weeping, put her bathrobe on over her jeans and brassiere, and sat down on the couch where she wept still.

He was curiously unmoved by the sight. He thought odd things. When she moves out, will she take the curtains? She was entitled to them. She had made them, but he loved them more than she did. He saw the morning light coming through the fabric's rough weave, and thought, Once we were like those threads, so close, and now we are not. Will she take Figaro, our small black-and-white cat? He had been her cat, but now the cat cared only for him. Figaro was nowhere to be seen, probably asleep on the dining room table in the back room. He had an image, so vivid as to be a hallucination, of two people, himself and Marie, coming into an empty laboratory. Each of them carried a white bakery box tied with string. The string had been made by twisting together red and white strands of thread. In each box was the love each one felt for the other. The love itself, its substance, was ensconced in the box, and rested on a white paper doily cut to look like lace; it resembled a cake. Its substance was crystalline and it was very clear, but it was sticky to the touch and somehow unformed. It reminded him of sap on the bark of a tree, sap that had not yet hardened. Except for a huge black table, the room was empty. At each end of the black table was a gold scale, and he knew immediately that they were to take their boxes and weigh them, thus settling once and for all the question of who loved whom more. Outside, the wind had picked up strength, and blew the curtains in and up once again. They rose suddenly, like a flock of startled pigeons. Perhaps if pigeons were deep blue, not battleship gray, people might love them more. He turned his attention to the gold scales. Each placed his box on the scale, and as Marie looked at her scale, and then her box, she began to weep. Did her box weigh more or less than she had hoped? It occurred to him that he was so tired he was dreaming with his eyes open. He waited for her to say, "You never loved me." Once she uttered those words, this scene would come to an end. She would stop weeping. Either they would begin to discuss what came next, or one of them would fall asleep, but in any case, Marie would move, get up, decide whether she wanted to be dressed for day or for night; they would not be frozen in their poses forever. Or, he thought, she might try to kill me. She was looking at him now out of narrowed eyes. The eyes of snakes, he thought, must look like that. "You never loved me," she said. In the laboratory, the bakery boxes turned into pigeons—or perhaps they were doves, they were so white—flew up from the scales and out of sight. The laboratory had no roof.

He smiled at Marie. He was always pleased when events confirmed his expectations. It was a satisfactory outcome, as when an experiment confirmed a hypothesis. Next she would say, "Why are you smiling?" and she was beginning to say something when the phone rang. "I'll get it," she said, jumping up to answer the telephone, as if to say, I'm still of some use here. Once I'm gone, you'll have to answer your own phone and make your own excuses. You better think twice. She always covered the phone with her hand and whispered the name of the caller so that, should he so desire, he could shake his head, and she would say that he had not yet come in, was asleep, would call back later, but now she stood still, her white robe over her jeans, the receiver of the telephone thrust out in front of her. She had become inanimate.

He took the receiver from her. His mother's voice came through the small holes. What was she saying? He felt Marie's hand on his arm. With her other hand, she was vigorously drying her eyes. "Dead?" he said aloud. "Dead?" His mother was saying disconnected words, *sudden, no pain, a blessing,* and then parts of sentences, "so sudden he didn't have time to ask for you," "tomorrow, someone will pick you up at the airport, just tell me what flight you're taking, he wants to be buried in Florida. That's where he lived," and he thought, Why not Chicago? It's colder in Chicago. He'll last longer. He said some things. They must have been satisfactory because his mother let him hang up. "I'll go with you to the funeral," Marie said.

"No," he said. "I'll go alone."

"Oh," she said. "You'll go alone." She knew his dread of death. She sat down on the couch. Not again, he thought. We're not starting that again. "So," she said, "if it's over, you'll want me to move out." She watched him. "I'll start packing," she said. When he nodded, she shook her head. "You bastard," she said, getting up and going into the bedroom, from which, in seconds, issued the sounds of drawers yanked open. He knew, without getting up, that the bed was now covered with her possessions. He lay down on the couch, on his back, looking at the cracks in the ceiling. "The trouble with you," his mother used to say, "is that you're too sensitive. You're too sensitive and too fussy. You have to compromise. You can't be such a perfectionist." He didn't know if he was sensitive or if he was a perfectionist, but in that instant, he knew there was something wrong with him, something missing.

"I'm sorry about your father," Marie said, standing over him.

"Mmmmm," he said. The higher the sun rose, the colder it became.

"Oh, well," Marie said.

"So that," he told his mother, "was the end of Marie." He thought his mother would do more than smile or nod; she had liked Marie, but Marie was not Jewish and was therefore unacceptable. He looked at his mother, disappointed, but then reminded himself that his father had just died and that his mother was now a widow. Who knew how widows reacted to anything? And this might not be the best time to tell his mother about Marie, not while they sat in the second seat of the black limousine driving to the cemetery. His mother's hot, dry hand rested on his wrist. She stared straight ahead. He looked out the window and thought how ugly it was here in Florida, flat and green and hot, the frying pan of the country, while in Chicago it was cold and at night frost nipped at the earth. If his father had to die, then he had died at a good time. The semester had not yet begun; there were no exams or papers. His father's death had rescued him from Marie. She could not very well ask him to stay with her and miss his father's funeral. Altogether, his father had picked a most convenient time to expire. He suspected his mother did not think so, but then she seemed calm. All her conversation had, so far, concerned finances, although she had said that she intended to stay in Florida because she had built a life here. Built a life! What was she, a mason? But then his mother always tended to talk in cliches. *Don't throw out the dirty water until you have new.* Of course it was not right to be annoyed at his mother, who was now a widow. When she stopped being a widow, then he could become annoyed at her. But did people ever stop being widows? It occurred to him he was not thinking properly.

The cemetery shocked him. Proper cemeteries had headstones that stood at right angles to the ground, mausoleums, statuary, winged angels carved from marble; they resembled little cities, had, from the highway, silhouettes of great cities. A cemetery seen from the highway defied your sense of scale, or at least disturbed it. This cemetery had stones set in the earth, a name and a date carved on each; flat, shiny gray stones he at first mistook for paving stones so that he tried to walk on them to avoid the muddy earth. It must have rained the night before. He hadn't noticed. His mother, who saw him stepping on the stones, jumping from one to another, said nothing, as if she saw nothing odd in his behavior. Perhaps she thought this was the way sons behaved whose fathers had just died.

The rabbi was saying something, but then rabbis always said something and in any event, he couldn't hear him. He felt the pressure and heat of his mother's hand on his arm, and he began to see a line of people coming in to a low gray granite cottage where a dead man was laid out on a large oval mahogany table. "Sorry for your trouble," said each visitor as they passed the widow and her daughters. "Sorry for your trouble," until it became a chant, and watching, he was outraged. "Sorry for your trouble," as if the visitors were commenting on a toothache rather than a death. When his mother tugged at his arm, he understood the funeral was over and that they were to return to the car, and as they walked, he wondered why he had just attended a funeral in Ireland, one that someone had described to him some months back, instead of his own father's funeral, at which he had been, as anyone who could read minds would know at once, absent.

His mother was regarding him, smiling sadly. "It hasn't hit you yet," she said.

"It hasn't?"

"It hasn't hit me either."

"I think it's hit you," he said.

He didn't like the way she looked at him now. "If it doesn't hit you, you'll be sorry," she said. Wasn't that wrong? Wasn't she supposed to say, "If it hits you, you'll be sorry?" The heat had unhinged him, the heat and these stepping stones. His mother would be all right. She was one tough cookie.

Marie had gone. There was no trace of her. It was as if she had viciously scoured herself from the apartment. She had, however, left the curtains, and Figaro was asleep in the middle of the bed waiting for him. The neighbor had fed him in his absence. He sat down on the bed and contemplated Figaro.

He had never had a pet before Figaro. His mother, who often boasted that her kitchen floor was so clean that a brain surgeon could operate upon it, and whose tragedy, in his opinion, was that no such surgeon had ever come to her door saying he had an emergency and needed a sterile kitchen floor, had feared dust, germs, animal hair, the sharp claws of animals shredding the beautiful tapestry fabric of her chairs. He had once brought home a parrot, and for the few weeks it lasted in the house, he had sat next to its cage, trying to teach it to say, "Hello, Daddy," so that, when his father came home from work, the parrot could greet him. He knew his father well enough to understand that a bird with a kind word for him at the end of the day would have a permanent place beneath their roof. However, the bird did not learn quickly, and after several weeks, his mother read an article about a recent outburst of parrot fever in Jamaica, and the bird was returned to the store.

Figaro had arrived with Marie, the Mother Teresa of cats. She found him when she took her cat into the veterinarian's to be put to sleep. "This is a wonderful kitten," the vet said, bringing out a black kitten he held by the neck. The cat hissed and spit and struggled while Marie inspected him. He had an asymmetrical streak of white fur which bisected his face and cut across his nose. He looked, as everyone noted, demented. Marie picked up the cat and he walked across her arm, used his nose as a wedge to lift her coat, and went to sleep above her breast just beneath her shoulder. She had decided to take the cat when the vet reminded the receptionist that the woman who had brought in the kitten and who had paid its bills had asked to approve the person who would adopt it. The woman was duly called and within fifteen minutes came in, brushing snow from the collar and chest of her coat.

"Where *is* the cat?" she asked.

Marie opened her coat. Only the cat's rear end and tail were visible. At the sound of the woman's voice, the cat turned, peered out from the depths of Marie's coat, and then retreated.

"Oh, well, he loves you already," the woman said.

"I love cats," said Marie.

"Her cat just died," said the receptionist. "Of diabetes."

"Diabetes?" the woman said. "I didn't know cats got diabetes."

"They do," said Marie. The kitten was absentmindedly chewing on one of her fingers.

"You know why he's here?" the woman said. "There's this gray cat who leaves her kittens in our boiler room. We found him down there. He was sneezing, his eyes were gummy, he was a mess, so we started feeding him. We wanted to bring him in here but he wouldn't let us near him. So we waited until his eyes stuck together and we dropped a carton on him. We got him here just in time."

"Just in time," said the receptionist. "He had pneumonia."

"So he's not such a friendly cat," the woman said. "I mean, first it was a boiler room, and boxes dropped on him, and then it was a cage and things stuck in his rear end and needles through his skin. You know."

"A survivor, that cat," said the receptionist. "If you see what I mean."

Marie took the cat home. For the first week, it hid beneath her legal bookcase, coming out to eat when she left the room. Then it began to lie down on the living room rug, as far from her as possible.

She always spoke to the cat, said hello when she came in, told the cat she would be back soon when she left. Occasionally, she read aloud to the cat. One morning when she awakened, she was surprised to find the cat wedged into her side, asleep on its back. When she tried to scratch its stomach, the cat attacked her wrist and she walked around with Mercurochrome stains and Band-Aids for a week. She named the cat Figaro.

He met Marie when the cat had begun to sit, cautiously and suspiciously, on the couch with her. Its fur was now so shiny the light reflected from it and the fleas that had bitten Marie so hungrily were long gone. It was no longer a kitten, but neither was it a cat. It was thin and long and leggy and its only interest, as he saw it, was in food. When they fed the cat, it would eat until the plate was clean and then cry for more. They fed the cat incessantly and ignored its cries only when the cat's stomach bulged ominously. At such times, the cat looked as if it had swallowed a shoe box.

"*Can* cats explode?" he asked Marie.

"Don't give it any more," she said.

Marie usually fed the cat, although he often stood over Figaro and watched him eat. Still, he was the one the cat followed, the one onto whose lap the cat jumped, the one of whom Figaro was jealous. If he read a book, he had to hold it high in the air so that the cat could not lie down on it, and when he held it up, tiring his arms, the cat would stand up on his hind legs and pull the book down with his front paw. When he went to bed, the cat came with him. When it was cold, the cat tunneled under the covers and slept on his ankle. If he went into the bathroom, the cat scratched at the door until he let him in.

"Why me?" he asked.

"It's love," Marie said.

"I don't love him," he said.

"But you will," she said.

He looked at Figaro, lying on the bed. He had come to adore the cat. The cat seemed to him, in its calm surveillance of all that occurred, almost omniscient. Its green glass eyes, so clear and transparent, were like pools of the purest water, so deep that, when he looked into them, he thought he could almost see into the brain that perceived the world. When he spoke to the cat, he believed there was nothing the cat could not understand. When he gave the cat commands, it obeyed them. If he told the cat to flip over on its back, the cat did, waving its paws in the air, waiting for its stomach to be scratched. If he held his hand over the cat's head and said, "Stand up," the cat stood up and held onto his fingers. He explained his experiments to the cat and the cat understood them. He knew the cat was a pure soul. He knew beyond a shadow of a doubt that the cat loved him. Once Marie had pretended to hit him with a newspaper and the cat had jumped on her leg and begun to rake at her skin with its back claws.

As he stroked the cat, it seemed to him that the cat did not look well. He tried to remember: Was it feed a fever, starve a cold? Starve a fever, feed a cold? Until the cat seemed healthier, he would not feed it. Figaro stretched, yawned, and as if approving of his decision, climbed onto his lap. He lay back on the bed and the cat crept onto his stomach, rising and falling as he breathed.

When he came home from the lab the next day, the cat seemed better but more nervous. Figaro flew around the room. He crept into the paper bag he put down on the floor and sprang out waving his front paws. He would crouch down in the middle of the rug and then run madly around the room, his wide, round eyes on him. He thought, He is more playful because he feels better. He considered feeding the cat, but decided that, to be on the safe side, he would wait until morning.

In the morning, Figaro once again seemed unwell. He decided that his lab assistants had the experiment he was running well under control. He would stay home with the cat. As the days went by, he read book after book. For the first few days, the cat protested, as was his habit, either lying on the book or standing up to drag it down, but eventually, the cat grew resigned and lay across his legs without disturbing him. By the end of the week, he had to carry the cat over to his dish of water, and as Figaro drank, he would look up at him from the floor, reproach in his eyes. His lab assistant called and said things were going well. He decided to remain at home with the cat until he was better.

"You have your whole life ahead of you," said his mother. "I have nothing. All I have left of him are his golf clubs. You could call more often. I'm always here."

"What's the weather like?" he asked his mother.

"What's the weather like?" his mother asked, her voice rising to a shriek. "This is Florida! What should the weather be like? It's hot! It's always hot!"

"No hurricanes?" he asked.

His mother hung up. He stared at the receiver in disbelief. He was making conversation. She always liked to talk about the weather. Why did she only have his father's golf clubs? What had she done with his clothes? If she'd given away his clothes, why didn't she give away his golf clubs and make a clean sweep of it? But then she was a widow. He didn't understand widows.

"I'm not a widow!" his mother shouted at him when he next called her. "I'm still your mother!"

"You're a widow and you're my mother," he said. Widows, apparently, were irrational. His mother hung up. Perhaps widows did that —lost their tempers, hung up on their sons.

Figaro, meanwhile, absorbed all his attention. The cat was listless. His ribs showed through his fur. When he pulled back the cat's lower lip, his gums looked pale. When he went into the kitchen or to the bathroom, the cat sighed and got down from the couch, following him, but when he first landed on the floor, his legs seemed to wobble beneath him. Lately, he seemed to stagger as he walked. He took to picking up the cat and carrying him wherever he went. When he lay on the bed, the cat sucked at his fingers or licked his skin. Occasionally, the cat, as if apologizing for his weakened state, reached out to pat his arm.

"Why can't you come down for Christmas?" his mother demanded. "All the other children are coming down for Christmas. It's not as if these are normal circumstances!" His mother, he believed, kept actuarial tables of the number of visits children made to their parents in Florida. He said something to that effect and the line went dead. When she ceased being a widow, he thought, she would cease hanging up.

When it became apparent to him that the cat was going to die, he spent every moment with the cat. He no longer read or watched television. He watched the cat. He wanted to observe the exact instant when it ceased to breathe. He wanted to know when the cat went from being something living and warm to something dead and cold. He began drinking cup after cup of coffee in order to stay awake. The cat now slept most of the time. When it awakened, it would look around, turning its head from side to side, but not lifting it, to see where he was. Then the cat would stretch out its small hot paw and rest its paw on his arm. He stroked the cat rhythmically and incessantly, and softly, because the cat's ribs now showed so prominently through its fur. He imagined the full weight of his hand on the cat would be painful and so, when he touched the cat, he did so lightly and carefully.

The doorbell rang one day and when he opened the door he saw Marie standing on the landing. She waited, expecting him to invite her in, and he thought, Figaro was her cat, too; I should let her see the cat, but then he thought, The cat is so weak the excitement would kill him immediately. He muttered something about having someone in the apartment, but if she'd wait a minute everyone would be decent. Marie flushed and said she had better be leaving. He went back in to the cat. Figaro had managed to pick up his head and was staring fixedly at the door as if he were hoping for rescue, but of course had been too weak to go to the door. Figaro had no choice. That was what it meant to be dying, he thought. The dying had few choices and then they grew weaker and had no choices. They wanted to live and they struggled to live but they could not choose to live. "She's gone," he told the cat, and the cat lowered his head and lay still. He was still breathing. He lay down next to the cat and fell asleep. When he awakened, the cat was still breathing.

As it happened, he was awake when the cat ceased to breathe. He pressed his ear to the cat's chest and could not hear his heartbeat. He saw that the eyes of the cat no longer focused. Still, the cat moved, odd, convulsive movements. Wake up, he told the cat. Get up. I'll give you something to eat. But the cat did not wake up and he understood the cat had died. As he stroked the cat's stiffening body, he began to cry, and he sat on the edge of the bed through the night, stroking the cat and weeping. In the morning, he put Figaro in a carton and took him to the lab where he would be cremated.

When he went home, he called his mother and said perhaps he might come to Florida for Christmas after all. He asked his mother whether or not she still had his father's golf clubs, and if so, could he use them. As he talked to her, his eyes wandered to the almost-full carton of cat food next to the refrigerator. How long had it been since he'd fed the cat? Almost two weeks. It was astonishing to him that an animal could go that long without food.

"So," said his mother, "it's finally hit you."

"What's hit me?" he asked.

"Look, I don't want to talk," his mother said. But she did not hang up.

He thought of this now because he was staying for the weekend with friends in Maine. They had a huge fieldstone house and when he had driven up to it, his two children fighting in the backseat, his wife still reading the directions scribbled on the back of an envelope, a black cat had been sitting on the front step. A lightning-like stripe zigzagged from its nose to its chin and when he saw the cat he felt a surge of joy that rose like a warm tide from his stomach and flooded his chest. He helped the children unload their suitcases and he carried in the golf clubs in their old red leather golf bag—the leather had cracked and had the texture of old, weatherbeaten skin—and then went back for the boxes of cake his wife had baked, but his attention was fastened to the cat. As soon as everyone was inside, he announced that he had a headache and asked if anyone would mind if he went up to bed. No one minded. The children were running down the road to the ocean and his wife was running after them. The cat was standing in front of him, and he swooped down upon the cat and carried it with him to the bedroom his hostess had pointed out. He took the cat inside and closed the door. He put the cat down on the braided rug and lay down. He pulled the brass bed's feather comforter over him. Milky white light poured in through the curtainless window. He lay on his back, his hands folded beneath his head. Eventually the cat jumped up on the bed and lay down on his chest, staring into his eyes, just as he had known it would.

"It's you," he said to the cat. "You're back."

The cat purred and flexed his claws. "My mother died," he told the cat. "Not long ago, but long enough." The cat crept forward until his cold nose touched his own. He began to stroke the cat, and as he did, he began to weep. "I'm sorry," he told the cat. "You're not angry?" The cat reached out, touched his cheek, and flexed his claws. He tapped the cat's paw gently and the cat, purring louder, retracted his claws. "She's been dead eight weeks," he said, and the sound of the cat's purr, ever louder, made him sob, so loudly he had to turn on his side and bury his face in the pillow. It seemed to him that the least thing made him cry, and he remembered his mother saying, not long before her death, that when he was younger he never cried and she had worried what would become of him. She was old; she spoke in non sequiturs. *You look like your father,* she said. The cat, as if he were walking on a rolling log, managed to stay on, settling on his hip. He thought, as he wept, that from a sufficient distance he might look like a grave covered in snow, and the cat the carving on top of the stone. It is because of Figaro that I have anything, he thought, poor

Figaro, who starved to death, and as he thought that, he felt sleep settling on him, erasing him, and he understood the fog wanting to erase him, as he understood how the houses, the lawns, and the sea would feel when the fog gathered its strength, thickened, and erased them all.

Taking Care

KATINKA LOESER

We are alarmed. The Makepeaces are not. But they have never been ripped off. When Tom and Jean left for the islands this winter, Tom telephoned the police, who ought to be used to his calls by now: the Makepeaces are always going to islands—one in the summer, a group in the winter. It is obvious

74

to our friends that, with Gladstone for a husband, I'm lucky to get to Manhattan Island and back, and then not so many times that I feel compelled to seek a rest cure. Anyway, when Tom Makepeace called the police recently to say that he and his wife were going away for a few weeks and that he would appreciate police surveillance of the house, he talked to a new desk officer. As Tom reports it, the new man took down the basic information—name, address, etc.—and then said, "Is your house alarmed?" Tom, who has a way with words, looked around, thought about it briefly, and said, "No, not alarmed, but you might say a bit twitchy." The desk officer cleared his throat. "Take care," he said, and hung up.

We've been robbed twice. The first time was on a perfectly lovely day when I had left a window open to let in fresh country air; someone came in through the window and went away with my jewelry case. I was furious, because, among other things, my medal was in it, and I knew I'd never get another. I threatened to buy a gun, but Gladstone said no—no guns in this house, absolutely not. Without further ado, I bustled out to the car and drove down to a local animal shelter to case the supply of savage dogs, one of which I would train to protect and attack. When I got there and wandered woefully over the recently hosed cement floors, I knew I had made a serious mistake. Not one dog or puppy looked like attack material. They crowded their barriers and cried out to me; those that had tails wagged them and those that didn't wagged anyway. I could not bear to think of their watching me leave; they would go back to a corner and lie down with their noses on their paws and be silent. I aimed myself at the nearest door and found myself in a hall stacked with cages of kittens and cats, who all saw me at once and shrieked for attention. Going through these shelters where people have dumped unwanted animals is a devastating experience. Unbalanced with rage, I got to the exit just as an attendant brought in a carton containing two white kittens. My own white cat had been killed on the road some weeks before. The kittens went home with me, although I do not recall the details of the transaction. I had had something to do with the unwanted before and been shaken by it. When I was young and lived in a Midwestern city, I spent one summer doing volunteer work at an orphanage (it was Catholic, I was not)—a dumping ground where there wasn't a chance of matching babies to adoptive parents in any systematic way. I worked hard to help feed, dress, hold, and in general assist in salvaging the detritus of alleys, garbage cans, what-have-you for Adoption Day, that time designated frequently by the staff for viewing the merchandise, when the supply got relatively well cleaned out and nobody fretted about taking in someone who might not scintillate dangling from the family tree. At the end of the summer, as I was saying good-bye to the nurses, I felt a hand on my shoulder and turned to see the Mother Superior. She said, "I am glad to see you smiling. It means that you are happy, as you should be. You have given us strength and support this summer, and, what is more, a helping hand. You deserve a medal." I grinned foolishly and shuffled my feet and said it was nothing. She took my hand, placed something in it, patted my shoulder, and went her sober way. I looked at what was in my hand, and one of the nurses laughed. "You wouldn't know," she said, "but that's a St. Christopher medal." I said I had heard of him—that he was the patron saint of lost things. She shook her head. "No," she said, "that's St. Anthony. St. Christopher is the patron saint of travelers. He'll take good care of you." I still have a warm feeling for St. Christopher; it means little to me that he was removed from the Church Calendar in 1970. One Western legend has it that he went in search of Christ and met a hermit, who told him to pray. "That I cannot do," Christopher said. "Then," the hermit said, "you must carry travelers over the deep river." And so Christopher did. One night he heard a voice calling him and found a little child. He put the child on his shoulders to carry him over the deep river, but the child grew heavier and almost weighed him down. He said, "You seem to weigh as heavy as the whole world." "Well said, Christopher," the child answered. "I created the world, I redeemed the world, I bear the sins of the world."

And the child vanished. Thus Christopher saw that he had borne Christ over the stream. Christopher never lost status with me.

The kittens, White and White, never leave me. Because I recently had the kitchen floor done over in white tile, I am always close to trampling a White; in the dark, when I grope for my shearling slippers, my bare foot prods a White. By day I think I am seeing things as they trot along amiably beside me; when I stop they repose on the tops of my feet, like rosettes of whipped cream. They are quiet only at night. To give them a sense of security, of belonging, I treated them to crimson cushions to sleep on, but it didn't work; they sleep on me. When I lie on my left side, they sleep along the ridges formed by my arm, hip, and thigh; when I roll over, they take to treading me. If I bend down to pick up something, they leap onto my back and crouch there, beginning a leisurely bath. When I receive guests, they scale forbidden bookshelves before my eyes and swat houseplants. They once ate two ferns and shredded my terry-cloth robe. When I bark a command—"Heel!"—they collapse, roll over, and squirm with delight. When I stand quite still and look down at them in blank despair, they wind themselves about my ankles and croon and have no other gods before me. They hear things that cannot really be heard. But as watchdogs they are a total flop.

The second time our house was broken into, I got home from the supermarket (where I had spent some time collecting no-frills canned goods), unlocked the front door, and found White and White crouched on the red hall carpeting waiting for me, as usual. But instead of greeting me with an invitation to romp, they simply knelt on folded legs like sacred cattle in a foreign land, each with a tiny tuck of disapproval in the corner of the mouth. "Holy cow!" I said, staggering past them to the kitchen, where I let down a bag of groceries from each arm, sighing over the effort it takes simply to exist: woman's work is never done, etc. I stretched my arms, rubbed them, and went upstairs to change into my work clothes. At first I couldn't think why the place looked worse than usual, than when I had gone out. Drawers and closets were open, and the contents were strewn over the floor. Then I realized that intruders had been there and had not had time to put everything back neatly. What kind of homes could they have come from? I called Gladstone at his office and then the police, who came right over and found the splintered door in back, which I had locked securely before I left. The police wanted to know what was missing. We could not find the television, which would not have been easy to miss, as it was as big as the washing machine. They had also taken the vacuum cleaner, and a digital clock that Gladstone had given me for my birthday and that I had scarcely been able to take my eyes from; it gave me the hypnotic though sweat-producing experience of not only realizing that time goes by but also watching it go. While Gladstone sat with the police listing missing articles, I wandered through the hall and bedrooms mewling and riddled with tics. There was so much stuff lying around which I failed to recognize that I began to wonder whether the intruders might have brought with them items of their own that *they* didn't know what to do with, to add to mine. In the room that used to be a child's and is now my retreat, used largely for writing importunate notes to the Conservation Commission protesting the new raised ranch that is too close to wetlands, the closet takes the place of an attic, which we have never had, as I have been fearful that it would too soon be filled with what I would only have to go through and sort out. The burglars had hit that closet like a hurricane.

I am no good at straightening up the house in lousy weather. Wait till the sun shines, Nellie, I say, and the clouds go drifting by. Now I am sitting at my desk on a foul spring day writing my Last Will and Testament in case I should begin to flounder, mortally, while I am tidying up—in case the strain should prove too much for me. It is a perfect day for this composition—gray, windy, clammy, like night turned inside out and showing its seamy side. The thermostat has been turned down all winter, leaving the house with an irreversible chill, and I am wearing my Pasadena Playhouse sweatshirt, given to me years ago by No. 1 son (in order of appearance). My spirits are good, as they always are when I put together this document—which I do frequently, until I get to the place where, being a conscientious member of society, I must dispose of my component parts when they are no longer working for me; then I look around for something to take my mind off my work.

It is at this moment that Gladstone appears at the door to my room, carrying a flashlight and candle in one hand and in the other his transistor radio, which he is holding close to his ear. "Wind's coming up," he tells me briskly. "And the radio says it's gusting to gale force. In case the power goes off you'll want these. The flashlight seems weak, so you better hang on to the candle as well; here's matches, too." He peers at his feet, which are isolated among little islands of material possessions. "Why don't you put some of this stuff away while you can still see where it goes?" He has been saying this for some weeks, and it is not really a question. But that's all right; it has been a gloomy season.

"I'm too busy," I say quickly. "What about the alarm? How can it work if the power goes off?" He explains that there is a backup system, and pads out of the room. I hear him in the bathrooms running water in tubs and basins so that we will have plenty if the power does go off, although I do not understand what we will do with it. Will Gladstone appear with a washboard for me? Has he a vision of me on my knees beside a tub, scrubbing the laundry, up to my elbows in suds while bellowing ethnic folk songs into clouds of steam? As I sit staring at the typewriter, Ms. White dances into the room, pirouettes, and lights in my lap. I rise and dump her; she rushes into the empty closet, hides behind the sliding door, and grumbles. All I can see is her long white tail—longer than necessary and oddly flat on the floor. I get up and stumble over to the closet. "Don't be a sorehead," I tell her. The tail twitches. I go back to the desk, to my wearisome task, and scan what I have written, wondering if it seems too impersonal.

Gladstone appears at the door of the room again, this time quite soiled from having been in the garage, where he has been starting the power mower. This is something he does often all winter—to keep the machine limber, as he says, and to be sure it is still able to start. When the day comes for the first grass-cutting, the mower starts, stops, starts, sends out a cloud of smoke, and has to go into the shop, where it is diagnosed as needing professional attention, is tagged, and takes its place in an endless line of machines, while we get in touch with a neighbor, who is in command of a sickle.

"Why did you want to know about the alarm?" he asks.

"I was just thinking," I say. "If we go out to dinner and the electricity goes off, we might not be guarded."

He folds his arms and I look out the window, where the sky is falling.

"We *aren't* going out to dinner," Gladstone says. "Not in this. I'm not getting tangled in live wires, even if I am in a car—or having trees drop on me. And something is bound to happen."

After the second break-in, we had to protect ourselves. The alarm system took some getting used to. There is a main alarm and alarms to alarm it—beams, bugs, strategically sensitized areas of carpeting, and panic buttons generously distributed throughout the house; I can scarcely turn around without being alerted to possible disaster. When the system was first installed, friends came to inspect it and shook their heads in dismay; they could not, they said, live in a fortress. A jittery woman tried to convince me that one cannot live with fear, and hinted that I ought to go to the next meeting of Emotions Anonymous with her, but I'm not about to spill the beans in front of an audience, am I. The system was installed by a crowd of scruffy, shaggy young men in jeans and statemental T-shirts, who looked as if they themselves might have been casing the premises with plans to make away with the plate but who were cozy in a system of electronics which I hardly believe exists. When it was all done, they gave me lessons with great kindness and encouragement, and they left with a wave and a cheerful "Take care." I was convinced that being safe was a snap. In the evening of their departure Gladstone turned the alarm on and, sighing in total security, we went our separate ways. I wandered through the living room and enclosed porch, where we keep potted plants, and where the setting sun gilded window boxes and fading sofas and trickled down the flowered wallpaper. Outside on the terrace, Robert White yowled that he wanted to come in. I opened the door and the alarm went off, clattering through the house like a rusted chariot coming for to carry me home. I clutched my head, hands over ears; Robert White spun twice in the air, lit sprawled, and whisked himself under a sofa, and Gladstone, who had been taking a shower, came pounding down the stairs in the bathrobe that I had just given him—one with kimono sleeves that flap like a crow's wings. He turned off the alarm and reset it. I tottered to the telephone and called the police. A deskman answered.

"Oh, *hi!*" I said. "This is Mrs. Gladstone Fairchild calling? I just wanted to tell you not to be upset because our new alarm went off by mistake." I listened. Then I said, "You don't have to bother. You see, I was only letting the cat in and . . ." I listened. "Well, O.K.," I said and hung up.

"Yes?" Gladstone said. He stood with his arms folded, a cat in each sleeve, resembling the Prophet Muhammad, who, it is written, when he preached from the tallest minaret in Mecca was seen to carry his white cat, whom he called Muezza, asleep in the sleeve of his robe.

"They're taking it seriously," I told him. "The cops are coming."

Still shaky, I went back to the porch to be sure I had locked the door. A begonia seemed listless; I moved it to a place where it would get more winter sun and the alarm charged through the house. Gladstone got to it just as the doorbell rang. Opening the door, we caught glimpses of the darkening front yard chopped to fragments by flashing lights of patrol cars. Two young officers stood on the welcome mat. "I'm so sorry," I began. "You see, I was just letting the cat in, as I told your captain and . . ."

"Yes, ma'am," one of them said. "The other men are looking around outside and we'll just have a look at the house." He disappeared with Gladstone while his partner paused to say to me, "You see, we don't know that someone isn't standing there with a gun at your head *forcing* you to say that it was a mistake."

As he spoke he threw open the door to the hall closet; two rain hats drifted out, an umbrella flopped across his shoes, and one of Gladstone's galoshes fainted at his feet.

"I'm sorry," I said. "I've been trying to get to that closet."

They left after a thorough inspection. "Take care," one of them said pleasantly.

"By the way," Gladstone says as I frown at the typewriter ribbon, which is crumpling. "Since we're not going out to dinner, what's *for* dinner?"

"I don't know," I tell him. "I hadn't planned for this kind of day; there was nothing about it in the *Times*. There's probably a can of tuna fish on the shelf. We could have a salad."

He stares at me. "That's *lunch.*"

The telephone rings. "I'll get it," he says, and, a moment later, "It's for you."

It is my friend Louise, who has cancer. "Honestly, I'm so depressed," she says. "I thought I'd call you before the phone goes."

"What's the matter?" I ask.

"My new wig is itchy," she says. "And my other one is at the hairdresser's. *And* I'm supposed to go out to dinner."

"In this?"

"What do you mean?" she asks.

"This weather," I say. "There could be live wires and branches and trees falling; you could get hurt."

There is a silence. Then she says, "I think I hear someone at the door. I'll call you tomorrow."

"O.K.," I say. "Take care."

I go back to my desk and hear Gladstone shuffling around the kitchen. He won't starve. We went out to dinner last night—very filling. We don't dress for dinner Saturday night anymore—not out here; perhaps it's a sop to the times, but it's also the result of a condition arranged, I am convinced, by prowling designers who the instant I have a good long skirt shorten all skirts or dismiss them altogether and bring on floaty dresses with appendages to the neck or sleeves that, if I should wear such a garment, would get in the soup or salad. Last night was the usual party where after three days in the kitchen the hostess is barely able to reel out to greet her guests, but it is always a superb dinner; husbands forget middle-age spread, wives forget middle-age sag. (Recalling fallen friends, however, we have gone back to measuring our alcoholic consumption in the cocktail hour.) After dinner the women retired to our hostess's bedroom to repair the ravages of chattering and chewing and time; we were getting on with it when I happened to glance across the hall to another room that had been a child's but was empty now, and, as in a trance, found myself at a window there, where the first chalk-white moths of March soared around a glaring arc light that warned away intruders and limned a bare Kousa dogwood against the darkness beyond—moths that might have been the wavering spirits of past spring nights come back like little ghosts from another time, only briefly, only to see if they might have been missed.

Now what? The typewriter ribbon has come out of the little hooks that hold it in place; it is an old, tired ribbon. I try to put it back, do, and continue my Last Will and Testament, but the ribbon slips out again and my last words remain unwritten, for heaven's sake. "What were her last words?" the curious will want to know, and never will. The page is smudgy, too, with carbon from my fingers. It's nothing that I can possibly leave for my heirs, loved ones, and God knows what professional Paul Prys. Here is an impasse.

I get up and go over to the yellow lounge chair that I haven't used for some time, as it has been otherwise occupied—by books, by magazines, by the hat I bought because hats were back but keep forgetting to wear. All these things go temporarily—on the floor, of course; I will dispose of them later. I do not put the hat on the floor, as that is no place for a hat, is it. I put it on my head experimentally, to see how long I can wear it without mashing my hair. If I were in town I might be going to "21" for lunch. Or something.

Ms. White has edged out of the closet and is sitting at the window, accommodating herself to the small sill. The wind is gusting with no nonsense now; the branches of the white birch clump are beginning to sweep the ground, as if seized by a sudden spell of housekeeping, and farther out in the yard the sugar maples are flustered by the weather, not knowing which way to turn. A burst of rain spatters the windows and Ms. White draws back in revulsion, turns toward me, and in one leap arrives at my side. I inch over to give her room. She blinks at me, turns her head, and stares into the room as the day darkens and drowns.

It is her time for musing, for story-telling, and with trembling lips she begins those small sounds of time remembered, lifting her head again and again as if there were a whispering in the air to remind her of this and that and long ago, not mourned but simply remembered. I understand; the only difference between us is that I must put everything into words and she has none. In my own past time there was my grandmother Elizabeth, who sat in her wheelchair and stared out the window toward the country south of town, where she had been raised. She was winding strands of hair over her Jim Twisters; my own had been put up in rags, and tomorrow we would both be curly. While I looked at my grandmother, I thought of what I had been told —that she was going to die soon—and from funerals of her friends I recalled one word. "Abide with me! Fast falls the eventide. . . ." "Eventide"—a word I had never heard until that summer, and one that never left me. Was she looking into the eventide that was fast falling over the farm where she had been a child, like me? I cannot say "eventide" to the little cat, but in her own terms she is mentioning it to me; she has no tones of imprecation or adulation or rue but only: This is the way it seems to be. I, who must have words and in their proper places—I think of a lass six years old who sat in profound dejection on a flagstone step, her head hanging, her yellow hair falling limply about her face, her hands dangling hopelessly between her knees. I am on my way to the clothesline with a basket of sodden laundry. I stop and question her; why isn't she playing with the other children?

"I'm sad," she says liltingly.

I boost the laundry basket with one knee. "Nonsense," I say. "You don't know what sad is, at your age. Go run around and you'll feel better." And I go on to the clothesline. In a tree out of sight a cardinal says, *"Tst!"* The cat and the cardinal know that words are not all. How can anyone say why she is sad? There is no reason. You do not take instruction in it; it has nothing to do with morning, noon, or night, and it cannot be cured; like a small cloud it will drift away. And my grandmother sat looking toward the farm south of town, putting Jim Twisters in her long brown hair and singing a funny country song to me: "Go tell Aunt Rhody the old gray goose is dead. . . . She died in the millpond from a toothache in her head." I stared at my grandmother in the eventide, and in my bed at night I wept for the old gray goose that was dead.

As Ms. White crowds closer to me, I scrutinize the massed objects on the floor and begin to recognize some things that are not mine and yet have not been abandoned by intruders; a Victorian dress, a folded practice pad for a drummer, a wire hanger from which had dangled the assorted limp headbands that are now a tangle at the edge of the heap. These go back some years to the days of children now gone— from when they began to get married, at sunrise or high tide or whatever. The sun set, the tide went out, and before you knew it they had made commitments, brought leftovers from their single lives home, and gone away again, leaving us uncommitted but with ample storage facilities remaining, should they be needed. Hadn't my Sign convinced everyone that I was a born housekeeper and homebody, and wasn't I the last to know? Were these keepsakes? I had some of my own. "Before you go," I said, "let me show you Grandmother's footed creamer again." But they had gone already.

I glance out of Ms. White's window at the ripening storm and see our neighbor, Chuck, jogging past the top of the driveway on his way home. Chuck is a psychiatrist; we meet at neighborhood parties now and then. Not very long ago I found myself next to him with a drink in my hand; there was also one in his. "I've been thinking I ought to be analyzed or something," I told him. "Well, don't look at me," he said, backing away and slopping a martini on his clean ascot. "Then how about somebody you knew at med school?" I said, following him. "I was a loner," he said, and got lost in the crowd.

Who will save me? Not since when all else failed and it became apparent that I was college material have I been in such a dilemma. I think of this cold morning, before the day went awry, before the wind came up and the sky darkened. I went out early to check the progress of the year, went alone to look for the beginning of squill, for buds, for anything that would assure me that the world had not run down. As I looked up I saw a gray bird sitting on the branch of a bare tree. I stopped. The bird stretched down a leg and instantly drew it back and under a wing, as if it had dipped too soon into spring. "Dummy," I said. It looked down at me soberly. "Not *yet,*" I said. It flew away and the raw wind began to come up, and I went back into the house. But what is there to do here except put everything back in the closet? Nothing works on a day like this: my Last W. & T. will have to be done over neatly after I get a new typewriter ribbon.

It *has* been a dismal season. Last week somebody I knew died. She had phoned to tell me where she was. "Come see me," she said. When I called back to say we'd be down very soon, she was gone. Now she stammers again, in my memory: "Call this a re-ha-bil-i-ta-tion center? Some re-ha-bil-i-ta-tion. Conked out, didn't I?" Here we are, civilized, and I must tell the news of her death to the civilized who knew her, who speak of death in slightly lower tones than those used on the courts or around the pool, or of high prices or rainy Caribbean holidays—the muted voices of those who accept the inevi-table, that we all have to go sometime, which those of us whose rough edges still show are not at all sure of, or which makes us raise our voices in heart-thumping, blood-racing outrage for which there is no medication. She may not be widely mourned, but I remember when she lived in our town, on our road, when she strolled toward our house with a basket of red raspberries slung over her arm, freshly gathered from the masses of tangled bushes in her yard, all the scents of summer in them. After she had moved away, the house was sold; the new tenants had the raspberries ripped out and replaced with the glittering flowering trees of May that bear no edible fruit. And then I recall a summer day when the Whites were very young, when I went out to the flagstone walk to check some houseplants that were summering there. As I glanced back to make sure the screen door was closed, I saw two small white heads and the tips of four white paws poised in the lower panel of the screen. I went about my work, feeling soil, pinching back blossoms, and removing yellowed leaves from a scarlet geranium. A few leaves slipped through my fingers, and one whirled away and lit on a flagstone near the door. I looked at it curiously; it was not curled at the edges like the other faded leaves. I took one step toward it; it fluttered away and dropped again. I sat down and stayed still; the Whites' heads were pointing at the leaf, which I now saw was a toad. It was thin and flat and golden, not burnished but of that true color of the unrefined and unalloyed metal. It was perhaps an inch long, and its narrow head was half the length of its body. It had the slanted, luminescent eyes of an Egyptian god. Its skin was almost transparent, scrawled with delicate, opalescent veins and shimmering like a dew-spattered spiderweb in the earliest morning. And so we all, we four things together, paused in a tenuous awareness of each other that had nothing to do with friends or enemies or kinds or species but only the sharing of living and differences, the pulsating veins, the unreliable heart, while at my back and over my head a small cloud moved in and sent a scattering of precise raindrops down, dappling the flagstones. The toad whirled and fluttered and disappeared behind a laurel next to the house. I got up and went in and closed the front door.

·   ·   ·

There go the lights! No—they are only flickering. I hope we will not have a brownout—a disaster for electrical appliances. (Once, when we did have one, the refrigerator broke down. I called the repairman, who came over and said, "Nope. Can't be fixed. Too bad, you'll have to get a new one, and they don't make them like this anymore—not to last.") If a tree goes down in the storm, or branches, and a high-voltage wire goes along with it, the company will turn off the power when they have been notified. That means I have to go down and turn off the refrigerator. I get up, and Ms. White, who had drifted into dreams, moves over into the warm spot I have left, stretches, yawns, goes back to sleep; it's not her problem, is it. I go down to the kitchen, where I see Gladstone opening the can of tuna fish while the electric can opener is still working. "Here we go," I say. "Don't forget your candle and flashlight," he says, but I have. He stands wistfully regarding the can on the palm of his hand, the radio crackling on a counter top by his side. "There ought to be olives, too," I say, "to go with the salad." I turn off and unplug the refrigerator as he watches. "How long before the ice cubes melt?" he wants to know. But the lights flicker again. I see a candle on the kitchen table and I light it, and at that instant I hear a car churning in the driveway and someone begins to pound on the door. Clutching the candle, I turn on the alarm and move into the hall. "Yes, who is it?" I call out, not about to offer a haven to a stranger. I peer through a glass panel at a huddled figure, both fists flailing the house. A voice floats in the wind: "There's a tree down on the road and live wires are sparking; call the power company!"

At that moment, the lights really go out. Through the dark Robert White leaps down the stairs to see who is here and lands in a sensitive area. Alarms clang through the house; Robert White does two backflips and snakes under a striped cotton rug. I shut off the alarm and open the door to say thank you, but the figure at the door scuttles to his car and splashes away. Gladstone passes me—trailing behind the light from his flashlight, which is tucked under his arm—on his way upstairs. He is carrying a tall glass full of ice cubes and an amber liquid, and his transistor radio is streaming with news: ". . . winds gusting to gale force, with power outages being reported in parts of Westchester and lower Fairfield County. This late report has been brought to you by Harrison's Convalescent Home. Do you have an aging parent who needs proper diet, medical attention, and love and tenderness? Bring him to us, the people of your caring community. . . ." And I am quite alone by the open door—at last, la!, wearing my new hat in public, alone with candle wax spotting my hand and the cuff of the Pasadena Playhouse sweatshirt. Police-car headlights and spotlights begin their phantasmagoric dissection of the night, slashing and shredding the dark lawn and woods, tearing at the sky. The wrath of weather reaches the flame of my candle, which trembles like a good deed in a naughty world, and once again, if only by mistake, my last words unwritten, perhaps even my last song unsung, I brace myself to be saved.

The Cat in the Picture

WRIGHT MORRIS

On retiring from the service, the Captain rented a
studio near the river, overlooking the harbor, and
took up painting in watercolors. He arose at seven,
put on the water for coffee, prepared the still life of
fruit he would paint that day, then called his wife
for a leisurely breakfast. The Captain's wife, a frail

woman in her forties, wrote book reviews for an Indiana paper and passed the day reading and listening to classical programs on the radio. At four o'clock the Captain served tea, with either lemon or cream in the English manner, which he drank from a large china bowl that he held cupped in his hands. The steam from the tea fogged his glasses and gave a ruddy glow to his face. While the Captain relaxed, his wife would sometimes read from the book she was reviewing, as his tastes were wide for a military man. He favored travel books that touched on the places he had been. He would often interrupt the reading to point out some small error of fact. The Captain himself had traveled widely in both the Near and the Far East, but his wife had not been out of the States. He didn't care for the wives of other Army men and the lives they led. His own wife was free, as he liked to say, to go on with the book she was writing and pass the time between her home in Indiana and New York.

While his wife read aloud to him, the Captain would sit and gaze at his painting, as it was characteristic of him not to waste a moment's time. Having turned to painting so late in life, he had a lot to learn. As he lacked both talent and imagination, he had taken a lively interest in painting when he discovered these faculties were not necessary. The Captain's wife, and his friends, admired his painting as they had all worried for years about what a man of his temperament would do when he retired.

As the light was not good for painting in the evening, the Captain and his wife would visit friends or attend some theater where the better foreign films were shown. The Captain enjoyed seeing old familiar sights again. He would point out to his wife the buildings that had been destroyed. Later he would have a small glass of brandy, which he sipped while his wife was undressing, and if the night was clear he would gaze across the river at the lights of New York. When his wife spoke to him he would open the skylight and come to bed.

A sound sleeper, the Captain had learned to adjust himself to the fact that his wife, a very poor sleeper, often lay awake. She rested more than she slept. She lay on her back, her eyes focused on the stains on the ceiling, red or green according to the corner traffic light. Years ago this had troubled the Captain, as he was sensitive to small movements, and the habit she had of stroking the covers at her hips. But he had learned to tolerate that. If he now awoke from a sound sleep it was due to the fact that she had stopped moving, and lay there like a corpse, scarcely breathing, listening to something. Not long ago a bat had got into the room. On his own sweating face the Captain had felt the breath of its wings. His wife would lie there unable to move, her body stiff if he happened to touch her, and the Captain had learned there was little he could do. He accepted it, as he did the phases of the moon. So when he awoke, the first week in April, he didn't trouble to ask what was the matter, but reached for the flashlight that he kept under the bed. He trained the narrow beam around the room. He saw nothing at all at first, but he could hear an unusual noise, a soft, dragging sound, that seemed to come from the back of the room. That was where he painted, had his easel and the low table with his still life. In the basket with the fruit he now saw something move. Lights blinked on and off, like bobbing headlights far down a road. Rising on his elbow the Captain saw a large black cat coiled on the bananas.

"A cat," he said, matter-of-factly. "He probably came in through the skylight." When his wife didn't answer, he said, "You want him out?"

"How do you know it's a *him?*" his wife said.

That surprised the Captain, but he said, "He looks like a pretty big cat." The springs of the bed made a giggling sound. Was she laughing at him? "You want him in or out?" the Captain said.

"Can he get out if he wants to?" his wife said.

"If he got in," the Captain said, "I suppose he can get out," and turned the light beam on the easel, where it pointed toward the ceiling. There was a short jump from the easel to the skylight: not much for a cat.

"I think it's raining," his wife said. "He came in out of the rain."

Turning the beam on the skylight, the Captain could see that it was wet.

"Any port in a storm," he said, and went back to sleep.

Usually the Captain was the first one up, but early the next morning he heard his wife moving around. She was speaking in a high baby voice to the cat. When the Captain raised on one elbow he saw his wife, crouched like an Indian, watching the cat lap up a saucer of milk. His wife was a small, nearly birdlike woman, and the cat was long and thin with yellow eyes. He watched for a moment, then he said:

"Cats don't belong to people. They belong to places."

"You hear him purring?" his wife said.

The Captain lay back on the bed and thought over what he knew about cats. "They're not like dogs. They're very independent," he said.

"He's nice," his wife said.

The Captain recognized in himself a certain catlike independence. He appreciated this quality, respected it. He was thinking that if the cat wanted to stay it would be all right, as cats were not like dogs. Dogs made slaves of the people who owned them. Cats did not. A cat led its own life, and you were free to lead yours.

"He has the nicest purr," his wife said.

"They still don't know how they do it," the Captain replied, and put the coffee water on. As he stood there his wife called to him to come and look at the cat. "I got my hands full," the Captain said, stirring the coffee in the top of the Silex. Then he stopped stirring and waited for the coffee to come down.

"He wants to be in the picture," his wife said. "He wants to put a little life in the picture."

The Captain poured himself some coffee and came back into the room. The cat was back in the wooden bowl again, with his head resting on one of the bananas. His yellow eyes followed the string that the Captain's wife dangled above him.

"If you could paint that—*that* would be a picture," his wife said.

The Captain let the steam from the coffee warm his face. As his wife seldom commented on his painting, nothing that she said was lost on him.

"You're a bad, naughty boy," she said to the cat, picking him up tenderly, and it crossed the Captain's mind—just crossed it—that she had put the cat in the bowl herself. Not that she did, but somehow it crossed his mind.

"He's going to have to learn," the Captain said, rearranging the fruit in the basket, "that some places are all right, and some are not."

"You hear that?" his wife said. The cat made a noise. "You better learn that if you want to live around *here,*" she said. His wife said this in a joking manner, wagging her finger close to the cat's nose, but the Captain's wife was not the joking type. Even the cat seemed to know it. "You've hurt our feelings," she repeated and walked out in the kitchen with it.

A moment later the Captain thought he heard her voice. "I can't hear you," he said, and cocked his head to one side as if that would help him.

"We're not talking to *you,*" his wife replied. There was a note in her voice that distracted the Captain from what she had said. It was new. "We're not talking to him," she said, this time directly to the cat. "Are we?" The cat made a purring noise. When the Captain took another swallow of his coffee it was already cold.

So that the cat would be free to go in and out, a suitable gap was left in the skylight, and the Captain's easel served as a ladder, morning and night. Going out the cat made no sound, but coming in, around four in the morning, he would leap from the top of the easel to the foot of the bed. The thump always gave the Captain quite a shock. He never seemed prepared for it. Before he could get back to sleep again, the cat would curl up at the foot of the bed and wash himself. The stroking movement of the cat's head would communicate itself to the bed, the frame would creak, and there would be a sympathetic throb in the springs. Although the Captain was a sound sleeper, he was sensitive to small, persistent noises—just as his wife, a poor sleeper, seemed indifferent to them. The noises made by the cat did not trouble her. Quite the contrary. She seemed to miss it when it wasn't there. If the cat was five or ten minutes late she would get out of bed and raise the skylight, calling to him in a high falsetto voice. Sometimes he would answer. Other times there would be no sound. The Captain, who saw well at night, sometimes saw it seated on the skylight all the time his wife was calling. His wife, who was blind without her glasses, never seemed to know. Not that it mattered, as sooner or later the cat would stretch himself and come in.

All of this disturbance troubled the Captain. He passed the time gazing into the darkness. Many years of experience had taught him to lie quiet and let the storm blow over, but the night seemed very young at four o'clock. The cat would move, purring like a motor, from one spot on the bed to another, and his wife's nervous hand, sooner or later, would seek it out. The cat's fur would crackle as she slowly stroked its back. The Captain himself, unable to sleep, felt himself to be something of an intruder, a stranger in the bed whom his wife and the cat took pains to ignore. She spoke only to the cat. The cat, in turn, purred only for her.

One night, right out of the blue, like a man who dreams that he is drowning, the Captain's legs thrashed out and hurled the cat bodily across the room. But before the cat landed—as the Captain observed —his wife was out of the bed looking for him, calling to him in the high baby voice that he had come to detest. She moved about like a sleepwalker, stumbling against the furniture. When she found the cat it refused to purr, although she brought it back to the bed and held it in her arms while she stroked it. The Captain, wide awake, passed the rest of the night searching for the word to break this silence and listening to the whisper of his wife's hand on the cat's sleek coat. But he could think of nothing that would not make the situation worse. He had kicked out. It had been his own feet that struck the cat. He had heard the soft body strike the leg of his easel, but the terrible shock of what he had done failed to dull his glow of satisfaction.

The following day, while his wife was out shopping, the Captain made himself a place on the studio couch and early in the evening, a very tired man, he went to bed. His only comment was that he had to get some sleep. He mentioned no names, and let it be understood that his move to the couch was a temporary measure—he would give it up when certain details had been straightened out.

That night the Captain slept better than he had in weeks. There were no bad dreams and he did not wake up at four o'clock. In the morning, very early, he went to the city, leaving his wife a note that he had to pick up some painting supplies. He wanted her to have time to consider the problem, and figure it out. There would be less friction if she spent the day alone. As he figured it out for himself, he would make a cozy place for the cat in the kitchen, or, if she insisted, behind the screen on the studio couch. The Captain, of course, would return to his rightful place in the bed. That struck him as a very reasonable solution, but when he returned to the studio he found his wife and the cat curled up together on the bed, taking a nap. The studio couch, in the corner with his easel, had been neatly made up, and around it his wife had placed the painted Chinese screen. The Captain went behind it, lying on the couch until the evening sky had darkened and his wife, after having fed the cat, called him to eat.

Although the Captain passed a comfortable night on the couch and no longer heard the springs or felt the throbbing vibrations, he woke up, as usual, around four o'clock. Through the thin slats of the screen he could see the ghostly figure of his wife. She was very slender, nearly childlike in her loose, flowing nightgown. She would call to the cat, crouched on the skylight, and after five or ten minutes of coaxing it would climb down one leg of the Captain's easel and leap into her arms.

When his wife left the studio to do their shopping, the cat would follow her to the door, then crouch there, its back turned to the room, until she returned. At this time the Captain and the cat were in the room alone. There had been a time, of course, when the Captain ignored it, or smiled to himself with amusement, as he considered himself something of a student of animals, then go on about the business of painting watercolors in which the familiar fruit looked odd. But now he often turned from his work and stared at the cat. The cat, however, never stared back. The Captain would cough, or make the sounds in his throat that his wife sometimes made when she fed it, but the cat would remain with its back to the room, its eyes on the door. There was about this, the Captain decided, something personal. He admired independence, but the cat's indifference irritated him. The cat seemed to be unaware of the trouble he was causing, or that he might show, toward the Captain at least, a little gratitude. The Captain felt in the cat's rude manner an aloofness that bordered on snobbery. The cat's own feelings, in a catlike manner, he kept to himself.

One day, out of the blue, so to speak, the Captain picked up a paint tube and tossed it casually toward the door. When it struck the floor, the cat leaped high into the air. This reaction was something of a shock to both of them. The cat stalked the empty paint tube as if it were alive. It amused the Captain to see what a fool the cat was in such matters, and that it made no connection whatsoever between the Captain and the tube. The following day he tried this experiment again. The cat leaped again—but not so high. The third time he did not leap at all, but head thrust forward, as if listening, its long black tail switched on the floor. It still crouched, but its body was tense, as if to spring. By tossing just two or three tubes a day the Captain managed to keep him in this condition—taut as a spring, or a gun that is cocked.

"Now you know what it's like," the Captain would say, tossing another tube in the air, and the cat's long body would grow rigid as it dropped. But unlike the Captain, the cat did not thrash out. Not openly, at least, until one tube, tossed high in the air, came down with a soft thud on the cat's back. So rapidly the Captain failed to follow the action—he thought the cat was having a fit—the cat spun around, trapped the tube, and sank in its teeth. When the Captain tried to retrieve it—the paint in the tube was poisonous—the cat growled, and struck out at him. It took all of the Captain's skill to get the tube of paint from its mouth and wipe the stain from the teeth before his wife returned. The cat continued to growl, and the hair along his arched back was up.

The following day, curious to see what the cat had learned from the experience, the Captain rolled a small tube across the floor. Not toward the cat, nor anywhere near him, but he spun around and trapped the tube, sank in its teeth, and disappeared under the bed. Nothing the Captain could do, or say, would persuade him to come out. The bed was also too low for a portly man, like the Captain, to get down on his knees and crawl under it. When he used the broom the cat would hiss like a snake, and growl. That was the situation when the Captain's wife came home. The Captain was back at his easel, painting, but as the cat was not there at the door to greet her, his wife knew that something was wrong. She demanded to know where the cat was, and when the Captain stood there, saying nothing, she got down on the floor, without removing her hat, and crawled beneath the bed. When she crawled out, the Captain didn't see her face, but over her shoulder he saw the scarlet smudges on the face of the cat. His fangs were deep red, and he seemed to have a mouthful of fresh blood.

With the cat still in her arms, his wife sat down and called the nearest animal doctor, then rushed off without waiting for the Captain to explain. Not that it mattered, as what was there to say? He had rolled the tube across the floor, and the cat had eaten it. While his wife was gone the Captain sat on the couch staring at the painting on the Chinese screen, trying to think of what he would say when his wife returned. Every sensible angle left something unexplained. Every explanation only made the situation worse. The only thing for him to do, he decided, was to say nothing about the cat, but to speak very frankly about himself. To admit that the apartment was somehow too small for a man and a cat. If the cat were going to be part of the family—and he was prepared to admit that it was—what they were going to need was a little more sleeping space. A separate room for himself, perhaps, or one for the cat. The Captain wrote a long note to this effect, on a sheet of watercolor paper, then pinned it to his easel where his wife would certainly look. For the time being he would take a room in a nearby hotel. As he planned to be back in two or three days—the time it would take him to find a larger apartment—the Captain took nothing with him but his razor and his toothbrush. With a whole bed to himself he liked to sleep with nothing on.

As he always did after a critical decision, the Captain passed a comfortable night, and in the morning he lay in bed waiting for word from his wife. He had suggested that they might look for something together, in the afternoon. But as he had no word from her by noon, and being anxious to get the thing settled, he got up and went apartment hunting himself. He found himself talking, in fairly general terms, about his wife. What a stickler for certain details she was, and how she loved cats. It seemed to do him good to stand and chat with a perfect stranger about his wife or, more specifically, about his wife's uncanny way with cats. How she talked with them, the things they would do for her. This seemed to interest a good many women, landladies in particular, who either had, or had recently had, a most unusual cat.

The Captain found no apartment, but the many discussions had softened, in some fashion, his feelings about cats. He felt that he had not been disinterested enough. He had allowed his feelings to get the better of him. On his way back to the hotel he noticed that the light was on in their apartment, and in his mind's eye he could see his wife up there, talking to the cat. Perhaps they were lying on the double bed together, taking a nap. His wife had come to specialize in cat material, and on his way back to his room the Captain bought several postcards featuring posed photographs of cats. He planned to put stamps on the cards, and mail them to her. But when he asked the clerk at the desk for stamps, he was notified that a suitcase and trunk, the charges collect, had been delivered during the afternoon. The Captain readily recognized them as his own. On the trunk were the stickers of the celebrated places he had been. The trunk he left downstairs in the lobby, but the suitcase he carried to his room, where he pushed it, for the time being, under the bed. Although he had said nothing, the situation had taken a turn for the worse. Without troubling to take off his clothes, the Captain spent the night sprawled out on the bed, sleeping fitfully, until he awoke covered with sweat. He had dreamed the cat had leaped through the open window landing on his bed with a plop.

So much for the dream, so much for the fact that the Captain now sat facing the window—but how to explain, since this was no dream, that he thought he heard the purring of the cat. The sweat covering his body seemed to turn to ice, and within his damp clothes, like something withered, the Captain had the sensation that he could feel his body shrink. His mouth hung open, but from it came no sound. When the chill had passed he lay back on the bed, too weak to move or to wonder, and as the first breeze off the river stirred the curtains at the window he fell asleep.

He awoke from the dreamless sleep strangely refreshed. He shaved, then removed the clothes that he had slept in and opened the bag that his wife had packed for him. Several shirts were neatly spread out on top. He put the shirts in a drawer, then removed the layer of pajamas, shirts, and socks, and stood there with a pair of socks in his hand gazing at the long, flattened body of the cat. The bottom side of the socks he held were still warm. The bloody scarlet color from the tube of paint was still on the cat's teeth. A practical man, the Captain wondered if the cat had died while eating the paint, or if he had been stuffed into the bag with his shirts while still alive— the living part of that picture his wife had always wanted him to paint.

Company

ARTURO VIVANTE

He's on his way home for a weekend. It's a long
trip—250 miles—and the first part over mountains. Often there's fog, or ice. In the five years he's
been taking the drive he's gone off the road twice,
badly denting his car, the first time in the fog,
against a post; the second time, in frozen rain,

against a railing, when even the police cars were skidding. Sometimes he wonders why he goes home at all. Not that he goes very often. Maybe once a month. He teaches art at a college and lives alone in a campus apartment. His wife refused to go and live there. Their house is by the sea. The college is in the mountains. "Too cold," she said, and he didn't insist that she move. In some ways he needs to be alone. It seems to him they've been separating for years, gradually living more and more on their own. After their three children were born, one by one they displaced him, and he took to sleeping alone. Her visits to his bedroom became rarer and rarer, till, some ten years ago, they stopped altogether. Now the children are away from home for long periods—the two younger ones at college, the older one working, all in New York. But they go home once in a while. By telephone, letter, and visits they all keep in touch. They are a family yet, not split.

Still, he feels separate, if not separated. When he's home there's always plenty to fix—walls, furniture, plumbing. Little rest. No great comfort. Easier in the apartment. And more friends up at the college. More diversions. Movies, plays, concerts, shows, dances, dinners, drinks. Affairs. Down at the house now there's his wife and the cat. The two of them, alone. As he drives, he can almost see them—the cat on the sofa beside her, and she watching the news. "Well, she's very self-contained," he says to himself, "self-sufficient, too. Though hardly self-supporting." She hasn't had a job since he married her. "I'm busy every minute," she says if he ever complains about it. "Bills to pay, scholarship and income tax forms to fill, the house and the yard to look after. There's no end to it." Certainly, he ponders, nobody pays her, or even thanks her for the miles she sweeps; they take for granted the long miles she walks each day within her house. Miles upon miles, uncounted, unrecounted, all adding up to and labelled a life's journey—an undistinguished, unmeasurable trail. And yet more knowing than any other miles these miles that one travels in one's home, the unsung, homespun miles.

And her social life? Their house is in the center of town, off the main street, and a few people drop in from time to time. Nights she's alone. Her faithfulness—not exactly faithfulness, more like lack of enterprise—keeps him returning. It is like a bond. If she flirted, if she had lovers, he would feel freer. But she has only a cat, at her feet.

He's done the road so many times that he finds himself past certain places without his having noticed them. He's surprised to be way past the Sagamore Bridge, for instance. Such a landmark, and he can't remember crossing it. In fact, he's only about half an hour from home. It's midnight and he wonders if his wife is waiting up for him. Probably not. Probably fast asleep, so sound asleep she may not even hear him when he gets in. Only the cat will be sure to hear him, and blink and perhaps meow for food, the cat who at night is always confined to the kitchen so she won't wet the carpets, who is over twenty years old—twenty-four, his wife claims—so old anyway that each time he comes home he expects not to find her, but always does.

Finally he reaches the turn off the highway to the center of town. Town! Village, really, and this time of year—it's winter—almost uninhabited compared to summer, when the population increases six-fold. All but a few stores are boarded up. He meets no traffic and there's no one out. The church clock says 12:30. This was a whaling town and the bell still strikes the hour and half-hour as on ships of old, so that only a few people—his wife for one—can tell the time from the tolls. He learned the sequence once, but has forgotten. He turns off the main street up the short driveway to his house, and parks his car next to his wife's. Fortunately she hasn't forgotten to leave a space for him. Sometimes she reads till late, and then a light shows up in her bedroom, the master bedroom in the front of the house. But not tonight. The house is dark, except for the outside light over the kitchen door, thoughtfully left on. He takes his keys out of his pocket and looks for the right one. When she's alone she locks the door. Her courage is of the moral, not the physical kind.

And he steps in, turns the light on, gets himself a glass of wine, and sits by the kitchen table, in a none too comfortable armchair, with his eyes fixed on the cat, whose eyes are fixed on his. He tries to outstare her, but she's in no mood to play the game and he feels in front of someone older and wiser than he. She blinks twice, then, her interest in him at an end, she turns away and walks to a bench by the window. She jumps up to it, gingerly enters a large brown paper bag that has been left there on its side, and disappears from sight. He almost smiles. Yes, she has her cute moments all right. He remembers her being chased by a small poodle and running behind a cane rake in a corner of the porch, and, safe there, looking at the nonplussed dog. And he remembers her being very concerned when any of the children wept, and even jumping on their shoulders and licking them in an effort to console them.

But her cute moments are few and far between. He remembers also with horror and distaste the times when—years ago, in her nimble days—she would come back to the house like a proud hunter, with a bird or chipmunk, or even a small rabbit hanging from her mouth and deposit them on the kitchen threshold as if they were gifts. Those darling creatures, any one of which he much preferred to the cat herself, and, given a choice, would far rather have preserved. Oh, he supposed he couldn't blame her for her nature without blaming the whole order of things—the ugly, yet perhaps inevitable, arrangement whereby "every maw the greater on the less feeds evermore." And yet why did he have to subject himself to such spectacles? Now she wasn't up to catching anything anymore. But unfortunately there were other things—unpleasantnesses of a different sort, the infirmities that waited on old age, the body becoming almost mechanical in its needs, the dreary routine of ingestion and excretion more prominent than in youth when food is more a means than an end. Such a time they had with her. Again and again he had to move the furniture, roll up the oriental carpet in the living room, carry it to the lawn, spread it, hose it, and leave it in the sun, hoping to rid it of the telltale odor. "She was perfectly house-trained," his wife would say, "until that winter we rented the house and went to Italy. No one bothered to let her out or anything."

He sips from his glass of wine and sees the bag move as if by magic. Ah, yes, the cat, he thinks. "Are you going to outlive me?" he says. "Are you going to be with us forever?"

His wife, in slippers and pink robe, comes into the kitchen smiling. "Who were you talking to?" she says.

"The cat."

"Where is she?"

"In there."

"It was so funny hearing you say that."

"I don't see what's so funny."

"You, talking to the cat, in this old house, in the middle of the night."

She comes nearer and leans toward him to be kissed, brush cheeks really.

"Were you asleep?"

"I was just about to go to sleep when I heard the car. It's so quiet here you can hear every noise. The other night I thought I heard someone tapping and I called the police. Then I realized it was a branch. Only the wind."

"What did they say?"

"They didn't mind."

"Gives them something to do."

"In this out of the way place one feels almost suspended from the world. What are we doing here?"

"Well, you didn't want to live at the college."

"Oh, I don't want to go there. I'd go to Rome if anywhere."

"Rome," he says, "how could we live in Rome? What could I do? Teach where?" He sighs. "When I close my eyes I see the road coming toward me, the curb, the dividing line, lights."

"It's a long drive," she says.

The cat, as if unable to sleep, comes out of the bag and begins cleaning herself.

"You can say whatever you like about her," his wife remarks, seeing her lapping her white chest, her legs, in fact every remotest corner of herself, "but not that she isn't clean." And he must admit her chest is the purest white. Then she turns to the cat and says, "Yass, she's a clean kitty, yass," and the cat looks at her as if in acknowledgment, and goes on with her toilette like a workman who knows he's doing a good job. "Yass, yass, it's a clean kitty."

Again he stares at the cat, thoughtfully this time, not trying to outstare her. She had belonged to a friend who, eighteen years ago, rented their house. On their return, the cat decided to stay on, scared by a dog at the friend's new house. She was welcomed by the children, but not by him. Two or three times in fact he tried to return her, only to find her at the doorstep in a matter of hours. "What gets me," he says, "is we didn't even choose her. I would never have chosen her. She's not beautiful like some cats. Some cats are splendid, with fiery eyes, glowing orange, ember-like, and long, soft fur, mysterious looking. But she isn't. She's pretty ordinary."

"What's he saying about you, kitty? Yass, she is pretty too. Aren't you a pretty kitty?"

"It's not that I don't like cats. When I was a child we had a tiger cat. She would bask in the sun like a sphinx, and I'd lie next to her and dote on her. But this, this black and white thing—"

" 'Thing' now he calls her. You are not a thing, are you, my kitty?"

"Mind you, my inclination is to like them. After Baudelaire, Manet, Colette, one would be a fool not to. Cats, they are contemplative, independent, proud, passionate. But she came to us spayed, altered, fixed."

"Poor little kitty."

"They certainly fixed her. She never goes near another cat, and so she hasn't caught any diseases. It may account for her longevity."

"She is wise, my kitty."

"Old and mangy-looking. Young creatures are easier to take care of. In fact, I think nature made the young as pretty as they are so their parents will be more apt to take care of them."

"She certainly needs a lot of care. Ooops, there she goes coughing up a hairball. Quick, open the door."

They get her out just in time.

"The times I've had to clean after her," she says. "In the summer it's better; then she stays out a lot."

"What misery."

"Oh well, don't make it sound worse than it is."

"How differently age affects animals and man. She's the equivalent of a hundred, and yet she can still climb and jump—nothing like a man of a hundred. I suppose it's because animals can't both be alive and helpless. I mean, they don't help one another as we do. They help their babies, not their elders. Once they get helpless they die, unless we look after them."

"I look after her. Eighteen years. First the children, and now her. Cat hair all over the place. But she'll get her fur all back in the summer, and lie out in the sun, and be happy. Yass, she will, won't you, kitty?"

"Each winter, I say to myself, 'This will be her last.' But it never is. She'll go on and on."

His wife smiles. "Sometimes she stays out all night and doesn't return in the morning, and I wonder if maybe she went to die. I've heard cats do that. They just disappear. But, each time, she returns in the afternoon, walks in as if she'd just gone out for a minute."

The cat now scratches at the door and his wife lets her in. "You just watch the great horned owl don't get you," she says to the cat. "Oh, look at her, how bent her legs are, and hardly any fur on her back at all."

"The mange?"

"No, just age, I think."

"We could send her to the Animal Rescue League, and they'll put her to sleep," he says.

"If she would only die by herself it'd be easier, but she won't make anything easy for us."

They go into the library where his wife reclines on a sofa and he sits in an armchair. The cat appears at the door, stops, looks hesitant, inquiring, then walks in, climbs onto the sofa, arches her back, stretches out, and stalks forward as if to pounce on an inexistent prey. But her pouncing days are over, and she slowly crawls forward to his wife's feet, then to her knees, and finally lies down on her waist.

"No, you are too germy," she says, but lets her stay.

"I could call the Animal Rescue League tomorrow morning," he pursues. "Shall I?"

"No," she says. "With you and the children away, it helps me to have her here. Something alive. Otherwise I'm all alone. If she weren't here it'd be too lonely." She turns to the cat. "We are pretty much alike, aren't we? Two old ladies left alone. Poor soulie. Kitty. Yass. She's my kitty."

The words give him pause, and he thinks of when the wind howls and the house creaks and trembles as if it shivered in the cold, and the shadows of bare branches waving in the wind sweep across the walls, enlarged, beckoning like skeletal arms, and of her and the cat alone here. And on the other hand of himself at the college, of the hateful image of himself up there—his revels and the not so lonely nights. And he wants to narrow, bridge the gap that separates them, and he moves to the sofa and tries to lie down beside her, frightening away the cat. But, "No you don't," she says sharply, resisting him, making no room for him. Thwarted, he puts his feet back on the floor, rises, turns, and lets himself drop back in the armchair. Feet down, legs straight, hands clasped in front of him, and head thrown back, he slumps in it. He listens to the silence. Meanwhile, the cat, seeing him slouched in the armchair at a safe distance, climbs back onto the sofa and goes to lie beside her, just where he had meant to be.

"Poor kitty," she says, stroking her.

"Poor husband."

"Well, you wanted it this way."

"What?"

"You know what I mean, you and all your girlfriends."

"What girlfriends?" he asks, but so faintly she doesn't reply. They reel in front of him—those he loved who didn't love him, those who loved him and he didn't love. Then he just sits and listens to the deep silence of the house. "There's nothing to be done," it says. "Nothing."

Nothing? Nothing is no solution, and he tries to find one. "Nothing now," he says to himself, "but in a few years I'll retire. Then I'll come here to stay and we'll be close again—the way old people are close."

A Suite of Cartoons

ROZ CHAST

The Seven Ages of Cats

r. Chst

THE
FOUR CAT BREEDS

1. Domestic Pettables

These cats can take as much affection as you're willing to dish out. This includes squeezing by two-year-olds. Look for telltale "I'll do <u>anything</u> to please" expression and perky congenital bow.

2. Complete Paranoids

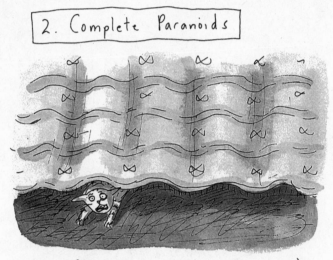

These felines are rarely seen except under furniture and way in the back of seldom-used closets. You might have one and not even know it.

3. Foreign Costabundles

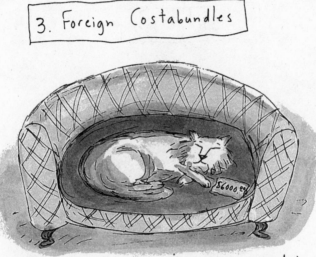

True Costabundles are recognized by their subliminal pricetags and nitwit owners. They sleep a lot and shed like mad, and also often have one tiny thing wrong with them like deafness in the right ear, etc.

4. Stranges

This unfortunate breed appears mainly in cat shows and in the dreams of people who think of themselves as "cat fanciers." Hairlessness, wrinkly skin, ratty tails and peculiar facial expressions are just a few of their traits.

n.Chst

FELINE
BRAIN TEASERS

1. Who is your owner?

A

B

C

D

2. Which of the following is inedible?

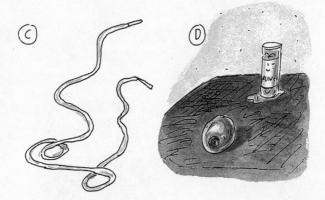

3. Name the scratchpost.

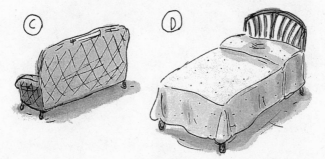

4. Whatever happened to your little mouse - toy?

(A) Under couch

(B) Behind bookcase

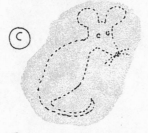

(C) Turned into a ghost

(D) I don't know and I don't care

r.Chst

THE WORLD'S MOST
UNFORTUNATE CAT

Only gets fed three times per day!

Often, no one is at home for <u>hours</u> <u>on end</u>!!

If a toy gets stuck under the sofa, <u>days</u> can go by before <u>anyone</u> bothers to retrieve it!!!

R. Chat

CAT JUNK FOOD

Nashville Gone to Ashes

AMY HEMPEL

After the dog's cremation, I lie in my husband's
bed and watch the Academy Awards for animals.
That is not the name of the show, but they give
prizes to animals for Outstanding Performance in a
movie, on television, or in a commercial. Last year
the Schlitz Malt Liquor bull won. The time before

that, it was Fred the Cockatoo. Fred won for draining a tinky bottle of "liquor" and then reeling and falling over drunk. It is the best thing on television is what my husband Flea said.

With Flea gone, I watch out of habit.

On top of the warm set is big white Chuck, catching a portion of his four million winks. His tail hangs down and bisects the screen. On top of the dresser, and next to the phone, is the miniature pine crate that holds Nashville's gritty ashes.

Neil the Lion cops the year's top honors. The host says Neil is on location in Africa, but accepting for Neil is his grandson Winston. A woman approaches the stage with a ten-week cub in her arms, and the audience all goes *Awwww*. The home audience, too, I bet. After the cub, they bring the winners on stage together. I figure they must have been sedated—because none of them are biting each other.

I have my own to tend to. Chuck needs tomato juice for his urological problem. Boris and Kirby need brewer's yeast for their nits. Also, I left the vacuum out and the mynah bird is shrieking. Birds think a vacuum-cleaner hose is a snake.

Flea sold his practice after the stroke, so these are the only ones I look after now. These are the only ones that always shared the house.

My husband, by the way, was F. Lee Forest, D.V.M.

The hospital is right next door to the house.

It was my side that originally bought him the practice. I bought it for him with the applesauce money. My father made an applesauce fortune because *his* way did not use lye to take off the skins. Enough of it was left to me that I had the things I wanted. I bought Flea the practice because I could.

Will Rogers called vets the noblest of doctors because their patients can't tell them what's wrong. The doctor has to reach, and he reaches with his heart.

I think it was that love that I loved. That kind of involvement was reassuring; I felt it would extend to me, as well. That it did not or that it did, but only as much and no more, was confusing at first. I thought, My love is so good, why isn't it calling the same thing back?

Things might have collapsed right there. But the furious care he gave the animals gave me hope and kept me waiting.

I did not take naturally to my husband's work. For instance, I am allergic to cats. For the past twenty years, I have had to receive immunotherapy. These are not pills; they are injections.

Until I was seventeen, I thought a ham was an animal. But I was not above testing a stool sample next door.

I go to the mynah first and put the vacuum cleaner away. This bird, when it isn't shrieking, says only one thing. Flea taught it what to say. He put a sign on its cage that reads *Tell me I'm stupid.* So you say to the bird, "Okay, you're stupid," and the bird says, real sarcastic, "I can talk—can *you fly?*"

Flea could have opened in Vegas with that. But there is no cozying up to a bird.

It will be the first to go, the mynah. The second if you count Nashville.

I promised Flea I would take care of them, and I am. I screened the new owners myself.

Nashville was his favorite. She was a grizzle-colored saluki with lightly feathered legs and Nile-green eyes. You know those skinny dogs on Egyptian pots? Those are salukis, and people worshiped them back then.

Flea acted like he did, too.

He fed that dog dates.

I used to watch her carefully spit out the pit before eating the next one. She sat like a sphinx while he reached inside her mouth to massage her licorice gums. She let him nick tartar from her teeth with his nail.

This is the last time I will have to explain that name. The pick of the litter was named Memphis. They are supposed to have Egyptian names. Flea misunderstood and named his Nashville. A woman back East owns Boston.

At the end of every summer, Flea took Nashville to the Central Valley. They hunted some of the rabbits out of the vineyards. It's called coursing when you use a sight hound. With her keen vision, Nashville would spot a rabbit and point it for Flea to come after. One time she sighted straight up at the sky—and he said he followed her gaze to a plane crossing the sun.

Sometimes I went along, and one time we let Boris hunt, too.

Boris is a Russian wolfhound. He is the size of a float in the Rose Bowl Parade.

He's a real teenager of a dog—if Boris didn't have whiskers, he'd have pimples. He goes through two Nylabones a week, and once he ate a box of nails.

That's right, a box.

The day we loosed Boris on the rabbits he had drunk a cup of coffee. Flea let him have it, with half-and-half, because caffeine improves a dog's trailing. But Boris was so excited, he didn't distinguish his prey from anyone else. He even charged *me*—him, a whole hundred pounds of wolfhound, cranked up on Maxwell House. A sight like that will put a hem in your dress. Now I confine his hunting to the park, let him chase park squab and bald-tailed squirrel.

The first thing F. Lee said after his stroke, and it was three weeks after, was "hanky panky." I believe these words were intended for Boris. Yet Boris was the one who pushed the wheelchair for him. On a flat pave of sidewalk, he took a running start. When he jumped, his front paws pushed at the back of the chair, rolling Flea yards ahead with surprising grace.

I asked how he'd trained Boris to do that, and Flea's answer was, "I didn't."

I could love a dog like that, if he hadn't loved him first.

125

. . .

Here's a trick I found for how to finally get some sleep. I sleep in my husband's bed. That way the empty bed I look at is my own.

Cold nights I pull his socks on over my hands. I read in his bed. People still write from when Flea had the column. He did a pet *Q*-and-*A* for the newspaper. The new doctor sends along letters for my amusement. Here's one I liked—a man thinks his cat is homosexual.

The letter begins, "My cat Frank (not his real name) . . ."

In addition to Flea's socks, I also wear his watch.

A lot of us wear our late husband's watch.

It's the way we tell each other.

At bedtime, I think how Nashville slept with Flea. She must have felt to him like a sack of antlers. I read about a marriage breaking up because the man let his Afghan sleep in the marriage bed.

I had my own bed. I slept in it alone, except for those times when we needed—not sex—but sex was how we got there.

In the mornings, I am not alone. With Nashville gone, Chuck comes around.

Chuck is a white-haired, blue-eyed cat, one of the few that aren't deaf—not that he comes when he hears you call. His fur is thick as a beaver's; it will hold the tracing of your finger.

Chuck, behaving, is the Nashville of cats. But the most fun he knows is pulling every tissue from a pop-up box of Kleenex. When he gets too rowdy, I slow him down with a comb. Flea showed me how. Scratching the teeth of a comb will make a cat yawn. Then you have him where you want him—any cat, however cool.

Animals are pure, Flea used to say. There is nothing deceptive about them. I would argue: think about cats. They stumble and fall, then quickly begin to wash—I *meant* to do that. Pretense is deception, and cats pretend: Who, me? They move in next door where the food is better.and meet you in the street and don't know your name, or *their* name.

But in the morning Chuck purrs against my throat, and it feels like prayer.

In the morning is when I pray.

The mailman changed his mind about the bird, and when Mrs. Kaiser came for Kirby and Chuck, I could not find either one. I had packed their supplies in a bag by the door—Chuck's tomato juice and catnip mouse, Kirby's milk of magnesia tablets to clean her teeth.

You would expect this from Chuck. But Kirby is responsible. She's been around the longest, a delicate smallish golden retriever trained by professionals for television work. She was going to get a series, but she didn't grow to size. Still, she can do a number of useless tricks. The one that wowed them in the waiting room next door was Flea putting Kirby under arrest.

"Kirby," he'd say, "I'm afraid you are under arrest." And the dog would back up flush to the wall. "I am going to have to frisk you, Kirb," and she'd slap her paws against the wall, standing still while Flea patted her sides.

Mrs. Kaiser came to visit after her own dog died.

When Kirby laid a paw in her lap, Mrs. Kaiser burst into tears.

I thought, God love a dog that hustles.

It is really just that Kirby is head-shy and offers a paw instead of her head to pat. But Mrs. Kaiser remembered the gesture. She agreed to take Chuck, too, when I said he needed a childless home. He gets jealous of kids and has asthma attacks. Myself, I was thinking, with Chuck gone I could have poinsettias and mistletoe in the house at Christmas.

When they weren't out back, I told Mrs. Kaiser I would bring them myself as soon as they showed. She was standing in the front hall talking to Boris. Rather, she was talking *for* Boris.

" 'Oh,' he says, he says, 'what a nice bone,' he says, he says, 'can *I* have a nice bone?' "

Boris walked away and collapsed on a braided rug.
" 'Boy,' he says, he says, 'boy, am I bushed.' "

Mrs. Kaiser has worn her husband's watch for years.

When she was good and gone, the animals wandered in. Chuck carried a half-eaten chipmunk in his mouth. He dropped it on the kitchen floor, a reminder of the cruelty of a world that lives by food.

After F. Lee's death, someone asked me how I was. I said that I finally had enough hangers in the closet. I don't think that that is what I meant to say. Or maybe it is.

Nashville *died* of *her* broken heart. She refused her food and simply called it quits.

An infection set in.

At the end, I myself injected the sodium pentobarbital.

I felt upstaged by the dog, will you just listen to me!

But the fact is, I think all of us were loved just the same. The love Flea gave to me was the same love he gave them. He did not say to the dogs, I will love you if you keep off the rug. He would love them no matter what they did.

It's what I got, too.

I wanted conditions.

God, how's that for an admission!

My husband said an animal can't disappoint you. I argued this, too. I said, Of course it can. What about the dog who goes on the rug? How does it feel when your efforts to alter behavior come to nothing?

I *know* how it feels.

I would like to think bigger thoughts. But it looks like I don't have a memory of our life that does not include one of the animals.

Kirby still carries in his paper Sunday mornings.

She used to watch while Flea did the crossword puzzle. He pretended to consult her: "I can see why you'd say *dog,* but don't you see —*cat* fits just as well?"

Boris and Kirby still scrap over his slippers. But as Flea used to say, the trouble seldom exceeds their lifespan.

Here we all still are. Boris, Kirby, Chuck—Nashville gone to ashes. Before going to bed I tell the mynah bird she may not be dumb but she's stupid.

Flowers were delivered on our anniversary. The card said the roses were sent by F. Lee. When I called the florist, he said Flea had "love insurance." It's a service they provide for people who forget. You tell the florist the date, and automatically he sends flowers.

Getting the flowers that way had me spooked. I thought I would walk it off, the long way, into town.

Before I left the house, I gave Laxatone to Chuck. With the weather warming up, he needs to get the jump on furballs. Then I set his bowl of Kibbles in a shallow dish of water. I added to the water a spoonful of liquid dish soap. Chuck eats throughout the day; the soapy moat keeps bugs off his plate.

On the walk into town I snapped back into myself.

Two things happened that I give the credit to.

The first thing was the beggar. He squatted on the walk with a dog at his side. He had with him an aged sleeping collie with granular runny eyes. Under its nose was a red plastic dish with a sign that said *Food for dog—donation please.*

The dog was as quiet as any Flea had healed and then rocked in his arms while the anesthesia wore off.

Blocks later, I bought a pound of ground beef.

I nearly ran the distance back.

The two were still there, and a couple of quarters were in the dish. I felt pretty good about handing over the food. I felt good until I turned around and saw the man who was watching me. He leaned against the grate of a closed shoe-repair with an empty tin cup at his feet. He had seen. And I was giving *him—nothing*.

How far do you take a thing like this? I think you take it all the way to heart. We give what we can—that's as far as the heart can go.

This was the first thing that turned me back around to home. The second was just plain rain.

Edward the Conqueror

ROALD DAHL

Louisa, holding a dishcloth in her hand, stepped out the kitchen door at the back of the house into the cool October sunshine.

"Edward!" she called. *"Ed-ward! Lunch is ready!"*

She paused a moment, listening; then she

strolled out onto the lawn and continued across it—a little shadow attending her—skirting the rose bed and touching the sundial lightly with one finger as she went by. She moved rather gracefully for a woman who was small and plump, with a lilt in her walk and a gentle swinging of the shoulders and the arms. She passed under the mulberry tree onto the brick path, then went all the way along the path until she came to the place where she could look down into the dip at the end of this large garden.

"*Edward!* Lunch!"

She could see him now, about eighty yards away, down in the dip on the edge of the wood—the tallish narrow figure in khaki slacks and dark-green sweater, working beside a big bonfire with a fork in his hands, pitching brambles onto the top of the fire. It was blazing fiercely, with orange flames and clouds of milky smoke, and the smoke was drifting back over the garden with a wonderful scent of autumn and burning leaves.

Louisa went down the slope toward her husband. If she wanted, she could easily have called again and made herself heard, but there was something about a first-class bonfire that impelled her toward it, right up close so she could feel the heat and listen to it burn.

"Lunch," she said, approaching.

"Oh, hello. All right—yes. I'm coming."

"*What* a good fire."

"I've decided to clear this place right out," her husband said. "I'm sick and tired of all these brambles." His long face was wet with perspiration. There were small beads of it clinging all over his moustache like dew, and two little rivers were running down his throat onto the turtleneck of the sweater.

"You better be careful you don't overdo it, Edward."

"Louisa, I do wish you'd stop treating me as though I were eighty. A bit of exercise never did anyone any harm.

"Yes, dear, I know. Oh, Edward! Look! Look!"

The man turned and looked at Louisa, who was pointing now to the far side of the bonfire.

"Look, Edward! The cat!"

Sitting on the ground, so close to the fire that the flames some-times seemed actually to be touching it, was a large cat of a most unusual colour. It stayed quite still, with its head on one side and its nose in the air, watching the man and woman with a cool yellow eye.

"It'll get burnt!" Louisa cried, and she dropped the dishcloth and darted swiftly in and grabbed it with both hands, whisking it away and putting it on the grass well clear of the flames.

"You crazy cat," she said, dusting off her hands. "What's the mat-ter with you?"

"Cats know what they're doing," the husband said. "You'll never find a cat doing something it doesn't want. Not cats."

"Whose is it? You ever seen it before?"

"No, I never have. Damn peculiar colour."

The cat had seated itself on the grass and was regarding them with a sidewise look. There was a veiled inward expression about the eyes, something curiously omniscient and pensive, and around the nose a most delicate air of contempt, as though the sight of these two middle-aged persons—the one small, plump, and rosy, the other lean and extremely sweaty—were a matter of some surprise but very little importance. For a cat, it certainly had an unusual colour—a pure silvery gray with no blue in it at all—and the hair was very long and silky.

Louisa bent down and stroked its head. "You must go home," she said. "Be a good cat now and go on home to where you belong."

The man and wife started to stroll back up the hill toward the house. The cat got up and followed, at a distance first, but edging closer and closer as they went along. Soon it was alongside them, then it was ahead, leading the way across the lawn to the house, and walking as though it owned the whole place, holding its tail straight up in the air, like a mast.

"Go home," the man said. "Go on home. We don't want you."

But when they reached the house, it came in with them, and Louisa gave it some milk in the kitchen. During lunch, it hopped up onto the spare chair between them and sat through the meal with its head just above the level of the table, watching the proceedings with those dark-yellow eyes which kept moving slowly from the woman to the man and back again.

"I don't like this cat," Edward said.

"Oh, I think it's a beautiful cat. I do hope it stays a little while."

"Now, listen to me, Louisa. The creature can't possibly stay here. It belongs to someone else. It's lost. And if it's still trying to hang around this afternoon, you'd better take it to the police. They'll see it gets home."

After lunch, Edward returned to his gardening. Louisa, as usual, went to the piano. She was a competent pianist and a genuine music-lover, and almost every afternoon she spent an hour or so playing for herself. The cat was now lying on the sofa, and she paused to stroke it as she went by. It opened its eyes, looked at her a moment, then closed them again and went back to sleep.

"You're an awfully nice cat," she said. "And such a beautiful colour. I wish I could keep you." Then her fingers, moving over the fur on the cat's head, came into contact with a small lump, a little growth just above the right eye.

"Poor cat," she said. "You've got bumps on your beautiful face. You must be getting old."

She went over and sat down on the long piano bench, but she didn't immediately start to play. One of her special little pleasures was to make every day a kind of concert day, with a carefully arranged programme which she worked out in detail before she began. She never liked to break her enjoyment by having to stop while she wondered what to play next. All she wanted was a brief pause after each piece while the audience clapped enthusiastically and called for more. It was so much nicer to imagine an audience, and now and again while she was playing—on the lucky days, that is—the room would begin to swim and fade and darken, and she would see nothing but row upon row of seats and a sea of white faces upturned toward her, listening with a rapt and adoring concentration.

Sometimes she played from memory, sometimes from music. To-day she would play from memory; that was the way she felt. And what should the programme be? She sat before the piano with her small hands clasped on her lap, a plump rosy little person with a round and still quite pretty face, her hair done up in a neat bun at the back of her head. By looking slightly to the right, she could see the cat curled up asleep on the sofa, and its silvery-gray coat was beautiful against the purple of the cushion. How about some Bach to begin with? Or, better still, Vivaldi. The Bach adaptation for organ of the D minor Concerto Grosso. Yes—that first. Then perhaps a little Schumann. *Carnaval?* That would be fun. And after that—well, a touch of Liszt for a change. One of the *Petrarch Sonnets.* The second one—that was the loveliest—the E major. Then another Schumann, another of his gay ones—*Kinderscenen.* And lastly, for the encore, a Brahms waltz, or maybe two of them if she felt like it.

Vivaldi, Schumann, Liszt, Schumann, Brahms. A very nice programme, one that she could play easily without the music. She moved herself a little closer to the piano and paused a moment while someone in the audience—already she could feel that this was one of the lucky days—while someone in the audience had his last cough; then, with the slow grace that accompanied nearly all her movements, she lifted her hands to the keyboard and began to play.

She wasn't, at that particular moment, watching the cat at all—as a matter of fact she had forgotten its presence—but as the first deep notes of the Vivaldi sounded softly in the room, she became aware, out of the corner of one eye, of a sudden flurry, a flash of movement on the sofa to her right. She stopped playing at once. "What is it?" she said, turning to the cat. "What's the matter?"

The animal, who a few seconds before had been sleeping peacefully, was now sitting bolt upright on the sofa, very tense, the whole body aquiver, ears up and eyes wide open, staring at the piano.

"Did I frighten you?" she asked gently. "Perhaps you've never heard music before."

No, she told herself. I don't think that's what it is. On second

135

thought, it seemed to her that the cat's attitude was not one of fear. There was no shrinking or backing away. If anything, there was a leaning forward, a kind of eagerness about the creature, and the face —well, there was rather an odd expression on the face, something of a mixture between surprise and shock. Of course, the face of a cat is a small and fairly expressionless thing, but if you watch carefully the eyes and ears working together, and particularly that little area of mobile skin below the ears and slightly to one side, you can occasionally see the reflection of very powerful emotions. Louisa was watching the face closely now, and because she was curious to see what would happen a second time, she reached out her hands to the keyboard and began again to play the Vivaldi.

This time the cat was ready for it, and all that happened to begin with was a small extra tensing of the body. But as the music swelled and quickened into that first exciting rhythm of the introduction to the fugue, a strange look that amounted almost to ecstasy began to settle upon the creature's face. The ears, which up to then had been pricked up straight, were gradually drawn back, the eyelids drooped, the head went over to one side, and at that moment Louisa could have sworn that the animal was actually *appreciating* the work.

What she saw (or thought she saw) was something she had noticed many times on the faces of people listening very closely to a piece of music. When the sound takes complete hold of them and drowns them in itself, a peculiar, intensely ecstatic look comes over them that you can recognize as easily as a smile. So far as Louisa could see, the cat was now wearing almost exactly this kind of look.

Louisa finished the fugue, then played the siciliana, and all the way through she kept watching the cat on the sofa. The final proof for her that the animal was listening came at the end, when the music stopped. It blinked, stirred itself a little, stretched a leg, settled into a more comfortable position, took a quick glance round the room, then looked expectantly in her direction. It was precisely the way a concert-goer reacts when the music momentarily releases him in the pause between two movements of a symphony. The behaviour was so thoroughly human it gave her a queer agitated feeling in the chest.

"You like that?" she asked. "You like Vivaldi?"

The moment she'd spoken, she felt ridiculous, but not—and this to her was a trifle sinister—not quite so ridiculous as she knew she should have felt.

Well, there was nothing for it now except to go straight ahead with the next number on the programme, which was *Carnaval*. As soon as she began to play, the cat again stiffened and sat up straighter; then, as it became slowly and blissfully saturated with the sound, it relapsed into that queer melting mood of ecstasy that seemed to have something to do with drowning and with dreaming. It was really an extravagant sight—quite a comical one, too—to see this silvery cat sitting on the sofa and being carried away like this. And what made it more screwy than ever, Louisa thought, was the fact that this music, which the animal seemed to be enjoying so much, was manifestly too *difficult,* too *classical,* to be appreciated by the majority of humans in the world.

Maybe, she thought, the creature's not really enjoying it at all. Maybe it's a sort of hypnotic reaction, like with snakes. After all, if you can charm a snake with music, then why not a cat? Except that millions of cats hear the stuff every day of their lives, on radio and gramophone and piano, and, as far as she knew, there'd never yet been a case of one behaving like this. This one was acting as though it were following every single note. It was certainly a fantastic thing.

But was it not also a wonderful thing? Indeed it was. In fact, unless she was much mistaken, it was a kind of miracle, one of those animal miracles that happen about once every hundred years.

"I could see you *loved* that one," she said when the piece was over. "Although I'm sorry I didn't play it any too well today. Which did you like best—the Vivaldi or the Schumann?"

The cat made no reply, so Louisa, fearing she might lose the attention of her listener, went straight into the next part of the programme—Liszt's second *Petrarch Sonnet*.

And now an extraordinary thing happened. She hadn't played more than three or four bars when the animal's whiskers began perceptibly to twitch. Slowly it drew itself up to an extra height, laid its head on one side, then on the other, and stared into space with a kind of frowning concentrated look that seemed to say, "What's this? Don't tell me. I know it so well, but just for the moment I don't seem to be able to place it." Louisa was fascinated, and with her little mouth half open and half smiling, she continued to play, waiting to see what on earth was going to happen next.

The cat stood up, walked to one end of the sofa, sat down again, listened some more; then all at once it bounded to the floor and leaped up onto the piano bench beside her. There it sat, listening intently to the lovely sonnet, not dreamily this time, but very erect, the large yellow eyes fixed upon Louisa's fingers.

"Well!" she said as she struck the last chord. "So you came up to sit beside me, did you? You like this better than the sofa? All right, I'll let you stay, but you must keep still and not jump about." She put out a hand and stroked the cat softly along the back, from head to tail. "That was Liszt," she went on. "Mind you, he can sometimes be quite horribly vulgar, but in things like this he's really charming."

She was beginning to enjoy this odd animal pantomime, so she went straight on into the next item on the programme, Schumann's *Kinderscenen*.

She hadn't been playing for more than a minute or two when she realized that the cat had again moved, and was now back in its old place on the sofa. She'd been watching her hands at the time, and presumably that was why she hadn't even noticed its going; all the same, it must have been an extremely swift and silent move. The cat was still staring at her, still apparently attending closely to the music, and yet it seemed to Louisa that there was not now the same rapturous enthusiasm there'd been during the previous piece, the Liszt. In addition, the act of leaving the stool and returning to the sofa appeared in itself to be a mild but positive gesture of disappointment.

"What's the matter?" she asked when it was over. "What's wrong with Schumann? What's so marvellous about Liszt?" The cat looked straight back at her with those yellow eyes that had small jet-black bars lying vertically in their centres.

This, she told herself, is really beginning to get interesting—a trifle spooky, too, when she came to think of it. But one look at the cat sitting there on the sofa, so bright and attentive, so obviously waiting for more music, quickly reassured her.

"All right," she said. "I'll tell you what I'm going to do. I'm going to alter my programme specially for you. You seem to like Liszt so much, I'll give you another."

She hesitated, searching her memory for a good Liszt; then softly she began to play one of the twelve little pieces from *Der Weihnachtsbaum*. She was now watching the cat very closely, and the first thing she noticed was that the whiskers again began to twitch. It jumped down to the carpet, stood still a moment, inclining its head, quivering with excitement, and then, with a slow, silky stride, it walked around the piano, hopped up on the bench, and sat down beside her.

They were in the middle of all this when Edward came in from the garden.

"Edward!" Louisa cried, jumping up. "Oh, Edward, darling! Listen to this! Listen what's happened!"

"What is it now?" he said. "I'd like some tea." He had one of those narrow, sharp-nosed, faintly magenta faces, and the sweat was making it shine as though it were a long wet grape.

"It's the cat!" Louisa cried, pointing to it sitting quietly on the piano bench. "Just *wait* till you hear what's happened!"

"I thought I told you to take it to the police."

"But, Edward, *listen* to me. This is *terribly* exciting. This is a *musical* cat."

"Oh, yes?"

"This cat can appreciate music, and it can understand it too."

"Now stop this nonsense, Louisa, and let's for God's sake have some tea. I'm hot and tired from cutting brambles and building bonfires." He sat down in an armchair, took a cigarette from a box beside him, and lit it with an immense patent lighter that stood near the box.

"What you don't understand," Louisa said, "is that something extremely exciting has been happening here in our own house while you were out, something that may even be . . . well . . . almost momentous."

"I'm quite sure of that."

"Edward, *please!*"

Louisa was standing by the piano, her little pink face pinker than ever, a scarlet rose high up on each cheek. "If you want to know," she said, "I'll tell you what I think."

"I'm listening, dear."

"I think it might be possible that we are at this moment sitting in the presence of—" She stopped, as though suddenly sensing the absurdity of the thought.

"Yes?"

"You may think it silly, Edward, but it's honestly what I think."

"In the presence of who, for heaven's sake?"

"Of Franz Liszt himself!"

Her husband took a long slow pull at his cigarette and blew the smoke up at the ceiling. He had the tight-skinned, concave cheeks of a man who has worn a full set of dentures for many years, and every time he sucked at a cigarette, the cheeks went in even more, and the bones of his face stood out like a skeleton's. "I don't get you," he said.

"Edward, listen to me. From what I've seen this afternoon with my own eyes, it really looks as though this might actually be some sort of a reincarnation."

"You mean this lousy cat?"

"Don't talk like that, dear, please."

"You're not ill, are you, Louisa?"

"I'm perfectly all right, thank you very much. I'm a bit confused—I don't mind admitting it, but who wouldn't be after what's just happened? Edward, I swear to you—"

"What *did* happen, if I may ask?"

Louisa told him, and all the while she was speaking, her husband lay sprawled in the chair with his legs stretched out in front of him, sucking at his cigarette and blowing the smoke up at the ceiling. There was a thin cynical smile on his mouth.

"I don't see anything very unusual about that," he said when it was over. "All it is—it's a trick cat. It's been taught tricks, that's all."

"Don't be so silly, Edward. Every time I play Liszt, he gets all excited and comes running over to sit on the stool beside me. But only for Liszt, and nobody can teach a cat the difference between Liszt and Schumann. You don't even know it yourself. But this one can do it every single time. Quite obscure Liszt, too."

"Twice," the husband said. "He's only done it twice."

"Twice is enough."

"Let's see him do it again. Come on."

"No," Louisa said. "Definitely not. Because if this *is* Liszt, as I believe it is, or anyway the soul of Liszt or whatever it is that comes back, then it's certainly not right or even very kind to put him through a lot of silly undignified tests."

"My dear woman! This is a *cat*—a rather stupid gray cat that nearly got its coat singed by the bonfire this morning in the garden. And anyway, what do you know about reincarnation?"

"If his soul is there, that's enough for me," Louisa said firmly. "That's all that counts."

"Come on, then. Let's see him perform. Let's see him tell the difference between his own stuff and someone else's."

"No, Edward. I've told you before, I refuse to put him through any more silly circus tests. He's had quite enough of that for one day. But I'll tell you what I *will* do. I'll play him a little more of his own music."

"A fat lot that'll prove."

"You watch. And one thing is certain—as soon as he recognizes it, he'll refuse to budge off that bench where he's sitting now."

Louisa went to the music shelf, took down a book of Liszt,

thumbed through it quickly, and chose another of his finer composi-
tions—the B minor Sonata. She had meant to play only the first part
of the work, but once she got started and saw how the cat was sitting
there literally quivering with pleasure and watching her hands with
that rapturous concentrated look, she didn't have the heart to stop.
She played it all the way through. When it was finished, she glanced
up at her husband and smiled. "There you are," she said. "You can't
tell me he wasn't absolutely *loving* it."

"He just likes the noise, that's all."

"He was *loving* it. Weren't you, darling?" she said, lifting the cat in
her arms. "Oh, my goodness, if only he could talk. Just think of it,
dear—he met Beethoven in his youth! He knew Schubert and Men-
delssohn and Schumann and Berlioz and Grieg and Delacroix and
Ingres and Heine and Balzac. And let me see . . . My heavens, he
was Wagner's father-in-law! I'm holding Wagner's father-in-law in my
arms!"

"Louisa!" her husband said sharply, sitting up straight. "Pull yourself together." There was a new edge to his voice now, and he spoke
louder.

Louisa glanced up quickly. "Edward, I do believe you're jealous!"

"Oh, sure, sure I'm jealous—of a lousy gray cat!"

"Then don't be so grumpy and cynical about it all. If you're going
to behave like this, the best thing you can do is to go back to your
gardening and leave the two of us together in peace. That will be best
for all of us, won't it, darling?" she said, addressing the cat, stroking
its head. "And later on this evening, we shall have some more music
together, you and I, some more of your own work. Oh, yes," she said,
kissing the creature several times on the neck, "and we might have a
little Chopin, too. You needn't tell me—I happen to know you adore
Chopin. You used to be great friends with him, didn't you, darling?
As a matter of fact—if I remember rightly—it was in Chopin's apartment that you met the great love of your life, Madame Something-or-
Other. Had three illegitimate children by her, too, didn't you? Yes,
you did, you naughty thing, and don't go trying to deny it. So you

shall have some Chopin," she said, kissing the cat again, "and that'll probably bring back all sorts of lovely memories to you, won't it?"

"Louisa, stop this at once!"

"Oh, don't be so stuffy, Edward."

"You're behaving like a perfect idiot, woman. And anyway, you forget we're going out this evening, to Bill and Betty's for canasta."

"Oh, but I couldn't *possibly* go out now. There's no question of that."

Edward got up slowly from his chair, then bent down and stubbed his cigarette hard into the ashtray. "Tell me something," he said quietly. "You don't really believe this—this twaddle you're talking, do you?"

"But of *course* I do. I don't think there's any question about it now. And, what's more, I consider that it puts a tremendous responsibility upon us, Edward—upon both of us. You as well."

"You know what I think," he said. "I think you ought to see a doctor. And damn quick, too."

With that, he turned and stalked out of the room, through the French windows, back into the garden.

Louisa watched him striding across the lawn toward his bonfire and his brambles, and she waited until he was out of sight before she turned and ran to the front door, still carrying the cat.

Soon she was in the car, driving to town.

She parked in front of the library, locked the cat in the car, hurried up the steps into the building, and headed straight for the reference room. There she began searching the cards for books on two subjects—REINCARNATION and LISZT.

Under REINCARNATION she found something called *Recurring Earth-Lives—How and Why,* by a man called F. Milton Willis, published in 1921. Under LISZT she found two biographical volumes. She took out all three books, returned to the car, and drove home.

Back in the house, she placed the cat on the sofa, sat herself down beside it with her three books, and prepared to do some serious reading. She would begin, she decided, with Mr. F. Milton Willis's work. The volume was thin and a trifle soiled, but it had a good heavy feel to it, and the author's name had an authoritative ring.

The doctrine of reincarnation, she read, states that spiritual souls pass from higher to higher forms of animals. "A man can, for instance, no more be reborn as an animal than an adult can re-become a child."

She read this again. But how did he know? How could he be so sure? He couldn't. No one could possibly be certain about a thing like that. At the same time, the statement took a good deal of the wind out of her sails.

"Around the centre of consciousness of each of us, there are, besides the dense outer body, four other bodies, invisible to the eye of flesh, but perfectly visible to people whose faculties of perception of superphysical things have undergone the requisite development. . . ."

She didn't understand that one at all, but she read on, and soon she came to an interesting passage that told how long a soul usually stayed away from the earth before returning in someone else's body. The time varied according to type, and Mr. Willis gave the following breakdown:

Drunkards and the unemployable	40 / 50	YEARS
Unskilled labourers	60 / 100	"
Skilled workers	100 / 200	"
The bourgeoisie	200 / 300	"
The upper-middle classes	500	"
The highest class of gentleman farmers	600 / 1000	"
Those in the Path of Initiation	1500 / 2000	"

Quickly she referred to one of the other books, to find out how long Liszt had been dead. It said he died in Bayreuth in 1886. That was sixty-seven years ago. Therefore, according to Mr. Willis, he'd have to have been an unskilled labourer to come back so soon. That didn't seem to fit at all. On the other hand, she didn't think much of the author's methods of grading. According to him, "the highest class of gentleman farmer" was just about the most superior being on the earth. Red jackets and stirrup cups and the bloody, sadistic murder of the fox. No, she thought, that isn't right. It was a pleasure to find herself beginning to doubt Mr. Willis.

Later in the book, she came upon a list of some of the more famous reincarnations. Epictetus, she was told, returned to earth as Ralph Waldo Emerson. Cicero came back as Gladstone, Alfred the Great as Queen Victoria, William the Conqueror as Lord Kitchener. Ashoka Vardhana, King of India in 272 B.C., came back as Colonel Henry Steel Olcott, an esteemed American lawyer. Pythagoras returned as Master Koot Hoomi, the gentleman who founded the Theosophical Society with Mme Blavatsky and Colonel H. S. Olcott (the esteemed American lawyer, alias Ashoka Vardhana, King of India). It didn't say who Mme Blavatsky had been. But "Theodore Roosevelt," it said, "has for numbers of incarnations played great parts as a leader of men. . . . From him descended the royal line of ancient Chaldea, he having been, about 30,000 B.C., appointed Governor of Chaldea by the Ego we know as Caesar who was then ruler of Persia. . . . Roosevelt and Caesar have been together time after time as military and administrative leaders; at one time, many thousands of years ago, they were husband and wife. . . ."

That was enough for Louisa. Mr. F. Milton Willis was clearly nothing but a guesser. She was not impressed by his dogmatic assertions. The fellow was probably on the right track, but his pronouncements were extravagant, especially the first one of all, about animals. Soon she hoped to be able to confound the whole Theosophical Society with her proof that man could indeed reappear as a lower animal. Also that he did not have to be an unskilled labourer to come back within a hundred years.

She now turned to one of the Liszt biographies, and she was glancing through it casually when her husband came in again from the garden.

"What are you doing now?" he asked.

"Oh—just checking up a little here and there. Listen, my dear, did you know that Theodore Roosevelt once was Caesar's wife?"

"Louisa," he said, "look—why don't we stop this nonsense? I don't like to see you making a fool of yourself like this. Just give me that goddamn cat and I'll take it to the police station myself."

Louisa didn't seem to hear him. She was staring open-mouthed at a picture of Liszt in the book that lay on her lap. "My God!" she cried. "Edward, look!"

"What?"

"Look! The warts on his face! I forgot all about them! He had these great warts on his face and it was a famous thing. Even his students used to cultivate little tufts of hair on their own faces in the same spots, just to be like him."

"What's that got to do with it?"

"Nothing. I mean not the students. But the warts have."

"Oh, Christ," the man said. "Oh, Christ God Almighty."

"The cat has them, too! Look, I'll show you."

She took the animal onto her lap and began examining its face. "There! There's one! And there's another! Wait a minute! I do believe they're in the same places! Where's that picture?"

It was a famous portrait of the musician in his old age, showing the fine powerful face framed in a mass of long gray hair that covered his ears and came halfway down his neck. On the face itself, each large wart had been faithfully reproduced, and there were five of them in all.

"Now, in the picture there's *one* above the right eyebrow." She looked above the right eyebrow of the cat. "Yes! It's there! In exactly the same place! And another on the left, at the top of the nose. That one's there, too! And one just below it on the cheek. And two fairly close together under the chin on the right side. Edward! Edward! Come and look! They're exactly the same."

"It doesn't prove a thing."

She looked up at her husband who was standing in the centre of the room in his green sweater and khaki slacks, still perspiring freely. "You're scared, aren't you, Edward? Scared of losing your precious dignity and having people think you might be making a fool of yourself just for once."

"I refuse to get hysterical about it, that's all."

Louisa turned back to the book and began reading some more. "This is interesting," she said. "It says here that Liszt loved all of Chopin's works except one—the Scherzo in B flat minor. Apparently he hated that. He called it the 'Governess Scherzo,' and said that it ought to be reserved solely for people in that profession."

"So what?"

"Edward, listen. As you insist on being so horrid about all this, I'll tell you what I'm going to do. I'm going to play this scherzo right now and you can stay here and see what happens."

"And then maybe you will deign to get us some supper."

Louisa got up and took from the shelf a large green volume containing all of Chopin's works. "Here it is. Oh yes, I remember it. It *is* rather awful. Now, listen—or, rather, watch. Watch to see what he does."

She placed the music on the piano and sat down. Her husband remained standing. He had his hands in his pockets and a cigarette in his mouth, and in spite of himself he was watching the cat, which was now dozing on the sofa. When Louisa began to play, the first effect was as dramatic as ever. The animal jumped up as though it had been stung, and it stood motionless for at least a minute, the ears pricked up, the whole body quivering. Then it became restless and began to walk back and forth along the length of the sofa. Finally, it hopped down onto the floor, and with its nose and tail held high in the air, it marched slowly, majestically, from the room.

"There!" Louisa cried, jumping up and running after it. "That does it! That really proves it!" She came back carrying the cat which she put down again on the sofa. Her whole face was shining with excitement now, her fists were clenched white, and the little bun on top of her head was loosening and going over to one side. "What about it, Edward? What d'you think?" She was laughing nervously as she spoke.

"I must say it was quite amusing."

"*Amusing!* My dear Edward, it's the most wonderful thing that's ever happened! Oh, goodness me!" she cried, picking up the cat again and hugging it to her bosom. "isn't it marvellous to think we've got Franz Liszt staying in the house?"

"Now, Louisa. Don't let's get hysterical."

"I can't help it, I simply can't. And to *imagine* that he's actually going to live with us for always!"

"I beg your pardon?"

"Oh, Edward! I can hardly talk from excitement. And d'you know what I'm going to do next? Every musician in the whole world is going to want to meet him, that's a fact, and ask him about the people he knew—about Beethoven and Chopin and Schubert—"

"He can't talk," her husband said.

"Well—all right. But they're going to want to meet him anyway, just to see him and touch him and to play their own music to him, modern music he's never heard before."

"He wasn't that great. Now, if it had been Bach or Beethoven . . ."

"Don't interrupt, Edward, please. So what I'm going to do is to notify all the important living composers everywhere. It's my duty. I'll tell them Liszt is here, and invite them to visit him. And you know what? They'll come flying in from every corner of the earth!"

"To see a gray cat?"

"Darling, it's the same thing. It's *him*. No one cares what he *looks* like. Oh, Edward, it'll be the most exciting thing there ever was!"

"They'll think you're mad."

"You wait and see." She was holding the cat in her arms and petting it tenderly but looking across at her husband, who now walked over to the French windows and stood there staring out into the garden. The evening was beginning, and the lawn was turning slowly from green to black, and in the distance he could see the smoke from his bonfire rising straight up in a white column.

"No," he said, without turning round, "I'm not having it. Not in this house. It'll make us both look perfect fools."

"Edward, what do you mean?"

"Just what I say. I absolutely refuse to have you stirring up a lot of publicity about a foolish thing like this. You happen to have found a trick cat. O.K.—that's fine. Keep it, if it pleases you. I don't mind. But I don't wish you to go any further than that. Do you understand me, Louisa?"

"Further than what?"

"I don't want to hear any more of this crazy talk. You're acting like a lunatic."

Louisa put the cat slowly down on the sofa. Then slowly she raised herself to her full small height and took one pace forward. "*Damn* you, Edward!" she shouted, stamping her foot. "For the first time in our lives something really exciting comes along and you're scared to death of having anything to do with it because someone may laugh at you! That's right, isn't it? You can't deny it, can you?"

"Louisa," her husband said. "That's quite enough of that. Pull yourself together now and stop this at once." He walked over and took a cigarette from the box on the table, then lit it with the enormous patent lighter. His wife stood watching him, and now the tears were beginning to trickle out of the inside corners of her eyes, making two little shiny rivers where they ran through the powder on her cheeks.

"We've been having too many of these scenes just lately, Louisa," he was saying. "No no, don't interrupt. Listen to me. I make full allowance for the fact that this may be an awkward time of life for you, and that—"

"Oh, my God! You idiot! You pompous idiot! Can't you see that this is different, this is—this is something miraculous? Can't you see *that?*"

At that point, he came across the room and took her firmly by the shoulders. He had the freshly lit cigarette between his lips, and she could see faint contours on his skin where the heavy perspiration had dried in patches. "Listen," he said. "I'm hungry. I've given up my golf and I've been working all day in the garden, and I'm tired and hungry and I want some supper. So do you. Off you go now to the kitchen and get us both something good to eat."

Louisa stepped back and put both hands to her mouth. "My heavens!" she cried. "I forgot all about it. He must be absolutely famished. Except for some milk, I haven't given him a thing to eat since he arrived."

"Who?"

"Why, *him,* of course. I must go at once and cook something really special. I wish I knew what his favourite dishes used to be. What do you think he would like best, Edward?"

"*Goddamn* it, Louisa!"

"Now, Edward, please. I'm going to handle this *my* way just for once. You stay here," she said, bending down and touching the cat gently with her fingers. "I won't be long."

Louisa went into the kitchen and stood for a moment, wondering what special dish she might prepare. How about a soufflé? A nice cheese soufflé? Yes, that would be rather special. Of course, Edward didn't much care for them, but that couldn't be helped.

She was only a fair cook, and she couldn't be sure of always having a soufflé come out well, but she took extra trouble this time and waited a long while to make certain the oven had heated fully to the correct temperature. While the soufflé was baking and she was searching around for something to go with it, it occurred to her that Liszt had probably never in his life tasted either avocado pears or grapefruit, so she decided to give him both of them at once in a salad. It would be fun to watch his reaction. It really would.

When it was all ready, she put it on a tray and carried it into the living-room. At the exact moment she entered, she saw her husband coming in through the French windows from the garden.

"Here's his supper," she said, putting it on the table and turning toward the sofa. "Where is he?"

Her husband closed the garden door behind him and walked across the room to get himself a cigarette.

"Edward, where is he?"

"Who?"

"You know who."

"Ah, yes. Yes, that's right. Well—I'll tell you." He was bending forward to light the cigarette, and his hands were cupped around the enormous patent lighter. He glanced up and saw Louisa looking at him—at his shoes and the bottoms of his khaki slacks, which were damp from walking in long grass.

"I just went out to see how the bonfire was going," he said.

Her eyes travelled slowly upward and rested on his hands.

"It's still burning fine," he went on. "I think it'll keep going all night."

But the way she was staring made him uncomfortable.

"What is it?" he said, lowering the lighter. Then he looked down and noticed for the first time the long thin scratch that ran diagonally clear across the back of one hand, from the knuckle to the wrist.

"Edward!"

"Yes," he said, "I know. Those brambles are terrible. They tear you to pieces. Now, just a minute, Louisa. What's the matter?"

"Edward!"

"Oh, for God's sake, woman, sit down and keep calm. There's nothing to get worked up about. Louisa! Louisa, *sit down!"*

The Cat in the Attic

VALERIE MARTIN

Why, on the eve of his sixtieth birthday, was Mr.
William Bucks, owner and president of Bucks' In-
ternational, rushing down his own staircase on the
arm of his employee, Chester Melville? And why
was Mrs. Bucks, the entrepreneur's young and
beautiful wife, standing above them on the land-

ing, screaming her contempt at the spectacle of her husband and her lover in full retreat? And why, especially why, did Mr. Chester Melville turn to his mistress and, in a voice trembling with rage, cry out, "You killed that cat yourself, Sylvia, as surely as if you had strangled him with your own hands."

This story is difficult to tell; it has so little of what one might call "sensibility" in it. But it is possible to experience a certain morbid sort of epiphany by the prolonged contemplation of the inadequate gestures others make at love, and, in fact, such an epiphany has of late been proved a fit subject for a tale. Chester Melville's failure to love was matched, was eclipsed, was finally rendered inconsequential, by the calculated coldness of the woman he failed to love, though at the moment we first see them here, this observation would have been small comfort to Chester. He understood, at last, that there was something in Sylvia Bucks that no man could love, something not right; I hesitate to say "evil," but perverse, organically amiss. He had felt something for her, nonetheless. Pity, at first, and a devilish curiosity. She had inspired in him a spirit of fierce possession, and he was touched to the heart by the smoothness of her skin and the soft anxious cries she uttered in her search for the orgasm she could never find, no not, she had confided, since the day of her marriage.

Her husband, Mr. William Bucks, or Billy, as his intimates called him, was an unprepossessing man, tall, balding, his large features crowded in the center of his face anxiously, as if they intended to make a break for freedom. He had an eager, friendly, almost doglike manner that made you forget, when you spoke to him, that he was worth a fortune. His software company was one of the quiet superpowers of the computer industry. He had created it himself, by the power of his formidable will. His natural business acumen was extraordinary and no doubt accounted for some of his success, but it was his will that Chester noticed, even in their first interview. Billy Bucks liked Chester on sight and wanted him as an employee. He persuaded him to leave his secure, uninteresting niche at IBM to join in Billy Bucks' personal adventure.

Before Chester attended his first dinner party at the Bucks' home, he made subtle inquiries among his fellow workers as to what he might expect. He was told that the food would be bad, the drinks first-rate and plentiful, that his employer would be gracious, and his wife unpleasant. She was twenty years younger than her husband, and their marriage, which had survived the pitiful storms of only one short year, was not a pleasure to watch. Mr. Bucks, he was told, adored his wife and would neither say nor hear a word against her. Mrs. Bucks was flamboyantly rude to her husband, and (this last was confided to him by a nervous young man who appeared miserable at finding himself in the possession of such damaging information) she was hopelessly addicted to cocaine.

Chester went to the party with only mild trepidation. He did not expect to have his own fate altered by passing an evening in the same room with Sylvia Bucks. He considered himself invulnerable to attacks of lust, for he had recently recovered from a long love affair in which he had been driven to the limits of his resources by a selfish, obstinate woman who had made him swear more than once that he would not love her. She had destroyed some small desperate part of his natural self-consciousness, so that he thought he deserved a better fate than loving her would ever bring him. There are disasters in love that serve finally to increase one's own self-esteem; this failure was of that order. But Chester was bitter, overconfident, and unaware that his senses were wide open. Mrs. Bucks seemed to look directly into this odd mixture of indifference and vulnerability in the first moment they met. Superficially she was gay, charming; her voice was a little husky. She was, perhaps, too solicitous, but her eyes couldn't keep up the pretense. Like her husband, she was tall; her skin and eyes were as pale as her hair, so that she gave an impression of fading into the very light she seemed to emanate. Chester saw that she was sad, and a glance at his employer, who stood effusing cheerfully at her side, told him why. Though it had been very high, she had had her price, and it was her peculiar tragedy to be, while not sufficiently intelligent to follow the simple and honest dictates of her conscience, not stupid enough to be unaware of the moral implications of her choice. It was not until much later that he understood this and realized that the eloquent and pleading looks she directed at him several times on that first evening were not, as he thought, intended to evoke some response, but were meant to express her awareness of the acute ironies that constituted her situation.

The servants operated as slightly inferior guests in the Bucks' household and by the time they bothered themselves to get dinner on the table, the party was too raucous to care. It was just as well, for the hostess, who had disappeared into the bedroom at several points and whose teeth were chattering audibly from cocaine, could not decide where everyone should sit, though she was unshakable in her conviction that this choice was hers to make. The food, when at last the guests seated themselves before it, was cold and tasteless. The chef, Chester observed, specialized in a sauce created from ground chalk and cheddar cheese that congealed upon meat and vegetable alike. Mrs. Bucks paddled her fork contentedly in this mess. He watched her closely and observed that she never actually brought a bite to her lips. When dinner was over, the party adjourned to the living room for more alcohol. Mrs. Bucks disappeared again into her bedroom.

Why did Chester follow her?

He didn't actually follow her. The bathroom door was near her bedroom door, and after he had availed himself of the former, he found himself pausing outside the latter. How long did he pause? It was not a very long time, but as it was unnecessary to pause at all, it was clearly longer than he should have. After a moment the door opened and Mrs. Bucks stood facing him.

"Mrs. Bucks," he said.

She sank against the door frame. "You scared me to death, Mr. Melville."

"I wish you'd call me Chet," he replied.

She looked up at him, but her eyes hardly focused. She was wearing a strapless top, and from the smooth skin of her shoulders the scent of the perfume she wore rose and overpowered the air. It was a wonder to him that a woman of such wealth would choose such an oppressive scent; it didn't smell expensive. Perhaps it was some unwanted memory of another woman, a woman one would expect to wear too much cheap perfume, that caused Chester to move a little closer. Mrs. Bucks continued her unsuccessful effort to see him. He leaned over her, brought his lips to her shoulder, and left there several soft impressions. She did not resist, or even speak, and for a moment he was terrified that she would push him away, screaming for her husband, his employer. Instead she sighed and said his name, "Mr. Melville," very softly, nor did he correct her again.

"May I call you?" he asked as she turned away from him and took a few wobbly steps toward the dining room. "Yes," she replied, without looking back. "I wish you would."

So, because of a momentary lapse in his usually sound judgment, Chester Melville entered into a clandestine affair with his employer's wife. He knew she would be a difficult woman, and that he would not be able to trust her for a moment. He knew as well that she would never be content with him, for she was committed to her need, not for love, but for some distraction from what must have been a dreadfully empty and insensitive consciousness. But it was partly this insensitivity that attracted Chester, for it made him want to give her a good shaking. He was also, after that first awkward kiss in the hall, mesmerized by her physical presence. She had a feline quality about her, especially in the way she moved, that made him feel as one does when watching a cat, that the cool saunter strings the beast together somehow, that it is the sister to the spring.

Chester was gratified to find that Sylvia had no desire to speak ill of her husband. In fact, she rarely mentioned him. There was, however, someone who competed with Chester for his mistress's affections. Though Sylvia had not been wealthy long, she had adopted the absurd custom many wealthy people have of making a great fuss about small matters. The smaller they were, the more they might appear as vital cogs in the great machine of her life. One of these manias was her cat, Gino, who was a constant consideration in all her plans. It was as if, should she disappear in the next moment, there wouldn't be enough servants left behind to care for his needs or understand his temperament. In her imagination Gino was always longing for her company, always disappointed, even disapproving, when he got it.

One evening, while Billy Bucks was inspecting a new plant in Colorado, Chester Melville sat on an uncomfortable bar stool at the Bucks' establishment, drinking a glass of white wine and talking affably with his cantankerous mistress. Gino appeared suddenly in the doorway, as if to present himself for inspection. Sylvia squealed at the sight of him, pushed roughly past Chester, and scooped the cat up into her arms, repeating his name in a sensuous voice she reserved for him alone. Chester noticed that he was very large for a cat, and that his shoulders had the meatiness of an athlete's. He allowed himself to be squeezed and fussed over, turning his strong body slowly, sinuously, against his mistress's straining, perfumed bosom, but he kept his cold green eyes on Chester.

He seemed to size up the competition. "So you're here too," his eyes informed Chester. He had a wonderful deep frown, as if nothing could be more distasteful than what he contemplated. When he was released and set upon the counter, he walked quickly to Chester and, standing before him, considered his face, feature by feature.

"Oh, he's looking at you," Sylvia cried.

Chester was not moved to respond, and Gino, for his part, did not so much as turn an ear in her direction. After a few moments he strode away, not toward his anxious mistress, who stretched out her arms invitingly, but to the end of the counter, where he stopped, looked over his shoulder, and cast Chester one more penetrating, almost friendly look before he leaped soundlessly to the floor.

"That's an interesting cat you have," Chester observed.

"Oh, Gino," Sylvia replied. "Gino is wonderful. Gino is my love."

Chester was to see Gino many times. Each time he was so impressed with the animal, with his cool manner and athletic beauty, that he found himself looking at other cats only to see how poorly they compared with Gino. But he was to remember him always as he was that last afternoon, a few months after their first encounter, stretched out on Sylvia's bed, one heavy paw resting on a silken negligee, his long tail moving listlessly back and forth across the arm of a sweater. The bed was strewn with Sylvia's clothes; a suitcase lay open, half packed, at the foot; and Sylvia herself stood, half clad, nearby. She was fumbling helplessly with a silver cocaine vial, a gift from her husband, but she could scarcely see it through her tears. Chester stood leaning against the dresser. "It's not going to do you any good to run away if you take two bags of cocaine with you," he was saying. "You need to think things through, you need to be alone, and you need to leave the coke behind."

"I need to get away from you," she said. "Not cocaine."

"Sylvia." He sighed.

The vial gave way and she tapped a thin line of the white powder across her forearm.

"Sylvia," he said again. "I love you."

At this moment Gino stood up and began to stretch his back legs. Sylvia gathered him up. "No one loves me but Gino," she crooned to the indifferent animal. "Gino's going with me. I promised him a yard, I always promised him a yard, and now he'll have one."

The "yard" was, in fact, one thousand acres of Virginia pine forest. Sylvia was running away, but her destination was her husband's summer place, a building designed to house nine or ten male aristocrats intent on a return to nature. It looked rough, but it wasn't. There were servants, a wine cellar, a kitchen created to serve banquets. Here Sylvia proposed to spend a week alone, because, as she told her sympathetic spouse, the chatter and confusion of city life were wearing her down. She told Chester Melville that on her return she would give him the answer to his proposal that she leave her husband. At that moment in the bedroom, she determined to take Gino with her, nor could she be dissuaded from this resolution by any appeal, not about the impracticality of the plan or the unnecessary strain to the animal's health. No, Gino must go, and so he went. He was tranquilized, shoved into a box, and loaded into the airplane with Mrs. Bucks' suitcases. One can only imagine the horrors of the three hours spent in the howling blackness of the airplane, the strange ride along the conveyor belts to his impatient mistress, who pulled him out of the box at once and, cooing and chattering, carried him to the car. When they arrived at the estate, Gino was given an enormous meal, which he could scarcely eat, and then Sylvia carried him to the back terrace, overlooking a wilderness of extraordinary beauty, and set him free. "Here's your yard," she said.

In the week that followed, Gino took advantage of the outdoors, but Sylvia did not. She moved about restlessly from room to room, annoying whomever she encountered. She made a particular enemy of Tom Mann, the caretaker of the estate. Most of the year he lived alone on the property; he had a small cottage a hundred yards from the house, and he exhibited the silent humorlessness that comes of too much solitude. He loved the property and probably knew it better than its owner ever would. Sylvia's unexpected presence was an annoyance to him, and he couldn't disguise his personal distaste for her. She made the great mistake of offering him some cocaine, and the expression on his face as he declined to join her told her clearly what he thought of her.

She was miserable, but she tried to amuse herself. She made desperate late-night phone calls. She forced the cook to prepare elaborate meals she didn't eat. She played rock records loud enough to be heard on the terrace, where she danced by herself, or with Gino in her arms, until she collapsed in tears of frustration. She took three or four baths a day, watched whatever was on television, and tried, without success, to read a book about a woman who, like herself, was torn between her rich husband and her lover. At the end of a week, she had decided only that she must have a change. She packed her bags and inspected Gino's traveling box. An hour before she was to leave, she went to the back door and called her beloved pet.

But he didn't respond. She called and called, and she made the cook call. Then she enlisted Tom Mann in the search, and together they scoured the house and the grounds, but the cat was not to be found. At last she was forced to go without him. He would show up for dinner, they all agreed, and he could be sent on alone the next day. So she went to the airport, anxious but not hysterical. The hysteria started that night, when Tom Mann called to say Gino had not shown up for supper.

Sylvia's first response was to inform Tom Mann that he was fired, an action that brought down on her, for the first time in their marriage, the clear disapproval of her husband. "The man has worked for me for twenty years," he told her petulantly. "He's completely trustworthy and he can't be replaced."

"He finds Gino, he goes, or I go," she responded. "It's that simple."

But it wasn't that simple. Billy Bucks was forced to call his employee and apologize for his wife's behavior. "She's not herself," he explained, though he had begun to suspect the unhappy truth, which was that Sylvia was, at last, entirely herself. "She's so fond of that cat," he concluded limply. Tom Mann, who knew his own worth, told his employer that he would continue in his post on the condition that he be spared any future communication with Mrs. Bucks. Billy, humiliated and chagrined, agreed.

The staff at the estate was instructed to make the search for Gino their first priority. Two days after Sylvia's departure, the big house was searched, but since Gino was not found and no one was staying in it, Tom Mann closed it up, as was his custom, and retired to his own cottage. He was of the opinion that Gino had taken to the woods, and the only consolation he could offer his employer was the probability that, as the animal had not turned up dead, he might yet be alive.

Sylvia spent the next three weeks in a constant state of panic, and she poured out her bitterness upon the two men who, in her myopic view, were the authors of her woe. Chester Melville knew what Billy Bucks suffered, and though he could not openly sympathize with him, he found himself curiously drawn to his employer. The two men worked closely, like men under fire, bound together by the camaraderie of terror. Every evening Billy called Tom Mann and received his monosyllabic report while his wife stood nearby, her eyes filled with bitter tears, her cocaine vial clenched in her angry fist.

Then Gino was found. Tom Mann was bothered by a leak in his roof, and a cursory inspection revealed that a large section needed to be reshingled. He remembered that there were a number of shingles in the attic of the house, though how they had arrived there he didn't know. He walked hurriedly through the cold empty rooms, hardly looking about him, for there was nothing indoors that he really cared for. Up the stairs he climbed, his heavy steps echoing hollowly in the still, cool air. When he opened the attic door, the sick, sweet smell of death rushed over him, chilling him like a blast of cold air, and he remembered, all at once and clearly, that just three weeks ago he had come up here to store an awning he'd taken down for the winter, that he'd left the door open for a while, and now he knew that Gino, whose emaciated corpse lay before him, the death-frozen jaws coated with the plaster he'd chewed out of the wall in his futile struggle for life, Gino must have come in without his knowledge. Tom Mann was not a man easily moved, but the pitiful condition of the once power-ful animal brought a low moan to his lips.

Gino was buried within the hour. The caretaker chose a spot near his own house, at the foot of a weeping willow tree he himself had planted twenty years earlier. He marked the grave with a flat stone to keep the body from being disinterred by passing animals. When this was done he phoned his employer and told him of Gino's fate.

Chester Melville was sitting in Billy Bucks' office when the call came through. He knew the substance of the message at once, simply by observing the sudden pallor of Bucks' complexion and the feeble-ness with which he concluded the call. "I'll tell Mrs. Bucks at once," he said. "I appreciate your call, Tom." He placed the receiver carefully into its cradle and rubbed his eyes with the heels of his hands.

"Gino's dead," Chester said.

Billy lowered his hands slowly and stared at his employee. He had heard everything in those two words, and he knew, though he had never suspected it for a moment, that he was addressing his wife's lover. The two men looked at each other disconsolately. "I can't tell her over the phone," Billy said at last. "I'll have to go home. Will you come with me?"

"Sure," Chester said, "if you think it will help."

"I think it will help me," Billy replied.

So the two men left the safety of their office building and trudged wearily through the snowy streets to Bucks' palatial flat. Sylvia was drinking coffee and perusing a magazine when they came in, and the sight of their grim faces so unnerved her that she let the magazine slip to the floor.

"Tom Mann called," Billy said. "I'm afraid it's bad news."

The scene that followed went on for a long time. Gino, who had been in reality a hearty, handsome, greedy, and independent beast, who had probably not spent one moment of his intensely feline life longing for anything that might come to him in human form, who had tolerated his mistress as cats do, was now resurrected as the only real love Sylvia had ever known. In the midst of her furious accusations, Chester realized that he had been willing to put his happiness, his job, and his entire future on the line for a woman who, because she knew herself so well, could only scorn any man who was mad enough to love her. He also observed that Billy Bucks knew this as well, but had married her anyway. As the two men beat their retreat down the stairway, Chester, overcome by his sense of his own foolishness, shouted back to her, "You killed that cat yourself, Sylvia, as surely as if you had strangled him with your own hands."

When they were gone, Sylvia smashed her husband's heirloom crystal, but that, she thought, could be replaced. She took a large knife from the kitchen and slashed a small Corot landscape, a particular favorite of her husband's, until it hung from the frame in strips. Then she went to the bedroom and ripped his down pillow until the feathers rose about her like a snowstorm. All she could hear was her lover's parting remark. She began to stab and stab her marriage bed itself, calling out to Gino as she drove the knife deeper and deeper, but nothing she could do would bring poor Gino back to her, nothing she could ever do.

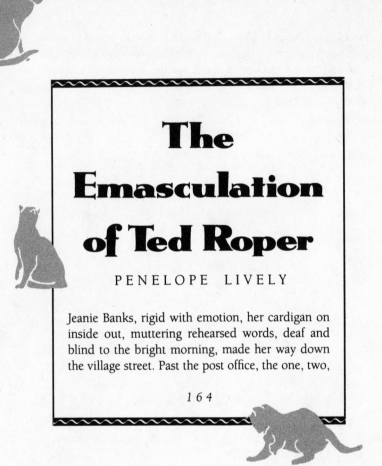

The Emasculation of Ted Roper

PENELOPE LIVELY

Jeanie Banks, rigid with emotion, her cardigan on
inside out, muttering rehearsed words, deaf and
blind to the bright morning, made her way down
the village street. Past the post office, the one, two,

164

three, four cottages, past the pub, Mrs. Halliday's, the garage, the one, two, three new bungalows, the Lathams', Cardwell's yard. She stopped outside Roper's, simmering, reached out to open the gate, lost her nerve, plunged on down to the lamp-post where the village ended, yanked up her resolution again, turned, aimed back, fumbled furious with the latch on Roper's gate.

The front garden a disgrace, as always, strewn with empty oil cans, plastic sacks, rusting iron objects, the excretions of Roper's hand-to-mouth odd-jobbing dealing-in-this-and-that existence. Furtive, unreliable, transacting in dirty pound notes, dodging his taxes without a doubt, down the pub every evening. Dirty beggar, cocky as a robin, sixty if he was a day.

Feeling swelled to a crescendo, and courage with it; she hammered on the door. Then again. And again. No answer. He'd be there all right, he'd be there, nine-thirty in the morning, since when did Roper go out and do a decent day's work? She shoved at the side gate.

He was round the back, fiddling about with a great pile of timber, good timber at that, planks all sizes and shapes and how did he come by it one would like to know? A whole lot of tyres stacked up in one corner, stuff spilling out of the shed, filth everywhere.

"Hello, Jeanie."

She halted, breathless now. Words fail you, they do really. They leave you huffing and puffing, at a disadvantage, seeing suddenly the run in your tights, seeing yourself reflected in the eyes of others—angry, dumpy, middle-aged widow, just Jeanie Banks. In the beady spicy nasty eyes of Ted Roper, stood there in the middle of his junk like a little farmyard cock. A randy strutting bantam cock.

"What can I do for you, Jeanie?"

She said, "It's not what you can do it's what's been done, that's what's the trouble."

"Trouble?" He took out tobacco, a grubby roll of cigarette papers. "Trouble?" His dirty fingers, rolling, tapping, his tongue flickering over the paper.

"My Elsa's expecting."

"Expecting?" he said. "Oh—expecting." A thin smile now, a thin complacent smile. Grinning away at it, the old bastard, pleased as punch. As if it were something to be proud of, as if it did him credit even, stood there with his thumbs stuck in his trouser pockets like those boys in western films. Some boy—Ted Roper. Boy my foot, sixty if he's anything.

"That's what I said. Expecting."

He put the cigarette in his mouth; thin smoke fumed into the village sunshine. Not trousers, she saw now. Jeans—jeans just like young men wear, slumped down on his thin hips, the zip sliding a bit, a fullness you couldn't miss below, stuck out too the way he stood, legs apart, thumbs in pockets.

"Well," he said, "I s'pose that'd be in the nature of things. She's getting a big girl now."

Grinning away there, wiry and perky and as blatant as you like. She felt her outrage surge.

"It's rape," she said. "That's what it damn well is. A little creature like that, a little young thing. Bloody rape!" The colour rushed to her cheeks; she didn't use language like that, not she, never.

"Now, now, Jeanie. Who's to know who gave who the come on."

She exploded. She shouted, "You take that blasted cat to the vet, Ted Roper, and get it seen to, the rest of us have just about had enough, there's kittens from one end of the village to the other and my Elsa was nothing but a kitten herself." She swung round and stormed to the gate. When she looked back he was still standing there, the cigarette laid on his lower lip, his jeans fraying at the crotch, the grin still on his face. "Or you'll find it done for you one of these days!"

All the way back to the cottage her heart thumped. It didn't do you any good, getting yourself into a state like that, it took it out of you, she'd be jumpy all day now. Back home in the kitchen, she made herself a cup of tea. The old cat, the mother, was sprawled in the patch of sun on the mat and Elsa was in the armchair. When Jeanie came in she jumped down and shimmied across the floor: pretty, graceful, kittenish and distinctly lumpy, no doubt about it, that unmistakable pear-shape forming at the end of her. And Jeanie, subsiding into the chair, drinking her tea, eyed her and eyed the old cat, not so old come to that, five or was it six, and as she did so a whole further implication leaped into the mind—why hadn't she thought of it before, how disgusting, if it were people you could have them slapped in prison for that.

"Fact is," said her sister Pauline, that afternoon, "there's probably hardly a one in the village isn't his. Being the only tom round about, bar him on Lay's farm and he's beyond it if you ask me. So you let Ted Roper have it? Good on you, Jeanie."

Jeanie, cooler now, calmer, righteous and ever so slightly heroic, went over it all again, word for word: I said, he said, so I said, and him as cocky as you like.

"He's a cocky little so-and-so," said Pauline. "Always was. I bet he got the wind up a bit though, Jeanie, with you bawling him out, you're bigger than he is." She chuckled. "Hey—d'you remember the time they got him in the girls' playground and Marge ripped the belt off his trousers so he had to hold 'em up all afternoon? God—laugh . . . ! Donkey's years ago . . .

"Funny, isn't it," Pauline went on, "there's four of us in the village still as were at school with Ted. You, me, Nellie Baker, Marge. Randy he was too. Remember?"

"Funny he's never married," said Jeanie.

Pauline snorted. "Out for what he can get, that one. Not that he'd get it that often, is my guess."

"Can't stand the man. Never could. 'Nother cup? Anyway, what I say is, he ought to be made to have something done about that cat. It's shocking. Shocking."

In the basket chair the old cat raucously purred; Elsa, in a patch of sunlight, lay flirting with a length of string.

"Sick of drowning kittens, I am," said Jeanie. "I'll have to get her seen to after, like I did the old cat. Shame."

"Shame."

The two women contemplated the cats.

"I mean, we wouldn't care for it, if it were you or me."

"Too right."

"Not," said Pauline, "at that time of life. That's a young creature, that is, she's got a right to, well, a right to things."

"Hysterectomy's the nearest, if it were a person."

"That's it, Jeanie. And you'd not hear of that if it were a girl. Another matter if it's in middle life."

"That cat of Roper's," said Jeanie, "must be going on twelve or thirteen."

Later, as she walked to the shop, Roper's pick-up passed her, loaded with slabs of timber, belting too fast down the village street, Roper at the wheel, one arm on the sill, a young lad beside him, one of the several who hung around him. She saw Roper see her, turn to the boy, say something, the two of them roar grinning across the cross-roads. She stood still, seething.

"Cardwell's boy, weren't that?" said Marge Tranter, stopping also. "With Roper."

"I daresay. What they see in that old devil . . ."

"Men's talk. Dirty stories, that stuff. Norman says he doesn't half go on in the pub, Roper. He's not a one for that kind of thing, Norman isn't. He says Roper holds out hours on end sometimes, sat there in the corner with his mates. Showing off, you know."

"Fat lot he's got to show off about," said Jeanie. "A little runt, he is. Always was. I was saying to Pauline, remember the time you . . ."

"Pulled his trousers down, wasn't it? Don't remind me of that, Jeanie, I'll die . . ."

"Not pulled them down, it wasn't. Took his belt. Anyway, Marge, I gave him an earful this morning, I'll tell you that. That cat of his has been at my Elsa. I went straight down there and I said look here, Ted Roper . . ."

A quarter of a mile away Ted Roper's pick-up, timber dancing in the back, dodged in and out of the traffic on the A34, overtaking at sixty, cutting in, proving itself. Cardwell's boy and Roper, blank-faced, bejeaned, the cowboys of the shires, rode the Oxfordshire landscape.

In the village and beyond, Roper's cat—thin, rangy, one-eyed, and fray-eared—went about his business.

And, according to the scheme of things, the ripe apples dropped from the trees, the *jeunesse dorée* of the area switched their allegiance from the Unicorn to the Hand and Shears, taking with them the chattering din of un-muffled exhausts and the reek of high-octane fuel, the road flooded at the railway bridge, and Jeanie's Elsa swelled soft and sagging, like the bag of a vacuum cleaner.

"Several at least," said Jeanie. "Half a dozen, if you ask me. Poor little thing, it's diabolical."

"There's a side to men," said Pauline, "that's to my mind just not like us and that's the only way you can put it. And I don't mean sex, nothing wrong with that when the time and the place are right. I mean . . ."

"It's a kind of men rather, I'd say. Harry's not that way, nor was my Jim. I mean, there's men that are normal men in the proper way but don't go on about it."

"In Italy," said Pauline, "all the men are the other kind. All of them. From the word go. Young boys and all. They wear bathing costumes cut deliberately so you can see everything they've got."

"Which is something you can take as read, in a normal man. It doesn't need shouting about."

"Exactly. If I were you, Jeanie, I'd give that cat a drop of cod liver oil in her milk. She's going to need all her strength."

Perhaps also according to the scheme of things, Ted Roper's pick-up, a while later, was involved in circumstances never clarified in a crash with Nellie Baker's Escort at the village cross-roads. No blood was shed and the pick-up, already so battle-scarred as to be impervious, lived to fight again, but the Escort was crippled and Nellie Baker too shaken and confused to be able to sort out exactly what had happened except for a strong conviction that aggression had been involved. At the Women's Institute committee meeting she held forth.

"He came out of nowhere and was into me before I knew what was happening. I was either stopped or the next best thing, that I'll swear."

"What does he say?"

"Whatever he's saying's being said to the police. He took off, without a word hardly. It was Mr. Latham ran me home and got the garage for me. I've told them my side of it, at the police station. It's up to them now."

"The police," said Jeanie Banks, "have been down at Ted Roper's more than once. Asking about this and that. They could do some asking just now, the stuff he's got there and one wonders where it all comes from."

"The police," said Pauline, "are men. Remember Ted Roper at school, Nellie? Jeanie and I were talking about that only the other day —how we used to take him down a peg or two."

And, according to a scheme of things or not, no case was brought against Ted Roper for careless driving or dangerous driving or aggression or anything at all. Those who failed to see how that pick-up could have passed its MOT continued to speculate; Ted Roper's insurance company ignored letters from Nellie Baker's insurance company.

Jeanie's Elsa had five kittens, two of them stillborn.

Ted Roper, wiry and self-assured as his cat, continued to cruise the local roads, to make his corner of the pub an area of masculine assertion as impenetrable and complacent as the Athenaeum. From it came gusts of hoarse laughter and anecdotes which were not quite audible, bar certain key words.

It may have been the stillborn kittens that did it, as much as anything, those damp limp little rags of flesh. Or the sight of the emptied Elsa, restored to a former litheness but subtly altered, wise beyond her years. Or months.

Jeanie, tight-lipped, visited Marge to borrow her cat basket.

"You'll take her to be done, then?"

"Have to, won't I? Or it'll be the same thing over again."

"Shame."

"Just what Pauline said."

Marge, lining the cat basket with a piece of old blanket, paused. "It's like with people. Always taken for granted it must be the woman. Pills, messing about with your insides . . ." She swung the door of the basket shut and tested the catch. "There's an alternative, Jeanie. Thought of that?"

"What do you think I was down Ted Roper's for, that time?"

"And much joy you got out of it. No, what I'm thinking of is we see to it ourselves."

The two women stared at each other over the cat basket. Marge, slowly, even rather terribly, smiled. "I wouldn't mind, I wouldn't half mind, giving Ted Roper his come uppance."

In a village, people come and go all day. Women, in particular— to and from the school, the shop, the bus stop, each other's houses. The little group of Jeanie, Pauline, Marge, and Nellie Baker, moving in a leisurely but somehow intent way around the place that afternoon, glancing over garden walls and up the sides of cottages, was in no way exceptional. Nor, unless the observer were of a peculiarly enquiring turn of mind, was the fact that they carried, between them, a cat basket, a pair of thick leather gardening gloves, and a half a pound of cod wrapped in newspaper.

Presently, the cat basket now evidently heavy and bouncing a little from side to side, they emerged somewhat breathless from the field behind the pub and made their way rather hurriedly to the garage of Nellie Baker's house, where an old Morris replaced the deceased Escort. The Morris drove away in the direction of Chipping Norton passing, incidentally, the very school playground where once, donkey's years ago, four outraged and contemptuous schoolgirls had a go at the arrogance of masculine elitism.

In a village, also, change is more quickly observed than you might think. Even change so apparently insignificant as the girth of a cat. In this case, it was habits as much as girth. A cat that has previously roamed and made the night hideous, and which takes instead to roosting, eyes closed and paws folded, in the sun on the tops of walls, idling away the time, will be noticed.

And the more so when the change eerily extends to the cat's owner.

At first it was just the paunch jutting below the sagging belt of Ted Roper's jeans. Then, balancing the paunch, came a fullness to the face, a thickening of the stubbly cheeks, a definite double chin. "Put on a bit, haven't you, Ted?" people said. "Have to cut down on the beer, eh?" And Ted would wryly grin, without the perky come-back that might have been expected. With physical expansion went a curious decline of those charismatic qualities: the entourage of youths dropped off. Some nights, Ted sat alone in the pub, staring into his glass with the ruminative and comfortably washed-up look of his seniors. A series of mishaps befell the pick-up: punctures stranding Ted on remote roads, a catastrophic fuel leak, a shattered windscreen. It was driven, presently, in a more sedate way; it no longer rode or cruised but rattled and pottered.

It was as though the old assertive stringy cocky Ted were devoured and enveloped, week after week, by this flabby amiable lethargic newcomer. The jeans gave way to a pair of baggy brown cords. He began to leave his corner of the public bar and join the central group around the fireplace; there, the talk was of onions, the ills of the nation, weather, and fuel prices.

And, in the village or outside his own gate, meeting Nellie Baker, say, or Marge or Pauline or Jeanie Banks, he would pass the time of day, initiate a bit of chat, offer small gifts by way of surplus timber, useful lino offcuts, the odd serviceable tyre.

"Poor old so-and-so," said Pauline. "They're easily taken down, aren't they? That's what comes of depending on the one thing. You can almost feel sorry for them."

Affection

CORNELIA NIXON

As a baby, my father claimed, I was a cat. I don't know what hard evidence he had, but at one time I played along with him to the extent that, when introduced to strangers, I fell on all fours (I'm not proud of this) and said meow. Later I acquired every known cat toy: stuffed cats, china cats, cat

173

books and posters, a cat pin, cat erasers, a cat lunchbox and tooth-brush, a blue felt circle skirt with appliquéd cats, and sheets with kittens printed out of all spatial sense. I also lobbied without cease for an actual cat, wearing my mother down until she suddenly agreed, apparently out of mere exhaustion, the year my third older brother joined the others in their loud and hungry teens.

Seymour spent his kittenhood in my room. My brothers were forbidden to approach my door, and I tried to stand guard around the clock, until my parents made clear that I would still have to go to school. When the bell rang in the afternoon, I was on my bike before most kids cleared their seats, racing home in panic, trying to beat my brothers. Soaked and panting, I didn't slow down until I made it to my door. But then I stopped, opened it a quarter inch at a time, in case he was behind it.

Sometimes he was hard to find in that wilderness of false cats. He'd be caught halfway up a curtain, big-eyed, mewing for help, or curled in a perfect circle on the bed, surrounded by the rubble of his day, torn magazines and lamps overturned on their shades. Impossi-bly small and light, at first he was no more than the idea of a cat, a loud purr in electrified fur, a dandelion with claws. Ten times a night I'd wake up afraid of crushing him, feel for him on the bed, and he'd start to purr. Once after dinner he was gone. I panicked, accused my brothers, forced a search of their rooms. Hours later, exhausted from weeping, I opened my bottom drawer and found him curled peace-fully on a sweater.

When my brothers were not at home, I introduced him to the backyard. Staggering across the lawn, he recoiled at grass blades, arched his back and hissed, or charged suddenly at nothing, scaring himself. For a long time he was relieved to go back to my room, purred loudly when he found the soft warm bed.

Then one day I saw him leap to the top of my bookshelf from a standing start. When he jumped off the bed, you could hear the thud from anywhere in the house. He sat for hours on the windowsill, lashing his tail as he stared outside, or into the closet with his ears perked, listening for mice. He was a big gray cat with a white belly and paws, like a fish designed to blend both with dark water, seen from above, and light sky, seen from below. The two-tone scheme extended to his nose tip and paw pads, which were half-black, half-pink. In his green eyes the black could be round and shiny as an eightball, tight as a stitch, or like a watermelon seed. When I opened the door of my room, he loped across the floor, making a break for the outside.

"*Yaaaaaaaaaa,*" my brother Charlie said, eyes crossed, tongue flapping while he jerked his body like Frankenstein, the first time he met Seymour on the lawn. Dropping to a crouch, Seymour eyed him, and fled sideways, out of the yard.

"What's a cat's favorite drink?" my father said and took the library card out of my book. Removing the pencil stub from behind his ear, he started doodling on it.

I didn't bother to answer. I was only out there on the deck, sitting in smoke and fumes from the barbecue, because inside Hank was torturing his saxophone, and a cat's favorite drink was a very old joke. If I gave the obligatory response (mice tea) there would be no stopping him. What do cats put in their lemonade? he'd want to know. What's their favorite dessert, their favorite weather, their favorite exercise? Where do they take their children on Saturday afternoons?

Solemnly he slid the card back into the pocket at the back of my book. Paying no attention, I secretly worked it out of the pocket to where I could see it. Drawn on the card was a ladybug meeting a Sugar Smack. They were the same shape, ovals, with spots. The ladybug had legs, the Sugar Smack didn't, but the resemblance was close enough. The ladybug gazed at the Sugar Smack, and a heart rose from it. The caption read "Love Stinks."

"So," my father said. "How's your cat?"

"Fine." As far as I knew, that was the case: he stopped by every day to eat, usually in the early morning before the boys were up. He no longer came home at night, and I had no idea where he was spending his time, but he seemed fine.

A boy yelled in the backyard, and David's hightops squeaked across the kitchen floor.

"You weenie!" he yelled, banged open the sliding screen and pounded down the steps to the yard.

"David!" my mother yelled from inside.

David dashed up the steps, giggling, ran into the kitchen, slammed the glass door, and locked it behind him. Charlie ran up panting, put his hands on either side of the door, and lifted it off its runner. He propped it against the wall and plunged inside.

Sounds of shouting, feet pounding the stairs. "Did not," we heard, and "Don't you ever." Doors slammed upstairs.

"I thought I saw him the other day," my father said, starting a doodle on a paper napkin. "Across the street. At the new people's house." He paused thoughtfully. "I could be wrong, but it looked as if he was pawing their front door."

"Oh, sure," I said. By no outward sign did I reveal that I had been shot through the chest with a hot dart. "He gets around. Cats have resources, you know—they're not like dogs. They make their own friends. It's an honor when they come around."

He raised his eyebrows without looking up from his drawing. "An honor. Yes, that's certainly true."

Inside, voices started again, my mother's and Charlie's. The front door banged open, and Charlie ran by in the driveway above us, headed for the garage. My mother was close behind him, his motorcycle helmet dangling by its strap from one hand, her arm straight down at her side. He pushed his motor scooter up the driveway to the street. She followed with quick graceful steps, shoulders back, head up, like a diver approaching the end of the board. He reached the sidewalk, paused to throw one leg over the bike. She swung the helmet over her head, straight-armed, slammed it into the concrete. It bounced with a sharp crack.

"That's what's going to happen to you, young man!" she said.

Charlie buzzed away without looking back. My mother walked quickly back to the house, head up, shoulders back. The helmet rolled over twice and stopped, teetering in the driveway. My father stood up and followed her inside.

The new people's house was just across the street, but it was hard to see from where I was. Like most of Berkeley, our street was on a steep hill. We lived on the downhill side, hanging out into air, and the top of our house was only about as high as the sidewalk on the other side. To see anything I had to cross the street, climb up into their yard.

Their red convertible was in the driveway, and most of the windows in the house were open, with curtains blowing out. I didn't have a plan. With anyone else I could have gone over to play with the kids, but the new people didn't have any, not even a dog or a cat. I considered them the most uninteresting family I had ever seen.

At the top of their driveway was a gate, but when I got to it I heard voices in back. Veering away, I crossed the front yard, searching the shrubbery as if for a lost ball. On the other side of the house was a new redwood fence, still smooth and faintly red, not gray and prickling with splinters like ours. Standing on a large ornamental rock, I could see over the top.

The last people that lived here had kids, and in those days the backyard was a dead lawn/dog bathroom, equipped with hula hoops, polo sticks and mole mounds, a tetherball pole in a bare circle. Now suddenly it looked like a picture in a magazine: a new deck, a tall hedge, massed flowers in orderly bloom.

The hedge blocked my view of the lawn, but through it I thought I saw a flash of gray and white. My heart started to pound. I hauled myself to the top of the fence, trying to see better, then dropped to the ground on the other side. I didn't care—let them catch me. I had to find out.

One corner of the deck met the house not far from where I landed. Maybe I could make it, maybe not. The deck was only about four feet off the ground, with azalea bushes planted around the edge. Getting through the azaleas without rustling would be tricky, and when I got there, I tried not to touch them at all.

The people were on the other side of the deck, talking and laughing loudly, and they didn't seem to notice me. Underneath, there was a hint of musty cat box, but the old dead grass was still in place, so I didn't have to crawl in the dirt. From there, I could see the whole yard.

It was Seymour, all right. Across the soft new lawn, in the shade of the hedge, he lay on his side like a lion, looking up, exposing his white underchin and belly fur. His head tracked a bug, he snapped at it, missed. Lowering his chin, he surveyed the yard.

I lifted my head above the azaleas, and he gave me a long intense look. Blinking, he turned away, licked his shoulder with sudden energy.

"So there we were, still in the cab, for God's sake—" a man's voice said, up on the deck. A woman gave a high quick laugh, and another man said "Oliver" in a warning tone.

I could see slices of them through the slats—it was the new people and another man. The new people were both tall and blond, the woman in a white sundress and the man in seersucker pants. The other man, the one named Oliver, was dark and had on white trousers. Through the slats, they all moved in flickers, like an old movie, up there in the yellow light.

"No, you have to believe me, I swear it," the man named Oliver said, and the new people laughed uneasily.

"If it's anything like the last one—" the man who lived there said.

"No, no, it isn't, believe me. So there we were, we'd hardly said eleven words to each other, and there we were—" He went on to describe several forms of torture I'd heard about on the playground, emphasizing how much the woman in the taxi wanted him to do those things to her. The new people's laughter got higher and thinner, with gaspy pauses, until his voice ran down. Nobody said anything for about a minute.

"Oh, kiss and tell, Oliver," the woman said.

Both men laughed quickly, as if surprised. She stood up, walked across the deck and down the steps to the lawn.

My heart was thudding so hard I could see it in my eyes as I shrank down behind the azaleas. Chin pressed to the dirt, I watched her cross the grass. Her dress was printed with red roses, her blond hair in a ponytail down her bare back.

I couldn't see her face, but I knew she was pretty, because I'd seen her once close up. I was passing their house on the sidewalk when she came running down the driveway, chasing the blond man, who was trying to get away from her, striding toward the red convertible, parked at the curb. She was inches behind him, half-laughing the way you do when you're playing a joke on someone, or chasing them and about to make the tackle. She had on jeans, a man's shirt, and loafers, hair pinned to the back of her head, while the man was wearing a suit and tie.

"Just tell me who she is," the woman said. "Just tell me how you met her!"

"No," the man said, opening the door of the convertible.

"Just tell me how you met her! Is she one of your patients? No, you have to—"

The man shrugged her off, closed the door, but she reached in and grabbed the shoulder of his jacket.

"Just tell me how you met her!" She was yelling but still keeping her voice down, quieter than it would have been, and half-laughing.

The man started to drive, the woman running along beside him, still gripping his jacket. As they passed me, he looked right at me and blushed. I was surprised to see that close up his face wasn't handsome at all, almost ugly as he grimaced at me. He drove off, breaking her hold on his jacket. She turned quickly, without glancing at me, and went into the house. I hadn't seen them again until now.

Seymour came out from under the hedge as she approached it and gave a pitiful meow, opening his pink mouth wide as a baby bird's. She stooped to pet his head, and he flopped onto his side, offering her the soft white fur of his belly. She stroked from his throat all down his underside, and he stretched his front legs forward and his back legs back, arching his neck. The tip of his tail started curling and uncurling. In a minute he would take hold of her wrist with his claws and teeth, play-biting, getting harder if she didn't stop.

When he grabbed for her, she laughed and scooped him up. She held him just right, his back supported on her arm, as she walked over to a bench under a low tree. She sat down, stroking his whole body, and he sprawled across her lap, kneading her with his paws. Taking a bit of dress between his teeth, he closed his eyes and kneaded her intently, a spot of cat drool spreading on her dress.

"Look at that, Oliver," the man who lived there said. "Isn't that an inspiring sight? Woman and child—it doesn't get better than that. You're looking at the goddamn inspiration of all great art. Don't you think it's an inspiring sight?"

"Woman and child," Oliver said, and ice clicked against glass.

I expected to be caught every second, but they walked right over me to dinner without seeming to notice. The next afternoon, no cars were in their drive, and I went over again, to see if he was still there. Nobody asked where I was going. These days, my mother said "What!" if I went near her, and once I saw her sitting with her elbows on the kitchen table and her hands over her eyes. She considered "Playing" enough of an answer for where I'd been.

Seymour was there, all right, making free with the house and grounds. I stayed back near the fence, where he wouldn't have to notice me, and he didn't seem to mind. He dozed on the deck, rolled in the flower beds, strolled along the top of the high fence. From an oak tree he leapt to an open window on the second floor. With one quick ripple of his back, he slipped under the sash, calling out a meow. After a while he came out, sat on the sill in the sunshine, and licked his paws. Jumping to the tree, he shinnied headfirst down the trunk. Pausing at the bottom, he blinked, stalked toward the hedge.

Hunched in the shadow, he waited, looking up. The hedge was in bloom, studded with red flowers, and a hummingbird hovered along it, sticking its needle-nose in every one. Flat along the ground, he crept up fast and launched himself into the air, all twenty claws aimed for the bird. The hummer darted just out of reach, chittering angrily, while he crashed down through the hedge, holding his position as if frozen, claws clutching air, and landed in a heap. Standing up, he shook himself and stalked away, thrusting his shoulders forward like a panther.

A car door slammed in the driveway. Seymour crouched under the hedge, and I made it under the deck one heartbeat before she came through the gate with bags of groceries.

Walking back and forth to the car, she paid no attention to Seymour. The third time she passed him with her arms full, he charged out, grabbed her calf with his paws, eyes black and round as if he had scared himself. She laughed, and he darted back under the hedge, drawing himself up fearfully. But when she went by again, out he charged, gave her a two-pawed bat and dashed back in. She crouched down, tried to tickle his chest.

"Am I dead yet?" she said. "Did you get me yet?"

He pulled back, staring at her hand as if she had a knife in it. Suddenly he pounced, grabbed her wrist, pawed her hand with his back feet, and leapt back under the hedge. He pounced, pawed, retreated, pounced, until she got tired of him.

She didn't let on that she saw me that day, but I was sure somehow she knew. When I saw her in the street, I rode away furiously on my bike, or went wild and yelled something stupid at the nearest kid. Even so, I couldn't stop. Whenever she drove away, I had to sneak up, climb the fence, snoop around their yard, whether he was there or not. If I tried to do something else, I had eyes in the back of my head, pointed at their house, until I forgot everything and raced toward it.

One evening, late that summer, I was near the front door when someone rang the bell. I opened it, not thinking much about it. My heart nearly stopped. It was the woman, and she had Seymour in her arms.

Someone grabbed my shoulders from behind. "Don't you ever open the door at night," my mother said and yanked me back into the hall.

I sat on the bottom stair, where I could watch through the banister. From the living room came boys' voices yelling, "Come on! Come on!" and a distant crowd roar.

"I'm sorry to bother you," the woman said hurriedly, adding her name and where she lived. She was dressed up, in high heels and a linen suit, her hair in a French roll.

"Yes, and you have our Seymour." My mother did not say her own name in return, and she reached for him, pulled him away from the woman before she started to hand him over. The woman looked startled and put her arms out, one second after it was no longer necessary to do so.

"Someone told us he might be your cat," she said in a flat, even voice, as if she were reading it. "And we were wondering—he seems to have some sort of abscess, on his paw—"

I stood up, tried to see around my mother's arm. She took hold of one paw, and he tensed, flipped over, climbed her shoulder. Behind us, my father came up to watch.

"The left rear," the woman said quietly. "We didn't like to take him to the vet without—"

"Thank you very much," my mother said and turned away. She started to close the door.

My father caught it over her head, and she ducked under his arm, carried Seymour to the kitchen. My father stepped into the doorway. He was so tall he had to stoop slightly to get under the frame. "So. Let's see. What shall we call it? Catnapping?"

The woman looked up at him and blushed. "We didn't exactly— I'm sorry, but you see, we didn't think he had a home." She examined my father. "He seemed to be throwing himself on our mercy."

"We thought someone must be keeping him in."

She gasped slightly. "You make it sound like we use little chains and handcuffs. It isn't exactly like that—he begs to come in. We've tried ignoring him, but he wakes us up at night, and he won't take no for an answer. Once he pawed our door for an hour and a half." She held up her hands, palms out, and paddled the air, as if begging to come into our house. "We thought he was hurting his paws."

My father took a step out onto the stoop, lowering his voice. "Alienation of affection, then. You've heard of that? You can sue the corespondent for it, in a divorce."

The woman smiled slightly, looking up at him. "Without of course being at fault oneself."

My father stepped all the way out, pulled the door closed behind him.

"Jesus, don't they know how to get rid of a cat?" Charlie said, laughing, in the kitchen. "There's nothing to it. You just go *yaaaaaaaaaaa.*"

In a flurry of white paws, Seymour shot around the corner. Casting me a black-eyed look, he put his nose to the bottom corner of the front door, batting with a soft paw.

"In a minute," I whispered, picking him up. "You can go back out in a minute. If you go right now they'll catch you, because they're both still out there."

I carried him up the stairs, and he watched nervously over my shoulder. At the window on the landing I showed him: my father and the woman were standing on the sidewalk in the fading light, blocking escape by the front door.

"Cat patrol," my father said a couple of weeks later, throwing down his napkin after dinner. "I'll just go get him, so Jane can have him for a while before she goes to bed."

I followed him out into the hall. "That's all right, Dad. Don't worry about it."

Seymour had been jailed in my room the whole time he was on antibiotics, on orders from the vet. He spent it sitting on the window sill, lashing his tail, or meowing at the door to get out.

"It's okay. I'll see him in the morning, when he comes over for breakfast."

"He's your cat."

"I know. But don't worry about it."

He put his hand on the doorknob. "You stay here. I'll be right back."

An hour later he brought Seymour up to my room and shut him in. Heading straight for the closet, he sat in the dark, wide-awake, eyes reflecting light when I opened the door to see how he was. I waited until the house settled down for the night, then let him out by the front door.

Soon we had the routine down: carried back after dinner, he went to sleep on my bed, until some dark and silent hour. Sleep was something he understood, and he woke me up as gently as it can be done: nose close to my face, he purred, or gave a soft chirp. Together we padded down the stairs in the dark, his fur brushing my leg under the gown. I only had to open the door a few inches, and in the fainter dark outside I watched him snake around it. Trotting away up the walk, his ears were alert, fur fluffed with excitement.

"But he comes back every night," the woman said, laughing on our front stoop with my father. It was the first rain of the year, and he and I were out there watching it when she drove up. She waved to him as she got out and called something I couldn't hear, then came across the street, smiling in a tan raincoat. Her hair was getting wet, and my father told her to come up under the eaves.

She smoothed her wet hair back out of her face. "He comes in the window about three o'clock in the morning and jumps on the bed, cheerful as can be. So glad to see us, and would we mind getting up and fixing him a snack? If we close the window, he sits in the tree and yowls, about five feet from our ears. That's a sound that could go through concrete. Cat from Mars, Sam calls him."

My father turned elaborately to look at me, but I was backing through the doorway, into the hall, out of reach.

Down in the darkroom my mother called his name. Soon she came up the stairs, two at a time. Headed for the study, she noticed the open front door and stood still, watching.

"Maybe if he had a way to get back in here at night," the woman said. "Maybe he comes here first, and can't—"

"A cat door," my father said. "We thought of that. But—the raccoons. Have you got raccoons? We've got raccoons, and skunks, and once in a while even—"

My mother stepped out the door. "You have to go get Hank this minute." She took hold of his arm, tried to pull him into the house.

"Okay," my father said, and she let go, stepped inside.

"But if he tries to come in here at night, and he doesn't have a way—" the woman said.

My mother stepped out, took hold of him again. "Right now. You can do this later." She was much smaller than my father but pulling so hard he had to step inside. She closed the door behind him.

"Jesus, Ella," he said.

She yanked his raincoat out of the closet and shoved it at him. "You said you were going twenty minutes ago! What does it take!"

From the window on the landing I watched the woman cross the street, flipping her collar up. When she reached their driveway, Seymour dashed out from under a bush and loped ahead of her with long easy strides. He got to their front door first.

My father ran across the street, holding his raincoat. He caught her arm just before she opened her door. Seymour pressed up against it, arching his wet back, meowing at them until they went inside.

My father didn't say anything to me, but he stopped going over after dinner to bring him back. It wasn't long after that before Seymour stopped coming over for breakfast. I was the only one who noticed at first, and I had time to figure out what had happened before anyone else.

Across the street, the woman's car was gone, and the windows in the house stayed closed for days. The man drove up at night in the red convertible and away again in the morning, always alone. After he left, I'd walk right up their driveway, open the gate and sit on the deck. Along the hedge, hummingbirds sipped the lowest flowers undisturbed.

Once I went over after a hard rain. Fat white clouds were sailing away, over the hill, leaving the sky empty and blue. Steam rose from their deck, shining in the sun. I lay down on the boards and rested my nose in a crack. The wood was warm and smelled of sweet spice, with gusts of cat box underneath. I thought about Seymour as a kitten, how he slept on my chest and mewed, heartbroken, if I put him down. Later he was so tender with my sleep.

Maybe I should have known. One summer morning as I walked by, pretending not to stare at the new people's house, I noticed something on their front stoop. Their curtains were still closed, and I went up quickly to see what it was.

Side by side on the doormat lay two dead mice. They were perfectly lined up, with each other and the door, stiff tails pointing the same direction. One's head was thrown back in agony, exposing a triangle of tiny teeth. The other lay on its side, glassy black eye open, paws curled. Both gray coats were matted with cat spit, but they were almost unmarked, a tiny drop of clotted blood on one, and nothing eaten.

Gardeners policed the new people's yard, packed redwood chips around authorized plants and left no leafy corners along the fence. The lower slopes of our yard, on the other hand, were a tangle of blackberry vines, nasturtiums and bindweed, home to salamanders, mice, and even snakes. After catching the first mouse, he must have carried it in his mouth while he climbed the steps to our deck, passed our kitchen door, climbed our driveway, passed our front door, crossed the street, climbed their steep yard, and placed it carefully on their doorstep. Then he had to go back down and do it all again.

I imagined Seymour on a beach. The woman held him on her lap, both of them in sunglasses. A cool drink was on the table and a bowl of cat food underneath. By now she must know what kind he liked: land animals were only worth a sniff, the dried stuff not even that. Most fish he would eat, though for some kinds he stayed on his feet, drawn up away from the bowl. Only for tuna would he sit all the way down.

Maybe there would be fishing boats pulled up to that beach. Maybe Seymour would meet them, leap aboard, rub the fishermen's legs. Maybe the boats caught tuna. Maybe Seymour stowed away on a tuna boat, lived with the fishermen, left that woman on the beach.

One night my father did not come home for dinner. My mother didn't say anything about it, and she didn't yell at Charlie or say much of anything else. She waited dinner until we were all half-starved, but none of us talked about it. We just lay around the living room, playing games and pretending to read, and even the boys were quiet. It got to be seven, seven-thirty, quarter to eight.

"Come to the table," my mother said.

"Aw, let's wait for Dad," Charlie said, but she was spooning food onto plates.

She left his place set, pans covered on the stove, and sat in the kitchen, writing Christmas cards, near the wall phone. It rang twice, both for Charlie. It was almost ten before she remembered to send me to bed.

The house was dark and still, and I must have been asleep a long time, when I suddenly woke up. I always slept with my door closed, but now it was open. A soft heavy object hit the floor. The door closed silently, the latch clicked and footsteps went down the stairs.

In the faint light from the window, I saw a shape like a shepherd's crook go by the bottom of my bed. A moment later it came back, twitching slightly. I thought I heard purring. Suddenly the bed compressed, and heavy soft feet stepped on my shins. Even in the dark I could see his white mask. He was purring louder than I'd ever heard, and kneading the bed at every step, claws catching in the comforter.

"No," I said. "You don't live here anymore."

The purr was deafening when he reached my face. He brought his nose close, touched my forehead, gave me one quick lick, as if to see who I was by taste.

"Forget it, Seymour. You made your choice."

Circling around by my chest, he kneaded the covers just right. He curled down against my side but kept his head up, ears pointed toward the door. Purring thrummed through the bed.

"Okay, look. It's late. But only for tonight. No promises. Understood?"

He didn't turn down that diesel purr one bit.

Felis catus

GINA BERRIAULT

When they awoke their first Sunday morning in
their very own house and slippered across their
sea-grass rugs to eat their breakfast on orange pottery, with the soft blue bay and the dark green
trees and the houses farther down the hill all blur-
ring together beyond the bamboo screen like an

189

impressionist painting; when now, after four years of apartments, they were settled at last, they talked together about finding a cat to live with them.

Mayda, chatting with the girls under her supervision at the telephone company, let it be known that she and her husband were in the market for a cat. After all, it was one of those homey, prosaic subjects that she was always looking for to maintain common ground with the girls, ground fast slipping away; for they were resentful, she knew, that her interest in the arts had procured for her, tall and homely as she was, a tall and cultured husband, and they suspected that he had sat down and planned with her, like a military strategy, a cultural life together that ruled out her fraternizing with the girls. But when one of the switchboard operators showed up in the morning with a gray-striped kitten in a shoebox, Mayda regretted having touched upon the subject. Unable to refuse it, she grew quite attached to it in the first week, for it did have a great deal of whirligig energy that one would never have anticipated from the *paleness* of it. Afraid, however, that their friends would think them indiscriminate, they drove up one weekend to a Siamese cattery near Guerneville and returned home with two seal points, adolescent brothers. Charles, watching the lean, beige brothers slide under the furniture and step high and bouncy upon the piles of cushions, said, with satisfaction, that they were losing no time in making themselves at home. But Mayda was a bit intimidated by the formality of their purebred bodies and went into the kitchen to get down on her knees and try to coax the gray one out from behind the stove.

In his browsing in the secondhand bookstore a few blocks from the London Men's Shop where he clerked, Charles came upon many a reference to cats in books that, topically, were in no way concerned with them, and he began to buy books that he would not otherwise have cared for—a Victorian era travel book on Italy because of some wonderful passages about the cats of the Forum Romanum, and a biography of a famous English surgeon because of the photograph it contained of that bearded gentleman with a huge tabby cat upon his lap. For the first time he was made aware of the predilection for cat companionship on the part of many renowned persons who had made their contribution to society in every field from entomology to religion, and the resemblance he bore to those persons in that respect increased his dissatisfaction with his job and reinforced the tantalizing idea, always in the back of his mind, of trying his hand as a novelist or an art critic. In Chinatown one afternoon he spied, in a window crowded with kimonos and carven teak boxes, a hanging glass shelf holding an assortment of tiny, painted ivory cats that overcame his antipathy for bric-a-brac, and he bought one—a yellow-striped tomcat on its haunches, a dazed, lopsided, pugilist's look in its face no bigger than an orange seed; and at the Museum of Modern Art one evening they bought two Fujita prints of feathery young cats, and Charles matted them on black silk.

When they had been living in their new home for six weeks, Mayda found time to reply to her sister Martha in Sacramento. She told how happy they were to be breathing what Charles called "green air," tending their garden and their cats, and told what a relief it was to drive out of San Francisco every evening, what a pleasure to drive back across the bridge to their charming hill town of Sausalito and contemplate across the bay the city where they worked all day; and she commented wryly that Charles's mother, in leaving him a sum of money large enough to make a down payment on a home, had finally contributed something to his comfort. Martha replied promptly, as usual, glad to hear they'd found a house "all cut out for them," and in uncomplaining comparison told them about the disrepair into which her own house had fallen. She'd taken a lot of time off from her work, she said, because she hadn't been feeling well for the past few months, and the money she had set aside for repainting and reroofing was used up. *Oh, well,* she wrote, *it doesn't look any worse than its neighbors, and that goes for me, too.* One of the items in her letter was about a college girl who had taken a room for a while in Martha's house. The girl had followed a state assemblyman to the capital, Martha wrote, but just before the assembly recessed the fellow must have broken everything off, because the girl cried all night long, so loudly that the children kept waking up and whimpering. *She was a strange girl,* Martha wrote. *The next morning she said she was going to Mexico and that we could have her cat. Then she packed her clothes and drove off in her foreign car. Peter tells me it's a Jaguar. You can have the cat if you want it. It's a handsome sir. She told me once what kind it was, something rare, but I can't remember. The kids always forget to feed the poor thing. Usually, I wouldn't mind seeing to it myself, but my chores seem to be piling up on me lately. Did I tell you I was down to 109 pounds?*

The following Sunday they drove up to Sacramento, leaving early in the morning and knocking at Martha's door at ten o'clock with tender surprise smiles on their faces. Martha, in a faded housecoat, was eating breakfast alone, the children having run out to play. She pushed aside the dishes and served the visitors coffee, repeating what a nice surprise this was—How long was it now since they'd visited last? A year come August? They said they had come because they were alarmed by her letter, and Mayda, pulling up a chair to the table, thought her sister's appearance gave them ample reason for a visit. And when Martha, her eyes rickracked by teary eyelashes, reached spontaneously across the table to pinch Mayda's cheek, to plump it out as one fondly does a baby's cheek, crying, "Maydine, you rascal!" utterly forgetting that her younger sister's every letter in the past four years had been signed by the new name Charles had chosen, even the displeasure Mayda felt over the discarded name was quashed by the pleasure the ailing woman took in saying it.

"Charlie," Martha said, when they had hardly lifted their heads from the first sip of coffee, "why don't you poke your head out the back door and call the kids? Just call loud, they're somewhere around."

He got up reluctantly. "Don't they come home for lunch?"

"But they've just had their breakfast," Martha said.

"Well, why can't we wait?" he asked querulously. "We're not leaving so soon." And he sat down again, frowning.

"Never mind!" Martha cried hastily. "If you'd rather just sit and talk that suits me fine. Once they come, we won't get a chance." Then with sincere concern she asked him, "And how is your asthma these days?"

He shrugged, surprised that he should be questioned about something that had not bothered him for almost four years, not since the early months of his marriage. But Mayda, perceiving that her sister was tracing his petulance to some lurking illness, cried with obliging cheer, "Oh, he's much better now. But we keep our fingers crossed."

The sisters took up again, as if their letters had been actual conversation between them, the news about themselves, and, stimulated by this sitting face to face with each other, they recalled their parents, recalled their friends, and soon Martha was recalling again that rainy day, six years ago, when her husband, a taxi driver, had lost his life in the streets not far from the capitol building. They had heard it all before, but, to Mayda, it was more tragic now than it had been even the first telling, because of Martha's thinly striving voice. And so she was dismayed when she felt Charles's hand upon her knee, and, glancing at him, saw that he was sorry about his disagreeableness. His hand was reminding her that he was always upset to the point of surliness by the suffering of others, by their physical deterioration. It was because he wanted so badly to express his sympathy and yet sympathy seemed so inadequate. *Darling, you know how it is with me?* his hand said. She did not respond. All this under the table apologetics was an affront to Martha, who could see that he was not listening. But when, a few moments later, a cat brushed against Mayda's ankle and was gone, her own eyes lost their listening, she moved her feet searchingly.

The cat leaped onto Martha's lap and from there onto the table, where it stepped knowingly among the dishes in the manner of a prince slumming along narrow, winding streets. Martha feigned a sideways brush-off, rising from her chair and crying, "Did you ever?" But Mayda reached for it, lifting it from the table and setting it down on the floor, not attempting to take it into her lap, for it had the inviolable weight of someone else's property. It belonged to the girl in the Jaguar.

"What kind is it, Charles?" she asked eagerly.

"Peter knows," Martha said. "He remembers brand names and things like that."

The cat elongated itself toward a cracked white saucer under the high-legged stove, found the food there not to its liking, and sat down with its back to everyone, musing in the heat that still remained in the region of the stove. Never had they seen a cat with fur of rich brown, and the combination of topaz eyes and glossy brown coat and long, thin legs was the height of elegance.

"How old is Peter now?" Charles asked, lifting the percolator from the hot pad and shaking it.

"Here, here, I'll make some more!" Martha cried, reaching for it.

"No, no! I can do it!" Charles rose, glancing up at her cupboards. "Just tell me where you keep the coffee."

"Peter's nine now," Martha said, while Charles was filling the percolator, jostling the aluminum parts around and making himself at home. "And Norine's seven. Could I borrow a cigarette, I wonder?" she asked, leaning back and smiling a pale flirtation. "I'm not supposed to smoke, and so I've got none in the house. Peter caught me smoking once and he really had a tantrum. He's terribly worried about me, that boy. They're both as nice as pie, it almost makes me cry. They're so tidy! But you know the way kids tidy things up? Everything looks kind of odd, like there were little shrines all over the house." She leaned forward to accept a light from Mayda, holding the cigarette clumsily to her lips. "They're angels, but I'm not going to brag about it."

"Suppose we call them?" Charles suggested, setting the percolator on the flame.

"Wait'll I finish this cigarette," Martha begged, and Charles put his hands into his pockets and strolled about the kitchen, gazing at trinkets and potted cactus plants on the windowsill, and he leaned against the door frame, gazing out through the screen and remarking about the huge fig tree in the yard. Then he was purposefully gone, and they heard him calling. A few minutes later he held open the screen door, and under his arm, as under a bridge, the children entered, and he came in after them, smiling.

"God, they've grown!" he exclaimed. "They didn't even remember me, they couldn't imagine who'd be calling them. You should have seen their faces when they came through the hedge."

"It's Uncle Charles," Martha assured them. "Don't you remember Uncle Charles and Aunt Maydine? How can you forget so fast?" she cried. "He got afraid of a man's voice," Martha explained. "He thought something was wrong, he thought it was the doctor calling."

"I'm sorry, old man," Charles said, and Mayda shot an unbelieving glance at him, never having heard him use that term before. The triteness of it must surely, she thought, go against his grain. "I didn't mean to frighten you, but your mother was telling me all about you. About how tall you are and what an enormous memory you've got. She said you know what kind of cat the girl left."

"That cat? It's a Burmese," the boy said, not yet able to look Charles in the face. Beckoned by the sound of the children, the cat, having wandered up the hallway, now wandered in again and poked its muzzle at the food in the saucer, this time eating it reluctantly, its tongue smacking a delicate distaste. Ambivalently, its slender body seemed to be backing away from the saucer, for its front legs were in a low crouch while its hind legs were up straight and shifting weight, as if the cat were unwilling to admit to spectators that it was finally accepting this gray, crumbly food.

"Its name is Rangoon," the boy said, warming up. "She called it Baby all the time, and I asked her if that was his real name, and she said it was Rangoon. I thought that was a funny name. I'd never call a pet of mine a goon like that. I didn't say that, I just asked her why she wanted to call it Rangoon, and she said Rangoon was the name of a river in Burma and Burma was where the cat's ancestors came from. She said a guy who loved cats, he was in Burma when a war broke out, and he escaped with the cats with bullets flying all around him and brought them to the United States." He had slid from his mother's knee and was standing in a pose of jaunty authority, his ankles crossed and his hand on his hip.

"I should think she'd want to keep it," Charles asked, "with all the history it's got."

"She was spoiled," Martha said.

"She cried all night," Norine told the visitors.

"That's because she was spoiled," Martha explained to the child, who was leaning against her. "Norine feels sorry for her, but I say it did her good to lose that man. You couldn't contradict that girl one little bit."

All at once Peter and the cat were wrestling amicably in the hall doorway, and no one knew whether Peter had intercepted the cat's flight or whether the cat had seen Peter moving toward it. After a moment the cat hung down from Peter's hands, the long body tentatively resigned, the tail swishing.

"If you want that cat you take him," Martha said to Charles.

A grimace wrinkled up Peter's face. It wasn't a prelude to a weeping kind of frown but had a senility to it. He looked, Mayda thought, like an old man attempting to read fine print.

"But you never take care of it," his mother reminded him.

"Never mind," Charles said. "We've got our hands full of cats."

"But this is a rare one," Martha insisted above the sudden rattling of the percolator as it shot up jets of steam.

Charles fumbled the pot to a cold grill, all the comfortable agility gone from his movements. "Rare, smare," he said. "At night all cats are gray."

"Take it! I don't want it!" Peter had dropped the cat and turned his back on them, and was standing rigid, shouting up the hallway as if to someone at the other end.

Not at all dismayed by her brother's shouting, the girl said recitingly, "Once we had a cat that ate clam chowder. But this one can't keep nothing on its stomach. Peter told me he'd rather have a tabby cat because they can eat anything. He said he didn't think this one could even eat a mouse. He said he wasn't sure it was a real cat."

"Well then, it's good riddance, isn't it, Peter?" his mother asked, and chidingly, "People like you more when you're generous."

The jagged atmosphere was soon dispelled by Charles's blandishments and by the children's desire to be swayed by him. After a while the girl took his hand and led him into the backyard to see her vegetable garden. Peter followed them out, and towed Charles back through the kitchen to examine the boy's collection of rocks and gems, and, emerging from the children's bedroom, Charles informed Mayda that Peter had given him the name of a firm that sold Arizona rubies for 25 cents a packet. At lunch they sat crowded around the kitchen table, and Charles made jokes, the halting way he had of relating an anecdote or posing a riddle interfering to no degree with the children's appreciation of him, expressed in whoops and sputtering attempts to tell as funny a joke. In the midst of it, Mayda wondered with an unpleasant shock if he appeared naturally comic to the children. Sometimes children saw things and people disproportionately, and perhaps they misconstrued his tall, thin body and the sharp contrast of his black crew cut with his large, pale eyes. Even the pink shirt, so popular in the city with young career men, might appear to the youngsters to be comically inappropriate for a grown man, and part of a clown's costume. After a time, the children got overexcited, and Martha's weary voice darted in among their cries. She clasped Peter's wrist, and to force him to pay attention to her, shook his hand until it was limp and tractable.

At three o'clock they left, after an hour or so of parlor sitting with Martha. Under his arm Charles carried Rangoon, and as soon as they were alone in the car and the cat was leaping in leisurely curiosity from Mayda's lap to the back of the seat and down again, they were immediately silenced by their feeling of uneasy gain. The fact that they were taking Rangoon home with them made their whole visit suspect, even in the stronghold of their mated minds, and there was nothing they wanted to say to each other.

. . .

Within a few days, Mayda wrote to her sister, addressing the letter
placatingly to Peter, too, and to Norine, and reported that Rangoon
was getting along famously, that a friend of theirs who was a reporter
for a daily paper and who had covered a cat show once had been over
for supper, and he thought Rangoon was championship quality. But
they weren't going to enter the cat in any competition, since they had
no record of its ancestry. Can you imagine?—there was a studbook
for cats wherein cats of known ancestry through four generations
were listed, and another listing called the Foundation Record for cats
of less than four generations of traceable ancestry. Wasn't that a kick?
The reply came from Peter. It was written with pencil on lined tablet
paper, and folded crookedly into the envelope, and he said that he
was writing because his mother thought he ought to because Rangoon had been his cat; he told them about his and Norine's trip to a
swimming pool and how they came home with their hair wet, and
closed the letter on the same page he had begun it, hoping it found
them in good health and signing it, *Your dear nephew, Peter.*

"Martha dictated it," Charles commented, and later, when the
bomb had exploded, he remembered that casual observation of his
and was able to say with sickly triumph, "What did I tell you?" Two
weeks later, a letter from Martha came, the longest she had ever
written to them, and following the news that her doctor had called in
a bone specialist for consultation and that they had persuaded her to
enter a sanitarium, *They think I'm such a rare duck, they don't want to
lose hold of me;* following the information that the few silver serving
spoons left to her by her mother, and the family photographs, were
being sent to Maydine railway express, for she didn't want to be
leaving precious things to the mercy of the tenants who'd be renting
the house; following the details of upheaval, and the prediction, *You
wait, Maydine, I'll bet my new boudoir slippers I'll be waltzing out of there
in no time,* she at last asked them, Charles and Maydine, to take her
two children into their home until she was well and could fetch
them.

As customary on their return from work, they had taken the mail from the box that stood at street level, and, climbing the long flight of brick steps, had opened first that which promised to be most interesting. On that evening their choice was a letter from a couple vacationing in Spain and from whom they had expected no letter at all, being, as they were, on the outer edge of that couple's circle, and they had paused halfway up the steps to read it, this recognition of them arousing on the instant a sharp delight in their home up ahead of them and the feeling of the bay at their backs. It was not until they were already in lounging clothes and sipping their wine that she opened her sister's letter. They ate their supper with no appetite, and Charles asked, picking at the casserole and green salad on his plate, "Do we have to decide tonight?"

"Don't be silly," she said, feeling an impending annoyance with him. "She's not leaving for three weeks yet. We've all that time."

She recalled to herself with a kind of pain, with a feeling of lameness, how plain the children were. If they were beautiful, they'd be a little easier to have around; the admiration of visitors would compensate for the trouble of caring for them, and their beauty would reflect, in a way, upon herself, for they were her sister's children. But they were as plain as the rest of the family, as she herself had been, and now that she had taken the edge off a bit with the way she bound up her dark hair, with the wearing of Mexican silver necklaces that sometimes seemed as heavy and eliciting of favor as a religious ornament between her breasts, did she want to be constantly reminded by the children of her own essential plainness? Idling her fork around her plate, she was overcome by an irrational anger against Charles, and drew her feet in farther under her chair. What was the matter with being plain? What was the matter with being big-boned, lanky, and plain, as long as your heart was in the right place? Why must he be so particular about how she appeared to other people?

"This place isn't big enough," he was saying.

"There's an extra bedroom," she said, not to be persuasive but simply to state a fact.

"That's not an extra bedroom," he bristled. "It's got a north light, and it's going to be my studio. There's no *bed* in it, is there?"

She made no reply, scourging herself for her rural mentality that called a room a bedroom just because it was empty. But at once she felt allied with Martha, with her own dear sister, her own dear, honest, and uncomprehending sister who continued to call her by her real name, and she stood up, choking on her misery.

He followed her into the front room and stroked her bowed head and made her get up a minute from the chair so he could sit down and take her onto his lap, and he comforted her and said he was sorry and if she wanted the children to come and live with them, it was all right with him. They were nice kids and old enough to take care of themselves after school. It was all right with him. But she didn't *know,* she wailed. She had a closeness with him, she told him, that she had never had with anyone, with her mother or father or even with Martha, and she didn't want it destroyed by any relatives of hers imposing on them, by the children who would probably shatter this affinity by denying it nourishment like time and seclusion and the indulgence of happy, little idiosyncrasies. She didn't know, she wailed. She didn't know.

Only once did they bring themselves to mention the problem, when one evening Charles, bending over to set down upon the floor the large blue platter spread with canned mackerel, asked Mayda, "Where'll they go if they don't come here?" and gently with his foot pushed aside the cats who were rising up on their hind legs or running against one another just beneath the descending plate.

"Go? They'll go to some neighbor, I guess," she said. "If there are any that generous."

"Will they wonder if we don't take the kids?"

"Who?"

"The neighbors, the neighbors," he said.

"They're not *your* neighbors," she replied acridly.

That night he came down with an asthma attack the likes of which he had not experienced since his childhood. He sat bolt upright in bed, his chest hollowed out by his long, hoarse breaths that drew her up beside him in terror. She switched on the lamp above their bed and saw that the four cats, bedded down over the expanse of comforter, had already been watching him in the darkness, their heads high and alerted. So frightened were the animals by the sounds he was making that when she slipped from under the covers and ran in her bare feet to fetch his nebulizer, they fled the room. She sat beside him on the bed, fervently kissing his shoulder, and when at last he had some relief and lay back, she asked him, "What could have done it, darling?"

"My life's slipping by," he replied in hoarse sarcasm. "It worries me."

"It might be the cats," she speculated.

"The cats?" he cried, tossing her cooling hand off his brow. "Why not pollen, or eggs, or anything? That little lost cat we smuggled up to our apartment that time—it slept on my neck all night, it liked to sleep there, and did I get an attack?"

Already shaken by his spell, she could only stare down at him timidly, her long hair falling around her arms like a shawl protecting her from his cruelty. He softened, stroking her arm and explaining to her that he was sick of his job, literally sick of it, that he didn't have it in him to be a salesman, no matter how well he was doing at it. He tried hard to be capable, he said, just because he hated it so. She agreed that it was time for him to quit the London Shop. If he wanted, she said, to take a few months off and look around for something more congenial, or even do a critical article, why they'd get along for a time with just her salary. They'd meet the house payments and the car payments all right, they just wouldn't be able to bank anything or buy clothes or things like recordings.

The next evening he told her that he could not bring himself that day to give his notice of resignation. Maybe he wouldn't have another attack for a long time, he told her. Maybe the one last night had been a fluky thing. But a few hours later, when he had barely laid his head on the pillow, he came down with an attack the nebulizer was not equal to, and she called in the local doctor, who gave Charles a shot and left some pills and told him to drop by for a checkup when he got the chance. In the morning he was too weak to rise, and he agreed to her proposal that she would phone his shop as soon as she got to work and inform the manager that Charles was suffering from asthma and suggest that, since she didn't know how long he'd be away from work, they'd better interview some other man for the job.

When she came home that evening she sprawled in the canvas butterfly chair. No words spoken, he brought her a whiskey and water as if she had ordered it, and sat down on some pillows on the floor, sat awkwardly, his long bones at odds with one another. Whenever, before, he had revealed a momentary fear of her, her vantage had put her into a panic, but now she took a cloudy pleasure in seeing him uncomfortable. He was leading her by the nose into a conspiracy against the children, and he *ought* to be uncomfortable about it. He *ought* to be feeling guilty. She slid farther down into her chair, stretching her legs out like a slattern into a position he had chided her about in the past and cured her of.

Not long after supper he retired to the bedroom as if he had been banished there. Until it grew dark she busied herself in the garden, troweling here and there, and three of the cats kept her company. Enlivened by the cool of the evening, they were scuffling together, or calling throatily, or darting at insects she could not see in the dimness. She had no view of the bay from this rear garden, but the absence only increased her appreciation of the place, for she knew the bay was there, waiting, while she occupied herself within this garden that was filled with absolving fragrances and enclosed by plum and madrona trees. Charles had closed the bedroom windows against the garden with as much finality as if a decree had been read to him, denying him the pleasures of the evening; the bamboo screens and tan silk curtains were both in use, and through this double film she saw only the glow of the lamp above the bed and that was all. She thought of him propped up by a mountain of colored pillows from the living room and suffering pangs of guilt, and her resentment of his maneuvering against Peter and Norine was dispersed by her gratitude to him for the composite gift he had given her —for marriage and this home and this garden. She troweled under the bedroom windows, thinking of her childhood and what she had learned of his. They hadn't been happy, either. No happier than Peter or Norine. Charles in military school, seeing his mother once a year and his father never, and herself going to work at fourteen, passing for eighteen because she was so tall and overgrown, and crying at night for all the things so bountifully possessed by the small-size girls. Now, for the first time, they were on compatible terms with life. They had each other and they had this house that, although it was built to the specifications of the previous owner, seemed built for themselves, and in its interior decoration expressed Charles's talents that had been so frustrated by his years spent in stuffy, small apartments. After an evening at a concert, they could return here and find a certain leisure in which to remember and assimilate. They had no more time than they had before, but they had room and graciousness in this little house that gave the impression of being time. And did they not deserve this?

She stood in the doorway of the bedroom, clasping the lapels of her sweater across each other as if she had caught a chill in the garden, and said to him, "I'll write Martha tonight. I'll say we're sorry, but we can't possibly take the children because we're having some trouble . . . you've got your asthma again, and this time it's so bad you've had to quit your job. I'll explain it as a kind of nervous breakdown, and say that we'll just be able to make ends meet for a while."

He said, "Oh, God, Mayda, I feel like a dog," and laid his book on the comforter and could not look at her, and then, in a moment, broke, bowing his head and rubbing his hand over his face, saying to her, "Come here, come here."

She went down on her knees by the bed, and they embraced, and he stroked her hair back to kiss her brow, while she assured him that it was not his fault he was laid low by his desire to do more than just sell clothes for the rest of his life. It was not his fault at all that they couldn't take the children. They wept together in relief, for now they were again in accord, and they wept for Martha and the kids and the whole tragic situation in that little family.

In the days that followed he set himself a regimen of reading and researching for the article on Paul Klee he had in mind, and this activity, and Mayda's enthusiasm about his project, had a calming effect upon his nights and he slept well. But on the fifth night he was again victimized by his asthma; not so severe a spell, but distressing enough, and he coughed, off and on, until morning. In the last gray hour before she arose, she suggested to him that he really ought to go down and see the doctor for some allergy tests, and, feeling that their accord was certain enough now that he would not think she was belatedly accusing him, she again brought up the possibility that the cats might be causing his spells. Lying upon his back, his hand spread appeasingly upon his chest, he considered this at length, and they agreed to experiment. They would prohibit the cats from entering the bedroom, and twice a week she would brush the cats thoroughly and throw away the brushings in a paper bag, precautions that would rid the air of the irritant, to an extent. And to further convince her of his amenability all along, he began to muse upon who, among their friends, would be most glad to receive the cats, if the experiment did not work and they might be forced to give the cats away. The Siamese brothers could go to that young couple who had bought the house on upper Broadway in the city and who said they were going to get around some day to buying a Siamese; they were just acquaintances, but at least he knew them well enough to see that they would be appreciative. The gray cat Grisette could go to the child next door, and Rangoon? Well, Rangoon could go to Lizbeth, that elderly photographer who kept the most exquisite cats. It was six months now since the evening they'd been introduced to her at her exhibit in the Museum and had gone up to her studio afterward. She hadn't been by to visit them, and they'd phone her once more and say they had a surprise for her.

So when, a few days later, Charles strolled down the hill to the doctor's office and the doctor told him to get rid of the cats that had been underfoot that night of his house call, Charles was able to say that Mayda and he were already experimenting. And when he told Mayda about it that evening, repeating what the doctor had said— that the asthma was only a symptom and that what he really had was an extravagant fondness for cats, a disease, said the doctor, called *Felis catus*—Charles laughed pleasurably in the manner of one recalling a compliment.

They needn't have fretted where to place Rangoon, for one Sunday afternoon, a few weeks after the experimenting was begun, while Charles was cutting away the grass from between the brick steps, a white Jaguar drew up in the street below and through the trees he saw a girl bend from under the low, sleek top and stretch her leg to the road. Turning to his cutting again, he heard a girl's heels on the bricks below him, and gazing around to her and prepared to tell her where this neighbor or that lived, he saw her paused below, her face lifted. "I'm looking for Charles Corbett," she told him, "or his wife."

At once he recalled the Jaguar of the girl who had roomed in Martha's house, and he smiled a sweet quirk of a smile, replying, "You flatter us. It's Rangoon you're looking for."

They laughed together, and he put his clippers aside and led the way up to the house, not in any hurry, moving with an erect ease in his long body to convey to her that they had her kind of visitor every day. Under the fuchsia bushes by the front door, one of the Siamese brothers was sitting drowsily. The girl bent to stroke it, but it sprang away from her and bellied out of sight, setting the little red flowers aquiver. "One has to introduce oneself, of course," the girl said.

Charles chuckled ruminatively, opened the door, and called Mayda. Fortunately, she had just freshened herself after a day in the garden and was in a crisp yellow frock and Japanese sandals.

"Mayda, this is Rangoon's mistress," he said, and they all laughed because the cat was given more importance than the girl.

Charles went in search of Rangoon, returned in a minute, when Mayda was asking the girl what drink she preferred, with the cat riding backwards in his arms, paws upon his shoulder, muzzle delicately examining his ear. He placed the cat in the girl's lap, and Rangoon stood for a moment startled, balancing on spindly legs. The girl cupped the cat's narrow face, cooed its name, and asked if it had missed her.

"They thought I'd forsaken it, can you believe it?" she cried to Mayda. "When I left I was so upset, I was mad at everybody, even Rangoon, and I said I didn't know when I'd be back." She had, Charles thought, the languidly clutching manner of the University Beauty, and he wondered if she'd left the cat with a certain design, a studied carelessness. "Believe me," she said, "I couldn't have gone back any sooner because I couldn't bear it. The town, I mean. Emotionally, you know. But yesterday I drove up, and there were absolute strangers in the house. The woman said there was no cat around like I described. She told me her landlady was in a hospital, and the kids were staying with friends down the street. She pointed the house out to me, and I went over and knocked on the door, and there were about six kids swarming to answer it, and I thought, Oh, my God, they've skinned it! And I recognized the boy and shook him and screamed at him, What have you done with my cat? Well, he told me you'd taken it, but he didn't know your address, so I had to put in a call to the hospital and get his mother on the line, and she told me where you live."

"And how is she?" Mayda asked, alarmed, and happening at that moment to be seating herself with drink in hand, she hoped that the activity of her body—the flouncing skirt, the crossing of legs—obscured her voice so that the girl would neither hear nor answer.

"She didn't say, she just said to give you her love and that she hoped Charles was better. She said she was awfully sorry to hear about Charles's breakdown . . ." The girl looked him over, and Mayda hastened to explain that it wasn't a breakdown, really. "It's only that the cats bring on his asthma," Mayda said. "He went through several awful spells of it and had to take a vacation from his work. We're so attached to the creatures that we really can't bring ourselves to part with them. You can't do it at the drop of a hat, you know," she said. "So we're in the midst of experimenting now, we're forbidding them to come into the bedroom, and I brush their fur ritually. If that doesn't work we'll simply have to give them away."

"Oh, for God's sake, Mayda," Charles protested, as if she were praising him, for the girl was gazing at him with glittering sympathy.

"But how selfless of you!" the girl cried at him. "Rangoon couldn't have asked for nicer folks to live with. He won't want to come home with me now. But things were so upset," she explained, and, bowing her head and stroking the cat alongside her hip, she was pouring out the story of the assemblyman and herself: that she had followed him to the capital and met him in an East Indian restaurant she'd discovered for them and that he had his opposition to her all jotted down on a card, like notes for a speech, and that she had prevailed against him. She was discreet enough to withhold his name and the part of the state she was from, but that was her only discretion in the rambling story.

With misgivings, Rangoon went along with the girl, cradled in her arms. Going down the brick steps, she felt her way with the pointy toes of her high-heeled pumps, for she had to bend her head to soothe him so he wouldn't bolt, and Mayda and Charles, following after her, were poised to catch him if he ran back up the steps. In the car Rangoon inhaled the odor of the red leather upholstery, and, standing on his hind legs, rediscovered the familiarity of the top of the seat. Leaping up there and stretching out, the cat gazed with mollified yellow eyes at Mayda and Charles, who had bent their heads under the top to gaze at him.

"Thanks again, awfully," the girl said, and her white cotton dress slipped back from her young knee as she put her foot to the clutch. They waited in the middle of the road until the car reached the turn that went downhill, where the girl slowed and waved to them. They stood waving back with an appealing awkwardness, like two wise persons attempting to be less serious, until the car was hidden by the trees.

A Suite of Photographs

TONY MENDOZA

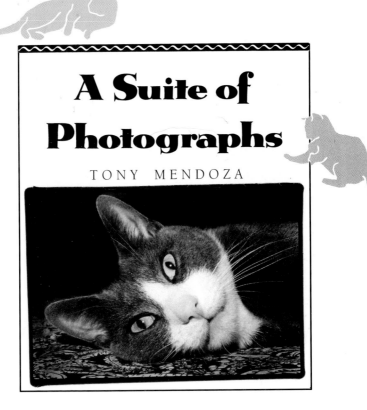

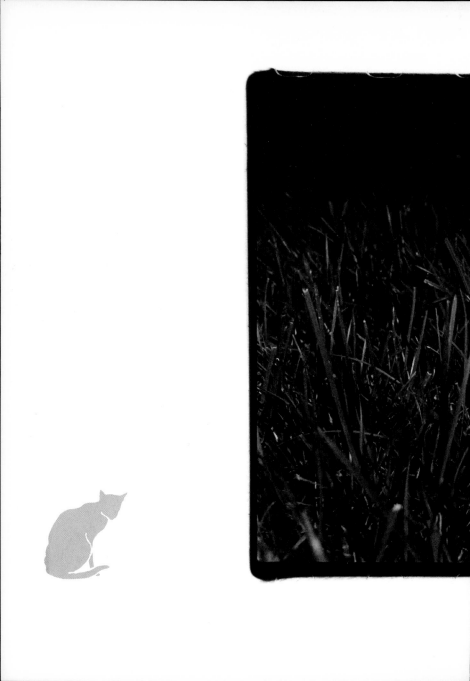

An Old Woman and Her Cat

DORIS LESSING

Her name was Hetty, and she was born with the twentieth century. She was seventy when she died of cold and malnutrition. She had been alone for a long time, since her husband had died of pneumonia in a bad winter soon after the Second World War. He had not been more than middleaged. Her four children were now middleaged, with grown children. Of these descendants one daughter sent her Christmas cards, but otherwise she did not exist for them. For they were all respectable people, with homes and good jobs and cars. And Hetty was not respectable. She had always been a bit strange, these people said, when mentioning her at all.

When Fred Pennefather, her husband, was alive and the children just growing up, they all lived much too close and uncomfortable in a council flat in that part of London which is like an estuary, with tides of people flooding in and out: they were not half a mile from the great stations of Euston, St. Pancras, and King's Cross. The blocks of flats were pioneers in that area, standing up grim, gray, hideous, among many acres of little houses and gardens, all soon to be demolished so that they could be replaced by more tall gray blocks. The Pennefathers were good tenants, paying their rent, keeping out of debt; he was a building worker, "steady," and proud of it. There was no evidence then of Hetty's future dislocation from the normal, unless it was that she very often slipped down for an hour or so to the platforms where the locomotives drew in and ground out again. She liked the smell of it all, she said. She liked to see people moving about, "coming and going from all those foreign places." She meant Scotland, Ireland, the North of England. These visits into the din, the smoke, the massed swirling people were for her a drug, like other people's drinking or gambling. Her husband teased her, calling her a gypsy. She was in fact part-gypsy, for her mother had been one, but had chosen to leave her people and marry a man who lived in a house. Fred Pennefather liked his wife for being different from the run of the women he knew, and had married her because of it, but her children were fearful that her gypsy blood might show itself in worse ways than haunting railway stations. She was a tall woman with a lot of glossy black hair, a skin that tanned easily, and dark strong eyes. She wore bright colours, and enjoyed quick tempers and sudden reconciliations. In her prime she attracted attention, was proud and handsome. All this made it inevitable that the people in those streets should refer to her as "that gypsy woman." When she heard them, she shouted back that she was none the worse for that.

After her husband died and the children married and left, the Council moved her to a small flat in the same building. She got a job selling food in a local store, but found it boring. There seem to be traditional occupations for middleaged women living alone, the busy and responsible part of their lives being over. Drink. Gambling. Looking for another husband. A wistful affair or two. That's about it. Hetty went through a period of, as it were, testing out all these, like hobbies, but tired of them. While still earning her small wage as a saleswoman, she began a trade in buying and selling secondhand clothes. She did not have a shop of her own, but bought or begged clothes from householders, and sold these to stalls and the second-hand shops. She adored doing this. It was a passion. She gave up her respectable job and forgot all about her love of trains and travellers. Her room was always full of bright bits of cloth, a dress that had a pattern she fancied and did not want to sell, strips of beading, old furs, embroidery, lace. There were street traders among the people in the flats, but there was something in the way Hetty went about it that lost her friends. Neighbours of twenty or thirty years' standing said she had gone queer, and wished to know her no longer. But she did not mind. She was enjoying herself too much, particularly the moving about the streets with her old perambulator, in which she crammed what she was buying or selling. She liked the gossiping, the bargaining, the wheedling from householders. It was this last which —and she knew this quite well of course—the neighbours objected to. It was the thin edge of the wedge. It was begging. Decent people did not beg. She was no longer decent.

Lonely in her tiny flat, she was there as little as possible, always preferring the lively streets. But she had after all to spend some time in her room, and one day she saw a kitten lost and trembling in a dirty corner, and brought it home to the block of flats. She was on a fifth floor. While the kitten was growing into a large strong tom, he ranged about that conglomeration of staircases and lifts and many dozens of flats, as if the building were a town. Pets were not actively persecuted by the authorities, only forbidden and then tolerated. Hetty's life from the coming of the cat became more sociable, for the beast was always making friends with somebody in the cliff that was the block of flats across the court, or not coming home for nights at a time so that she had to go and look for him and knock on doors and ask, or returning home kicked and limping, or bleeding after a fight with his kind. She made scenes with the kickers, or the owners of the enemy cats, exchanged cat lore with cat lovers, was always having to bandage and nurse her poor Tibby. The cat was soon a scarred warrior with fleas, a torn ear, and a ragged look to him. He was a multicoloured cat and his eyes were small and yellow. He was a long way down the scale from the delicately coloured, elegantly shaped pedigree cats. But he was independent, and often caught himself pigeons when he could no longer stand the tinned cat food, or the bread and packet gravy Hetty fed him, and he purred and nestled when she grabbed him to her bosom at those times she suffered loneliness. This happened less and less. Once she had realised that her children were hoping that she would leave them alone because the old rag trader was an embarrassment to them, she accepted it, and a bitterness that always had wild humour in it, only welled up at times like Christmas. She sang or chanted to the cat: "You nasty old beast, filthy old cat, nobody wants you, do they Tibby, no, you're just an alley tom, just an old stealing cat, hey Tibs, Tibs, Tibs."

The building teemed with cats. There were even a couple of dogs. They all fought up and down the gray cement corridors. There were sometimes dog and cat messes which someone had to clear up, but which might be left for days and weeks as part of neighbourly wars and feuds. There were many complaints. Finally an official came from the Council to say that the ruling about keeping animals was going to be enforced. Hetty, like others, would have to have her cat destroyed. This crisis coincided with a time of bad luck for her. She had had 'flu, had not been able to earn money, had found it hard to get out for her pension, had run into debt. She owed a lot of back rent, too. A television set she had hired and was not paying for attracted the visits of a television representative. The neighbours were gossiping that Hetty had "gone savage." This was because the cat had brought up the stairs and along the passageways a pigeon he had caught, shedding feathers and blood all the way; a woman coming in to complain found Hetty plucking the pigeon to stew it, as she had done with others, sharing the meal with Tibby.

"You're filthy," she would say to him, setting the stew down to cool in his dish. "Filthy old thing. Eating that dirty old pigeon. What do you think you are, a wild cat? Decent cats don't eat dirty birds. Only those old gypsies eat wild birds."

One night she begged help from a neighbour who had a car, and put into the car herself, the television set, the cat, bundles of clothes, and the pram. She was driven across London to a room in a street that was a slum because it was waiting to be done up. The neighbour made a second trip to bring her bed and her mattress, which were tied to the roof of the car, a chest of drawers, an old trunk, saucepans. It was in this way that she left the street in which she had lived for thirty years, nearly half her life.

She set up house again in one room. She was frightened to go near "them" to re-establish pension rights and her identity, because of the arrears of rent she had left behind, and because of the stolen television set. She started trading again, and the little room was soon spread, like her last, with a rainbow of colours and textures and lace and sequins. She cooked on a single gas ring and washed in the sink. There was no hot water unless it was boiled in saucepans. There were several old ladies and a family of five children in the house, which was condemned.

She was in the ground floor back, with a window which opened onto a derelict garden, and her cat was happy in a hunting ground that was a mile around this house where his mistress was so splendidly living. A canal ran close by, and in the dirty city-water were islands which a cat could reach by leaping from moored boat to boat. On the islands were rats and birds. There were pavements full of fat London pigeons. The cat was a fine hunter. He soon had his place in the hierarchies of the local cat population and did not have to fight much to keep it. He was a strong male cat, and fathered many litters of kittens.

In that place Hetty and he lived five happy years. She was trading well, for there were rich people close by to shed what the poor needed to buy cheaply. She was not lonely, for she made a quarrelling but satisfying friendship with a woman on the top floor, a widow like herself who did not see her children either. Hetty was sharp with the five children, complaining about their noise and mess, but she slipped them bits of money and sweets after telling their mother that "she was a fool to put herself out for them, because they wouldn't appreciate it." She was living well, even without her pension. She sold the television set and gave herself and her friend upstairs some day-trips to the coast, and bought a small radio. She never read books or magazines. The truth was that she could not write or read, or only so badly it was no pleasure to her. Her cat was all reward and no cost, for he fed himself, and continued to bring in pigeons for her to cook and eat, for which in return he claimed milk.

"Greedy Tibby, you greedy *thing,* don't think I don't know, oh yes I do, you'll get sick eating those old pigeons, I do keep telling you that, don't I?"

At last the street was being done up. No longer a uniform, long, disgraceful slum, houses were being bought by the middle-class people. While this meant more good warm clothes for trading—or begging, for she still could not resist the attraction of getting something for nothing by the use of her plaintive inventive tongue, her still flashing handsome eyes—Hetty knew, like her neighbours, that soon this house with its cargo of poor people would be bought for improvement.

In the week Hetty was seventy years old, came the notice that was the end of this little community. They had four weeks to find somewhere else to live.

Usually, the shortage of housing being what it is in London—and everywhere else in the world, of course—these people would have had to scatter, fending for themselves. But the fate of this particular street was attracting attention, because a municipal election was pending. Homelessness among the poor was finding a focus in this street which was a perfect symbol of the whole area, and indeed the whole city, half of it being fine converted tasteful houses, full of people who spent a lot of money, and half being dying houses tenanted by people like Hetty.

As a result of speeches by councillors and churchmen, local authorities found themselves unable to ignore the victims of this redevelopment. The people in the house Hetty was in were visited by a team consisting of an unemployment officer, a social worker, and a rehousing officer. Hetty, a strong gaunt old woman wearing a scarlet wool suit she had found among her castoffs that week, a black knitted teacosy on her head, and black buttoned Edwardian boots too big for her, so that she had to shuffle, invited them into her room. But although all were well used to the extremes of poverty, none wished to enter the place, but stood in the doorway and made her this offer: that she should be aided to get her pension—why had she not claimed it long ago? and that she, together with the four other old ladies in the house, should move to a Home run by the Council out in the northern suburbs. All these women were used to, and enjoyed, lively London, and while they had no alternative but to agree, they fell into a saddened and sullen state. Hetty agreed too. The last two winters had set her bones aching badly, and a cough was never far away. And while perhaps she was more of an urban soul even than the others, since she had walked up and down so many streets with her old perambulator loaded with rags and laces, and since she knew so intimately London's texture and taste, she minded least of all the idea of a new home "among green fields." There were, in fact, no fields near the promised Home, but for some reason all the old ladies had chosen to bring out this old song of a phrase, as if it belonged to their situation, that of old women not far off death. "It will be nice to be near green fields again," they said to each other over cups of tea.

The housing officer came to make final arrangements. Hetty Pennefather was to move with the others in two weeks' time. The young man, sitting on the very edge of the only chair in the crammed room, because it was greasy and he suspected it had fleas or worse in it, breathed as lightly as he could because of the appalling stink: there was a lavatory in the house, but it had been out of order for three days, and it was just the other side of a thin wall. The whole house smelled.

The young man, who knew only too well the extent of the misery due to lack of housing, who knew how many old people abandoned by their children did not get the offer to spend their days being looked after by the authorities, could not help feeling that this wreck of a human being could count herself lucky to get a place in this "Home," even if it was—and he knew and deplored the fact—an institution in which the old were treated like naughty and dimwitted children until they had the good fortune to die.

But just as he was telling Hetty that a van would be coming to take her effects and those of the other four old ladies, and that she need not take anything more with her than her clothes "and perhaps a few photographs," he saw what he had thought was a heap of multicoloured rags get up and put its ragged gingery-black paws on the old woman's skirt. Which today was a cretonne curtain covered with pink and red roses that Hetty had pinned around her because she liked the pattern.

"You can't take that cat with you," he said automatically. It was something he had to say often, and knowing what misery the statement caused, he usually softened it down. But he had been taken by surprise.

Tibby now looked like a mass of old wool that has been matting together in dust and rain. One eye was permanently half-closed, because a muscle had been ripped in a fight. One ear was vestigial. And down a flank was a hairless slope with a thick scar on it. A cat-hating man had treated Tibby as he treated all cats, to a pellet from his airgun. The resulting wound had taken two years to heal. And Tibby smelled.

No worse, however, than his mistress, who sat stiffly still, bright-eyed with suspicion, hostile, watching the wellbrushed tidy young man from the Council.

"How old is that beast?"

"Ten years, no, only eight years, he's a young cat about five years old," said Hetty, desperate.

"It looks as if you'd do him a favour to put him out of his misery," said the young man.

When the official left, Hetty had agreed to everything. She was the only one of the old women with a cat. The others had budgerigars or nothing. Budgies were allowed in the Home.

She made her plans, confided in the others, and when the van came for them and their clothes and photographs and budgies, she was not there, and they told lies for her. "Oh, we don't know where she can have gone, dear," the old women repeated again and again to the indifferent van driver. "She was here last night, but she did say something about going to her daughter in Manchester." And off they went to die in the Home.

Hetty knew that when houses have been emptied for redevelopment they may stay empty for months, even years. She intended to go on living in this one until the builders moved in.

It was a warm autumn. For the first time in her life she lived like her gypsy forbears, and did not go to bed in a room in a house like respectable people. She spent several nights, with Tibby, sitting crouched in a doorway of an empty house two doors from her own. She knew exactly when the police would come around, and where to hide herself in the bushes of the overgrown shrubby garden.

As she had expected, nothing happened in the house, and she moved back in. She smashed a back windowpane so that Tibby could move in and out without her having to unlock the front door for him, and without leaving a window suspiciously open. She moved to the top back room and left it every morning early, to spend the day in the streets with her pram and her rags. At night she kept a candle glimmering low down on the floor. The lavatory was still out of order, so she used a pail on the first floor, instead, and secretly emptied it at night into the canal which in the day was full of pleasure boats and people fishing.

Tibby brought her several pigeons during that time.

"Oh you are a clever puss, Tibby, Tibby! Oh you're clever, you are. You know how things are, don't you, you know how to get around and about."

The weather turned very cold; Christmas came and went. Hetty's cough came back, and she spent most of her time under piles of blankets and old clothes, dozing. At night she watched the shadows of the candle flame on floor and ceiling—the windowframes fitted badly, and there was a draught. Twice tramps spent the night in the bottom of the house and she heard them being moved on by the police. She had to go down to make sure the police had not blocked up the broken window the cat used, but they had not. A blackbird had flown in and had battered itself to death trying to get out. She plucked it, and roasted it over a fire made with bits of floorboard in a baking pan: the gas of course had been cut off. She had never eaten very much, and was not frightened that some dry bread and a bit of cheese was all that she had eaten during her sojourn under the heap of clothes. She was cold, but did not think about that much. Outside there was slushy brown snow everywhere. She went back to her nest thinking that soon the cold spell would be over and she could get back to her trading. Tibby sometimes got into the pile with her, and she clutched the warmth of him to her. "Oh you clever cat, you clever old thing, looking after yourself, aren't you? That's right my ducky, that's right my lovely."

And then, just as she was moving about again, with snow gone off the ground for a time but winter only just begun, in January, she saw a builder's van draw up outside, a couple of men unloading their gear. They did not come into the house: they were to start work next day. By then Hetty, her cat, her pram piled with clothes and her two blankets, were gone. She also took a box of matches, a candle, an old saucepan and a fork and spoon, a tinopener, a candle, and a rat-trap. She had a horror of rats.

About two miles away, among the homes and gardens of amiable Hampstead, where live so many of the rich, the intelligent, and the famous, stood three empty, very large houses. She had seen them on an occasion, a couple of years before, when she had taken a bus. This was a rare thing for her, because of the remarks and curious looks provoked by her mad clothes, and by her being able to appear at the same time such a tough battling old thing, and a naughty child. For the older she got, this disreputable tramp, the more there strengthened in her a quality of fierce, demanding childishness. It was all too much of a mixture; she was uncomfortable to have near.

She was afraid that "they" might have rebuilt the houses, but there they still stood, too tumbledown and dangerous to be of much use to tramps, let alone the armies of London's homeless. There was no glass left anywhere. The flooring at ground level was mostly gone, leaving small platforms and juts of planking over basements full of water. The ceilings were crumbling. The roofs were going. The houses were like bombed buildings.

But on the cold dark of a late afternoon she pulled the pram up the broken stairs and moved cautiously around the frail boards of a second floor room that had a great hole in it right down to the bottom of the house. Looking into it was like looking into a well. She held a candle to examine the state of the walls, here more or less whole, and saw that rain and wind blowing in from the window would leave one corner dry. Here she made her home. A sycamore tree screened the gaping window from the main road twenty yards away. Tibby, who was cramped after making the journey under the clothes piled in the pram, bounded down and out and vanished into neglected undergrowth to catch his supper. He returned fed and pleased, and seemed happy to stay clutched in her hard thin old arms. She had come to watch for his return after hunting trips, because the warm purring bundle of bones and fur did seem to allay, for a while, the permanent ache of cold in her bones.

Next day she sold her Edwardian boots for a few shillings—they were fashionable again—and bought a loaf and some bacon scraps. In a corner of the ruins well away from the one she had made her own, she pulled up some floor boards, built a fire, and toasted bread and the bacon scraps. Tibby had brought in a pigeon, and she roasted that, but not very efficiently. She was afraid of the fire catching and the whole mass going up in flames; she was afraid too of the smoke showing and attracting the police. She had to keep damping down the fire, and so the bird was bloody and unappetising, and in the end Tibby got most of it. She felt confused, and discouraged, but thought it was because of the long stretch of winter still ahead of her before spring could come. In fact, she was ill. She made a couple of attempts to trade and earn money to feed herself before she acknowledged she was ill. She knew she was not yet dangerously ill, for she had been that in her life, and would have been able to recognise the cold listless indifference of a real last-ditch illness. But all her bones ached, and her head ached, and she coughed more than she ever had. Yet she still did not think of herself as suffering particularly from the cold, even in that sleety January weather. She had never, in all her life, lived in a properly heated place, had never known a really warm home, not even when she lived in the Council flats. Those flats had electric fires, and the family had never used them, for the sake of economy, except in very bad spells of cold. They piled clothes onto themselves, or went to bed early. But she did know that to keep herself from dying now she could not treat the cold with her usual indifference. She knew she must eat. In the comparatively dry corner of the windy room, away from the gaping window through which snow and sleet were drifting, she made another nest—her last. She had found a piece of plastic sheeting in the rubble, and she laid that down first, so that the damp would not strike up. Then she spread her two blankets over that. Over them were heaped the mass of old clothes. She wished she had another piece of plastic to put on top, but she used sheets of newspaper instead. She heaved herself into the middle of this, with a loaf of bread near to her hand. She dozed, and waited, and nibbled bits of bread, and watched the snow drifting softly in. Tibby sat close to the old blue face that poked out of the pile and put up a paw to touch it. He miaowed and was restless, and then went out into the frosty morning and brought in a pigeon. This the cat put, still struggling and fluttering a little, close to the old woman. But she was afraid to get out of the pile in which the heat was being made and kept with such difficulty. She really could not climb out long enough to pull up more splinters of plank from the floors, to make a fire, to pluck the pigeon, to roast it. She put out a cold hand to stroke the cat.

"Tibby you old thing, you brought it for me then, did you? You did, did you? Come here, come in here . . ." But he did not want to get in with her. He miaowed again, pushed the bird closer to her. It was now limp and dead.

"You have it then. You eat it. I'm not hungry, thank you Tibby."

But the carcase did not interest him. He had eaten a pigeon before bringing this one up to Hetty. He fed himself well. In spite of his matted fur, and his scars and his half-closed yellow eye, he was a strong healthy cat.

At about four the next morning there were steps and voices downstairs. Hetty shot out of the pile and crouched behind a fallen heap of plaster and beams, now covered with snow, at the end of the room near the window. She could see through the hole in the floor-boards down to the first floor, which had collapsed entirely, and through it to the ground floor. She saw a man in a thick overcoat and muffler and leather gloves holding a strong torch to illuminate a thin bundle of clothes lying on the floor. She saw that this bundle was a sleeping man or woman. She was indignant—*her* home was being trespassed upon. And she was afraid because she had not been aware of this other tenant of the ruin. Had he, or she, heard her talking to the cat? And where was the cat? If he wasn't careful he would be caught, and that would be the end of him. The man with a torch went off and came back with a second man. In the thick dark far below Hetty was a small cave of strong light, which was the torchlight. In this space of light two men bent to lift the bundle, which was the corpse of a man or a woman like Hetty. They carried it out across the dangertraps of fallen and rotting boards that made gangplanks over the waterfilled basements. One man was holding the torch in the hand that supported the dead person's feet, and the light jogged and lurched over trees and grasses: the corpse was being taken through the shrubberies to a car.

There are men in London who, between the hours of two and five in the morning, when the real citizens are asleep, who should not be disturbed by such unpleasantness as the corpses of the poor, make the rounds of all the empty, rotting houses they know about, to collect the dead, and to warn the living that they ought not to be there at all, inviting them to one of the official Homes or lodgings for the homeless.

Hetty was too frightened to get back into her warm heap. She sat with the blankets pulled around her, and looked through gaps in the fabric of the house, making out shapes and boundaries and holes and puddles and mounds of rubble, as her eyes, like her cat's, became accustomed to the dark.

She heard scuffling sounds and knew they were rats. She had meant to set the trap, but the thought of her friend Tibby, who might catch his paw, had stopped her. She sat up until the morning light came in gray and cold, after nine. Now she did know herself to be very ill and in danger, for she had lost all the warmth she had huddled into her bones under the rags. She shivered violently. She was shaking herself apart with shivering. In between spasms she drooped limp and exhausted. Through the ceiling above her—but it was not a ceiling, only a cobweb of slats and planks, she could see into a dark cave which had been a garret, and through the roof above that, the gray sky, teeming with incipient rain. The cat came back from where he had been hiding, and sat crouched on her knees, keeping her stomach warm, while she thought out her position. These were her last clear thoughts. She told herself that she would not last out until spring unless she allowed "them" to find her, and take her to hospital. After that, she would be taken to a "Home."

But what would happen to Tibby, her poor cat? She rubbed the old beast's scruffy head with the ball of her thumb and muttered: "Tibby, Tibby, they won't get you, no, you'll be all right, yes, I'll look after you."

Towards midday, the sun oozed yellow through miles of greasy gray cloud, and she staggered down the rotting stairs, to the shops. Even in those London streets, where the extraordinary has become usual, people turned to stare at a tall gaunt woman, with a white face that had flaming red patches on it, and blue compressed lips, and restless black eyes. She wore a tightly buttoned man's overcoat, torn brown woollen mittens, and an old fur hood. She pushed a pram loaded with old dresses and scraps of embroidery and torn jerseys and shoes, all stirred into a tight tangle, and she kept pushing this pram up against people as they stood in queues, or gossiped, or stared into windows, and she muttered: "Give me your old clothes darling, give me your old pretties, give Hetty something, poor Hetty's hungry." A woman gave her a handful of small change, and Hetty bought a roll filled with tomato and lettuce. She did not dare go into a cafe, for even in her confused state she knew she would offend, and would probably be asked to leave. But she begged a cup of tea at a street stall, and when the hot sweet liquid flooded through her she felt she might survive the winter. She bought a carton of milk and pushed the pram back through the slushy snowy street to the ruins.

Tibby was not there. She urinated down through the gap in the boards, muttering "A nuisance, that old tea," and wrapped herself in a blanket and waited for the dark to come.

Tibby came in later. He had blood on his foreleg. She had heard scuffling and she knew that he had fought a rat, or several, and had been bitten. She poured the milk into the tilted saucepan and Tibby drank it all.

She spent the night with the animal held against her chilly bosom. They did not sleep, but dozed off and on. Tibby would normally be hunting, the night was his time, but he had stayed with the old woman now for three nights.

Early next morning they again heard the corpse removers among the rubble on the ground floor, and saw the beams of the torch moving on wet walls and collapsed beams. For a moment the torch light was almost straight on Hetty, but no one came up: who could believe that a person could be desperate enough to climb those dangerous stairs, to trust those crumbling splintery floors, and in the middle of winter?

Hetty had now stopped thinking of herself as ill, of the degrees of her illness, of her danger—of the impossibility of her surviving. She had cancelled out in her mind the presence of winter and its lethal weather, and it was as if spring was nearly here. She knew that if it had been spring when she had had to leave the other house, she and the cat could have lived here for months and months, quite safely and comfortably. Because it seemed to her an impossible and even a silly thing that her life, or rather, her death, could depend on something so arbitrary as builders starting work on a house in January rather than in April, she could not believe it: the fact would not stay in her mind. The day before she had been quite clearheaded. But today her thoughts were cloudy, and she talked and laughed aloud. Once she scrambled up and rummaged in her rags for an old Christmas card she had got four years before from her good daughter.

In a hard harsh angry grumbling voice she said to her four children that she needed a room of her own now that she was getting on. "I've been a good mother to you," she shouted to them before invisible witnesses—former neighbours, welfare workers, a doctor. "I never let you want for anything, never! When you were little you always had the best of everything! You can ask anybody, go on, ask them then!"

She was restless and made such a noise that Tibby left her and bounded onto the pram and crouched watching her. He was limping, and his foreleg was rusty with blood. The rat had bitten deep. When the daylight came, he left Hetty in a kind of a sleep, and went down into the garden where he saw a pigeon feeding on the edge of the pavement. The cat pounced on the bird, dragged it into the bushes, and ate it all, without taking it up to his mistress. After he had finished eating, he stayed hidden, watching the passing people. He stared at them intently with his blazing yellow eye, as if he were thinking, or planning. He did not go into the old ruin and up the crumbling wet stairs until late—it was as if he knew it was not worth going at all.

He found Hetty, apparently asleep, wrapped loosely in a blanket, propped sitting in a corner. Her head had fallen on her chest, and her quantities of white hair had escaped from a scarlet woollen cap, and concealed a face that was flushed a deceptive pink—the flush of coma from cold. She was not yet dead, but she died that night. The rats came up the walls and along the planks and the cat fled down and away from them, limping still, into the bushes.

Hetty was not found for a couple of weeks. The weather changed to warm, and the man whose job it was to look for corpses was led up the dangerous stairs by the smell. There was something left of her, but not much.

As for the cat, he lingered for two or three days in the thick shrubberies, watching the passing people and beyond them, the thundering traffic of the main road. Once a couple stopped to talk on the pavement, and the cat, seeing two pairs of legs, moved out and rubbed himself against one of the legs. A hand came down and he was stroked and patted for a little. Then the people went away.

The cat saw he would not find another home, and he moved off, nosing and feeling his way from one garden to another, through empty houses, finally into an old churchyard. This graveyard already had a couple of stray cats in it, and he joined them. It was the beginning of a community of stray cats going wild. They killed birds, and the field mice that lived among the grasses, and they drank from puddles. Before winter had ended the cats had had a hard time of it from thirst, during the two long spells when the ground froze and there was snow and no puddles and the birds were hard to catch because the cats were so easy to see against the clean white. But on the whole they managed quite well. One of the cats was female, and soon there were a swarm of wild cats, as wild as if they did not live in the middle of a city surrounded by streets and houses. This was just one of half a dozen communities of wild cats living in that square mile of London.

Then an official came to trap the cats and take them away. Some of them escaped, hiding till it was safe to come back again. But Tibby was caught. He was not only getting old and stiff—he still limped from the rat's bite—but he was friendly, and did not run away from the man, who had only to pick him up in his arms.

"You're an old soldier, aren't you?" said the man. "A real tough one, a real old tramp."

It is possible that the cat even thought that he might be finding another human friend and a home.

But it was not so. The haul of wild cats that week numbered hundreds, and while if Tibby had been younger a home might have been found for him, since he was amiable, and wished to be liked by the human race, he was really too old, and smelly and battered. So they gave him an injection and, as we say, "put him to sleep."

Ralph

WENDY LESSER

I have a cat without a nose.

This is the only extraordinary thing about
Ralph. He was intended from the beginning to be a
merely normal cat. I called him Ralph to signal
that—to reflect his ordinariness, and to ensure it.

Before Ralph I owned a cat named Melanctha,

227

named for Gertrude Stein's wandering black heroine. My Melanctha also wandered. She would take up residence for days or weeks with neighbors, and I too would have to wander in order to find her, knocking on the doors of strangers who lived one street over.

"Does she lie on your chest and lick your neck when you're going to sleep?" I would ask, to make sure this was the right black cat.

"Yes!" the children of the household would always say. So I would take her home, without looking back at them.

I think she did this licking thing because she was the runt of the litter, and never got enough of her mother. But what does it matter? Do we reject love because its intensity stems from early childhood deprivation?

When Melanctha wasn't wandering, she sat beautifully on my kitchen windowsill, a perfect Egyptian figurine. She sat very still and stared out the window at nothing I could see.

My best friend and I spent many hours in this kitchen, sitting catty-corner from each other at the built-in table, talking about our hopeless boyfriends. "I have no idea what goes through his mind," she would say. Once she added, looking at the cat, "It's like trying to read the inside of Melanctha's mind." "Melanctha's mind" became our shorthand for the whole subject of the obscurity of men.

One day Melanctha wandered too far. Or perhaps I romanticize the safety of home.

She was missing for weeks, and none of the neighbors had seen her. I would fall asleep at night thinking about the sandpapery scratch of her tongue on my neck. I found her body decaying in the bushes outside my house. "She must have been hit by a car," said my downstairs neighbor, who had run outside in response to my cry. "At least she came home to die," he added.

This made me weep harder. The children who lived next door, happening to be at that moment in their front yard, were embarrassed. "I'm sorry," I told their mother. "I'm all right," I told the children. "It's okay for grown-ups to cry." I made my downstairs neighbor take Melanctha's body to the SPCA for me. While he did it,

I scrubbed the grout between my bathroom tiles with an old tooth-brush. This is the only time I have ever done such a thing.

Ralph was explicitly Melanctha's replacement. My best friend was not reticent in her comparisons. "Well, he's certainly not the cat Melanctha was," she would say. "Look at those ridiculous white leggings. He looks like an amateur Shakespearean actor whose tights are falling down."

"Yes," I would admit. At first his shortcomings irked me—that he was not all black, that he lacked dignity, that he was male. I did not choose him, as I had Melanctha. He had been assigned to me randomly, the only remaining kitten in a litter owned by my sister's soon-to-be-ex-boyfriend, a sweet ne'er-do-well who disappeared from our lives, leaving Ralph as his only legacy.

But then I began to feel that the randomness, the ordinariness, was the whole point. I, who was not (to say the least) good at dealing with the unplanned, had unexpectedly been given an easy example of it. Ralph was my chance to learn to lend myself to circumstances. His name, which had begun as a kind of insult, became a term of endearment.

A decade later, Ralph was still essentially the same personality: affectionate to friends and strangers alike, happy with his small portion, unassuming. By this time I had married a man who was, among other things, allergic to cat hair. After a long period of resistance, I agreed to convert Ralph to an outdoor cat. Ralph was, as always, accommodating.

Friends who were slaves to their pets deplored but also admired my harsh decree. "We'd like to get our cats outside, too," they said. "We're trying to Ralphicize them." His solid name supported an exotic yet useful verb, halfway between "rusticate" and "ostracize."

My husband had a son already when I married him—a boy of five when we first met. Once, shortly after his father and I had started seeing each other, they came to my house for dinner. "Make hamburgers or hot dogs," said the father, my not-yet-husband. "He won't eat anything else."

"Nonsense," I said. I cooked cheese soufflé. The boy wouldn't eat. Very politely, he touched nothing.

Instead, he watched Ralph eating. We were all clustered in that same little kitchen where Melanctha had once adorned the window-sill. Ralph attacked his kibble ravenously and incompetently, spilling it in a mad circle around his dish.

"Soon you'll meet my sister," I told the boy conversationally. "She's coming up here for a visit."

"Is she a messy eater too?" he asked.

"Too?"

"Like Ralph. I wondered if everyone in your family is like Ralph."

My stepson is now sixteen, almost an adult, almost never at home. I have my own son now, a boy of five. It is on him that Ralph's noselessness has had an effect.

It began with a bleeding sore last winter. I waited for the sore to heal, as even the most severe cat scratches eventually do. But this didn't. As one always does in such cases, I correctly suspected the worst.

My regular vet, Dr. Berger, a charming man who spends half the year trekking with wolves, was away. His replacement was a young fellow with excellent diagnostic skills and no bedside manner.

"We'll have to do a biopsy to be certain," he said, "but I'm almost sure this is an extremely aggressive form of skin cancer. We see a lot of it here in California—the sun causes it. If you leave it alone he'll be dead in two months. It eats 'em up."

"What are my options?" I said, affecting rationality.

"Well, radiation is our top-of-the-line recommendation, but it's hard on the animal and it costs a lot."

"How much?"

"Oh—this is only ballpark, you know, I couldn't make any firm estimates—but somewhere in the $1500-to-$1800 range."

"And that's my only choice? Radiation or he dies?"

"Well, Dr. Berger has a friend in Arizona who's done some experimental surgery on cats with exactly this kind of cancer. He cuts off their noses. Seems to work in just about all the cases so far."

"How much does that cost?" I asked.

"Oh, say half as much—$700 or $800."

I didn't really have seven hundred dollars, let alone fifteen hundred—not to spend on "a cat," especially "an old cat." But when I stopped obsessing about the money, I realized I didn't have a choice: I couldn't just let him die. And I also realized that the money was a safe distraction, a screen for all the other things I was trying to keep myself from obsessing about.

"If we cut off his nose, he doesn't have to have radiation too?" I asked the young whippersnapper.

"Nope. See, in a cat this age, he's going to die of old age anyway before the cancer has a chance to recur. Now, if it were a child—"

"All right," I said. "Let me talk to Dr. Berger about it."

Back from his wolves, Dr. Berger assured me Ralph would be cute without a nose. That was the word he used: "cute." I cleared out my savings account. The operation was a success.

Cute is not the word that would have jumped to my mind when I first saw Ralph after the surgery. Horrifying, maybe. Repellent. Abnormal. There was a bleeding hole in the middle of his face. As I was leaving to take him home, other patrons in the vet's waiting room turned away in disgust or fear.

When I first came to Berkeley, fifteen years ago, I would sometimes run into a man on the street who had no face. He lived in one of the downtown hotels near the campus, and he could often be seen shuffling up and down Telegraph Avenue. Everyone who lived in Berkeley at that time remembers this man. I was told then—I never learned if it was true—that he was a former chemistry professor who had been in a terrible accident. I pitied this man, or thought I pitied the person I imagined him to be, and I tried not to look away when I passed him on the street. But I couldn't help it. My eyes flickered involuntarily. Once I wrote down, in a notebook I was keeping at the time, a metaphor: "His eyes, surprising in the corrugated face—like a car whose headlights still gleam out from the midst of a badly crumpled fender."

When Ralph came home from his operation, I took him to my office to live. (I say "office," but it was in fact my apartment, leftover from pre-marriage days, strenuously held onto as a remnant of my independent life.) I had two reasons for taking him there. One was that I wanted to keep him indoors, and I couldn't do that with an allergic husband at home. The other was that I didn't want my son to see him right away.

"You can see him when he's healed," I said.

"Will he ever get his nose back?" my son asked.

"No," I said. "But he'll look better when it heals." And he does.

But still not cute. "He looks kind of terrible," my son remarked when he first saw him. "Do you think he minds?"

"I don't think so," I said. "I don't think he knows." But just in case, I try not to mention the word "nose" in front of Ralph.

Other people are not so delicate. "What is *wrong* with that *cat?*" said someone who came by to make a delivery. "He looks like something out of the movie *Dick Tracy.*"

Recently my niece, a very sympathetic and gentle soul, visited us for Thanksgiving. "Do you want to come over to the office with me to feed Ralph?" I asked the children. My son told his younger cousin all about the operation. She agreed to come, but preferred not to see Ralph. While my son and I called him, she turned away her face. But by mistake she caught a glimpse. Then she reached down to pet him. "I was afraid at first, but really he's kind of cute," she later said.

On my son's kindergarten classroom wall is a poster the teacher has made for the children. In one column are things that make them happy, accompanied by a smiling face. In the other are things that make them sad, with a frown. "When somebody you love dies" and "When a pet dies" are two of the entries in the sad column. At the end of the happy column, my son has contributed: "When a pet gets well."

Ralph

For me, Ralph will never be completely well. I miss the nose. I miss the way it used to look—any cat has it, that beautiful Egyptian profile. When Ralph sits on my chest and purrs, I don't like looking up into those two rosy, gaping nostrils. And I hate the way he sounds when he sneezes. But I have learned to live with it remarkably well, for me. Accommodation was never my strong point; it was always Ralph's. Now we meet halfway.

Touching Is Good for Living Creatures

MERRILL JOAN GERBER

"Can't you put in mayonnaise?" Myra asked. "The baby birds won't like it that dry."

"Do you think birds eat mayonnaise in the wild?" Janet asked, mashing away. Bits of egg were

234

flying out of the bowl and landing in the clean glasses in the cabinet.

"Well, they don't eat hard-boiled egg in the wild either."

"All right," Janet said. "Put in mayonnaise. Put in ketchup. Put in sautéed mushrooms, for all I care. Here—you mash."

"I don't have time. I have to catch the school bus."

"But *I* have time?"

"You're home all day, Mom," Myra said. "It stands to reason." She wiped her hands on a dish towel and hurried down the hall to the bathroom. Janet heard her turn the barrette box upside down on the counter. Of course she would leave the box open. She would leave it there with ribbons and rubber bands and colored combs strewn about and Janet would have to put it away.

The baby birds must have heard her unscrew the top of the mayonnaise jar. *"Beep-beep! Beep-beep!"* They were craning their skinny little necks over the top of the shoe box, crowding together under the bulb of the gooseneck lamp for warmth and pleading to be fed.

"They're hungry again, Mom," Myra called down the hall. She appeared with her book bag over her shoulder, her hair held back with a red, white, and blue ribbon. "Be sure to feed them every hour. Don't give them bread—it expands in their stomachs. And stroke them so they can move their bowels."

"Anything else?" Janet asked. "Anything else you want me to do for you while I'm just home all day?"

"Would you feed the bunny?" Myra said. "And Creamy? I forgot to feed him. And the kitty too."

"The *kitty*? Is he still around? Didn't Daddy say not to encourage him? You *know* how Daddy feels about two cats. One is too many, as far as he's concerned."

"*You* gave the kitty milk last night, Mom. I *saw* you."

"Only because I don't want him dying on my doorstep. But Daddy doesn't want anyone feeding him. He'll be ours forever then."

"Yeah," Myra said. "Wouldn't that be super?"

"We *can't*, Myra. We're overextended. The vet bills, the cat food, the carrots, the eggs!" For emphasis, Janet tossed a spoonful of mashed egg in the air, and it landed in a clump on the floor. *"Me!"*

"You don't cost anything," Myra said. *"Luckily."*

They heard the brakes of the school bus squeaking down the hill.

"I've got to go. Would you open the door for me? I have to carry this poster to school."

Janet opened the front door for Myra, and leaned over to kiss her good-bye. Myra turned her head away.

"Hey," Janet said, "I just want a good-bye kiss. Touching is good for living creatures. You always tell me that when you spend hours petting Creamy."

"That's okay," Myra said. "You kissed me yesterday. And you touched me enough when I was a baby. . . ." She dashed out the door, running on her skinny long legs toward the bus stop.

As soon as the bus was out of sight, Janet pulled up a stool to the kitchen counter and began to croon to the baby birds. "Yes, little ones, food is coming. Be patient." She dipped her eyebrow tweezers into the mashed egg, pinching a morsel with the silver tongs. The babies peeped and screamed, reaching their open beaks in desperation toward her hand. Each beak, huge in proportion to the bird's frail body, was outlined in fluorescent yellow. "Bull's-eye," Janet whispered, poking food into one eager beak and then the other. "Yes, you love it, don't you?" The birds chirped and gobbled, vibrating the tweezers in her hand with the enthusiasm of their hunger. "One for you. Now one for you. Now your turn, now yours." The birds were like teaspoonfuls of life, all beak and fine new feathers, hollow bones, air. One day, having started life on her egg salad, they would fly over rooftops, soar into the blue sky. Myra had found them beneath the plum tree after a night of high winds; the cat and kitty were homing in on them like pointer dogs.

"Oh, no! Don't get involved in a rescue mission again," Janet had said when Myra carried them into the house. "You know how they always die. Anything can go wrong—it always does. Then you'll be depressed for a week. Let nature work it out."

"Do you want to see Creamy bite off their heads?" Myra asked. "At least we can *try* to save them."

"But you mean *I* can try. It's always me that does it. You go away to school and *I* feed them, *I* watch them, *I* pray for them . . . and then *I* bury them."

"What can I do, Mom? I didn't blow them out of the tree."

"No," Janet agreed. "You didn't."

Now that the children were no longer babies, were all in school, Janet had finally begun to relax her vigilance just a little bit. Even Danny had commented on it. One night, coming to bed in a soft new nightgown, she had simply closed and locked the bedroom door behind her.

"Are you leaving the door closed?" he asked quietly, looking up from his magazine.

"Isn't that okay?"

"Well, yes, of course," he said. "But I thought you liked to be able to hear the children."

"They'll be okay," she said. "I'm not worried about them anymore. They're healthy. They breathe perfectly well all night. They've outgrown their croup attacks. If they want me, they can call me."

"Well . . ." Danny said, with a smile, putting aside the magazine and holding out his arms. "That's *certainly* a good idea."

The gray kitty had wandered into the driveway while Danny was washing the car one Sunday afternoon. It had a tiny face, the bluest eyes imaginable, and eight toes on each front paw. Janet had two contradictory reactions at once. "We can't keep it," she said, sounding a stern warning to Myra, who was in the driveway shining her bike while Danny washed the car. For Danny's benefit she added, "It's definitely not going to live here." The kitty began pitifully lapping at the bucket of soapsuds. "It would need shots, it would need to be sterilized, it would need worming. It probably has fleas." And even as she said it, as Myra picked up the kitten and began to stroke it, Janet felt a profound softening in her breast, a sweet weakness, an over-whelming tenderness toward the beautiful mewing creature.

In a glance, Myra knew what she could ask for and get. Secretly she met her mother at the side door and together they gave the kitten milk. "But I mean it," Janet whispered to her. "We really can't go on this way. It's adorable, I know. But Daddy doesn't like all these pets taking over the house. He'll accept Creamy because we've had him for so many years, but not *another* cat. Daddy doesn't understand animals. He never had any when he was little—his parents thought they were messy and dirty."

"So are kids," Myra said.

"But Daddy likes kids."

"Who knows?" Myra said. "Maybe not." She walked away and Janet felt something different in her breast, a hollow shock, some kind of fear. Maybe she had given her children the wrong father.

The baby birds went to sleep, one on top of the other, cuddled together under the light bulb. With no one home to pretend for, Janet sat and watched them a long time, remembering the looks on the faces of her sleeping babies, the way their hands had fallen out limply between the crib bars, their delicious soft cheeks, the curve of their eyelashes resting on the rosy skin. Refusing to care for the pets was a stance Danny had forced her to adopt—he thought she did enough work for the kids as it was, more than she ought to, now that they were growing up and ought to do more for themselves. He wanted to claim her back—she knew that. He was tired of having to share Janet as generously with the children as he had all these years, and now he wanted her to come back to him, to give him at last the lion's share of attention, which he was more than willing to lavish upon her.

She knew she was supposed to show exaggerated relief: Thank

God, they're growing up. I have some peace now. She *was* glad to see them grow. Of course she was. But with it came Myra's turning her face away from her kisses.

Janet's anger at the birds, at the kitten, at the mess of bunnies and fish and frogs, had nothing to do with the creatures themselves but with Myra and her sisters, who no longer needed to be fed, teaspoon by loving teaspoon. If pressed, Janet would have had to admit that she really loved the animals, loved their needing her, their unbiased affection, their goodness. When she fed and petted them, she felt a transcendent sense of contentment.

Now she went out into the yard to feed the bunny, and the gray kitty mewed at her from the yew tree. His tiny, triangular face peered out from the thickly twined leaves and branches and he cried pathetically.

"Are you in there *again,* you little mischief head?" Janet said. "Come on, now—reach out to me and I'll put you down."

The kitty offered a paw, but when she moved to grasp it he pulled back, disappearing into the depths of the tree. She heard a scrambling and a rustling, and in a moment he appeared three feet higher, crying more loudly and desperately.

"Well," she said, "shall I wait till you figure it out or shall I get the ladder?"

She went inside and came out carrying the stepladder, and found that now the kitty was at the very top of the tree. She climbed up the ladder and reached perilously to get him; it was risky, she knew. No one was home and she could break her neck doing this. With both arms up in the air for him, she had no way to balance herself or to catch hold of anything. She hoped for the best and then pulled his front legs toward her. Tiny as he was, he resisted leaving his safe perch. They struggled; she caught him but lost her balance. Together they flew through the air, separated, and came down, each of them, on all fours. After a minute she managed to stand up and brush off her hands. A close call. Her heart was pounding. She scooped the ·

kitty up in her arms and carried him into the house, where she sat down on the couch, holding him close against her. She could feel the pulsing of his heart. Soon, though, he began to purr, a rough, sweet rumbling deep under his fur. His coat was smooth, electric, magnificent to stroke. She petted him till they both calmed down and dozed off. Later, when she woke up, she left him on the couch, still sleeping, till just before the children came home from school.

What's this?" Danny asked, holding something between his thumb and forefinger as they sat having their breakfast at the dining-room table. "And look! There's another one that just landed in my coffee!"

"Fleas!" Myra gasped.

Bonnie and Jill automatically lifted their feet off the floor. "Yuck!"

"Don't blame me, Daddy," Myra said. "I haven't let the kitty in once."

"Then who did?" Danny demanded, looking around the table.

"Not *I*," said Myra.

"Not *I*," said Bonnie.

"Not *I*," said Jill.

"What is this? 'The Little Red Hen'?" said Janet.

"Fleas don't have their own key to the house," Danny said, "do they?"

Just then something stung Janet's ankle. She looked down and saw four black dots digging into her tender flesh. When she leaned down to grab one of them, they all leaped as if on tiny springs to her other leg.

"My God," Danny said, "they're all over the place!"

"We *can't* have fleas," Jill said. "Creamy has a flea collar."

"The kitty doesn't have a flea collar," Bonnie said.

"The kitty doesn't come in the house!" Myra pleaded.

"Never mind how it happened—that's it!" Danny said. "No more cats in the house from now on. That means Creamy too."

"You can't do that," Myra said. "He'll be insulted. He *lives* here."

"Well, now he will live in the backyard," Danny said. "In fact, *only*

Creamy will live in the backyard. As for that kitten, you will just have to find someone to take it, or give it to the pound. You absolutely cannot keep it."

"You're cruel!" Myra cried. "Anyone who doesn't love animals is sick."

"With bubonic plague, which fleas carry, I'll be even sicker," Danny said, pushing away his contaminated coffee cup.

"Danny," Janet said quietly, "would you like me to pour you another cup of coffee?"

When they all had gone for the day, Janet went through the house and stood in the center of each room. Within seconds, fleas clung to her legs like iron filings to a magnet. It was her fault. She had let the kitty in every day, let it follow her around, let it sleep on the beds. Now she was in bad trouble.

She fed the baby birds their breakfast—mashed egg that was laced with cooked oatmeal—and then drove to the pet store in the mall and had a long talk with the proprietor.

"Aah, fleas," he said. "They're like wild armadillos on pogo sticks. You can't catch 'em, can't find 'em, can't kill 'em. *Unless* you're willing to go to war."

"I'm willing," Janet said. "Under these circumstances I can't conscientiously object."

He outlined a plan for her. She would have to vacuum every inch of the house, strip the beds, wash the blankets and bedspreads, seal the food boxes in plastic, remove the eating utensils and plants from the house, and buy insecticide bombs at the hardware store. The bombs would cover the fleas and everything else in the house with a poisonous mist. Luckily, human beings were bigger than fleas, so the chemicals that would kill the fleas would probably just give human beings cancer in thirty years or so—which was better than being eaten alive now. "Life is a trade-off," the pet-store owner said philosophically. Then he added that the cats would have to have a flea treatment on the same day as the bombing.

241

"Anything else?" Janet asked.

"Wear a gas mask," the man said.

At the hardware store Janet was told the bombs didn't work too well because they couldn't get the flea eggs. In a week the eggs would hatch and there'd be twice as many fleas in the house as there were to begin with. So instead of bombs, she was persuaded to buy "Murder 'Em Kennel Dust," which, if raked into the rugs, would get the eggs too. Coming home, she hid the lethal materials in the trunk of her car, determined to get rid of the fleas so that she wouldn't have to get rid of the kitten. She wasn't sure just how to work on Danny; he had spoken his final word on the subject. But she certainly couldn't approach him about keeping the kitten while scratching her shins!

The next morning, Janet fed the baby birds and then drove them— with all her houseplants and cereal boxes—a block away from the house, where she parked the car. Returning to the house, she put on plastic eye goggles, a surgeon's mask, rubber gloves, and an orange poncho (nonporous) and began skulking through the house, bent over, shaking "Murder 'Em Kennel Dust" over her pure-nylon rugs. When every room in the house was covered with a layer of powder, she got the red garden rake and began earnestly raking the stuff deep down into the rugs. She was worried. Ecologists had warned that by wiping out the snail darter, humanity might have changed the whole ecological balance. God only knew what would happen if fleas became extinct. She began to cough, sure that the poison was penetrating her surgeon's mask. She saw clusters of fleas holding on to the laces of her tennis shoes as if to a life raft. She was sweating under the poncho. Once she looked up into the mirror on the living-room wall and screamed in surprise.

"It's all right," she said to herself. "It's only me."

The doorbell rang and she opened the front door.

"Can I help you?" she said to the fleeing backs of two women and a child. They had left religious literature on her doorstep. Maybe they didn't feel that mutants needed to be given a conversion speech.

She walked from room to room through the powdery fog till she was convinced she had raked the seeds of destruction deeply enough. Then, gasping for breath, she ran out into the yard, where Creamy and the gray kitty lay in the sun, playing with each other's tails.

"Come over here, you guys—you're next. I bought you peppermint-scented 'Murder 'Em Pet Spray'—I'm doing this all the way!"

She didn't want Danny to know that the fleas had invaded the entire house, or that she could possibly be the cause of a cancer he might get in thirty years, so she vacuumed the powder sooner than she was supposed to. That night, collapsed, exhausted, in front of the TV, she ordered Myra up off the poisonous floor. "It's drafty," Janet said. "I don't want you to sit down there."

"We always sit on the floor," Myra complained.

"The TV gives off radioactive rays," Janet said. "Sit on a chair."

"Tell her the truth," Danny said. "Just tell her you don't want her to get bitten by fleas."

"I forgot to tell you," Janet said. "The fleas are all gone. Miraculously. There isn't a single one around. Maybe they weren't fleas. Maybe they were just ashes blowing out of the fireplace."

"*Biting* ashes?" Danny said. "By the way, where are the cats now?"

"Outside," Myra said. "Banned from their own home. Creamy is having a mental breakdown."

"Let him call the family-counseling talk show on KABC," Danny said.

"Phooey," Myra said, getting up off the floor and throwing her arms around her father's shoulders. "Who wants to watch TV anyway?"

"Mommy and I do," Danny said. "*Alone,* if you don't mind."

"You don't love me," Myra accused him. "It's obvious."

" 'Torn between two lovers,' " Danny sang, imitating one of Myra's favorite songs. " 'Breaking every rule. . . .' We have to try to keep it a secret from Mommy, sweetheart."

"Oh, shut up," Myra said, and stormed off to her room.

Janet was reassured. It was clear that they were friends. She wondered if she ought to tell Danny what a good father she knew he was, after all. But enervated from her day's labors, she lay there like a dead person, too weak to move, to speak, even to return the pressure of her husband's hand. Danny had been right. If the children were no longer exhausting her, now it was the pets who drained all her energy. Like the poisoned fleas in the carpet, her very libido was lying limp and impotent in her hidden crevices. If she weren't preoccupied with the fleas, it would be the birds, and if it weren't the birds, it would be the cats. Poor Danny—there never seemed to be a time and place for him. She would have to give up the kitten. It was her destiny. She lay there, beaten, sorrowful, while Danny switched channels with the remote-control device.

A program zipped by showing a woman giving another woman a sensual massage. Danny clicked back to it.

"This program will explore," the voice-over said, "the hidden meanings and power of human touch and the exquisite responsiveness of the touch-receptive cells in the human skin."

Danny ran his finger across Janet's upper arm. She wondered if he could tell it was made of numb rubber, the arm of a mannequin. A cluster of monkeys came on the screen, hugging and embracing one another. A mother and her baby were shown entwined, and then the little monkey was separated by a glass barrier from its mother and almost at once it displayed symptoms of extreme grief—first a desperate pawing at the glass and then, later, a slumped-over posture, head bowed, little hand to its forehead—classic sorrow. "Monkeys who are deprived of touch," the voice-over said, "eventually display signs of severe disturbance and aggression."

Now there were happier scenes—of an infant at his mother's breast, of parents cuddling a crying child, of an old woman playing with her cat, of a young man roughhousing with his dog, of a little girl rubbing noses with a kitten. "Pets," the voice-over said, "enhance the lives of those who live with them. The give-and-take of affection, particularly the cuddling, holding, and stroking of pets, has been shown to improve the quality of life for their owners. Touch is the matrix of our social and emotional relationships with others. People who own pets are calmer, more secure—and may even live longer."

Danny, still resting his arm on Janet's shoulder, reached up and gently stroked her cheek with his forefinger.

"Ummm," she sighed. Feeling seemed to be returning to her flesh. She shifted on the couch and embraced him, sliding her hand up his sleeve. As the TV screen flashed again to the restful expression on the face of the woman being given a massage, Janet massaged Danny's biceps muscle. As the picture returned to the monkeys, then panned to the old woman playing with her cat, to the young man with his dog and to the child with the kitten, Janet stroked Danny's skin with sweet sensuality. Then very quietly she stood up and excused herself for a second. She opened the patio door and returned with the gray kitten in her arms.

"Look," she whispered to her husband, placing his large hand on the luxurious fur of the kitten's back. "Feel that," she said. "When I stroke him, I feel calm, happy, full of well-being. All my senses come alive."

"They do?" Danny asked.

"Feel," she said softly, drawing his fingers through the fur. "It's almost electric." She placed her own hand over his and together they stroked the kitten, who had begun to purr loudly in contentment.

"He keeps me company when no one is home," Janet said. "He's so sweet, and when I pet him, I can hardly wait for you to come home so I can pet you."

"Ummm," Danny murmured. He had put his head back against the edge of the couch and closed his eyes.

"I love his rough little tongue," she said. "It's scratchy, just like your cheek when you kiss me and your whiskers rub my face hard."

"Oh, yes." Danny nodded.

"And people who love pets live longer," Janet whispered. "They're better lovers. . . ."

Danny was totally relaxed, given up to the moment. Janet reached over and switched off the TV. In the dark silence she continued to nourish the touch-receptive cells of the three of them, breathing in, as she did so, the sweet, peppermint aroma of the kitten.

I See You, Bianca

Bianca

MAEVE BRENNAN

My friend Nicholas is about the only person I
know who has no particular quarrel with the city
as it is these days. He thinks New York is all right.
It isn't that he is any better off than the rest of us.
His neighborhood, like all our neighborhoods, is
falling apart, with too many buildings half up and

247

half down, and too many temporary sidewalks, and too many doomed houses with big Xs on their windows. The city has been like that for years now, uneasy and not very reasonable, but in all the shakiness Nicholas has managed to keep a fair balance. He was born here, in a house on 114th Street, within sight of the East River, and he trusts the city. He believes anyone with determination and patience can find a nice place to live and have the kind of life he wants here. His own apartment would look much as it does whether he lived in Rome or Brussels or Manchester. He has a floor through—two rooms made into one long room with big windows at each end, in a very modest brownstone, a little pre-Civil War house on East Twelfth Street near Fourth Avenue. His room is a spacious oblong of shadow and light—he made it like that, cavernous and hospitable—and it looks as though not two but ten or twenty rooms had contributed their best angles and their best corners and their best-kept secrets of depths and mood to it. Sometimes it seems to be the anteroom to many other rooms, and sometimes it seems to be the extension of many other rooms. It is like a telescope and at the same time it is like what you see through a telescope. What it is like, more than anything, is a private room hidden backstage in a very busy theatre where the season is in full swing. The ceiling, mysteriously, is covered in stamped tin. At night the patterned ceiling seems to move with the flickering shadows, and in the daytime an occasional shadow drifts slowly across the tin as though it was searching for a permanent refuge. But there is no permanence here—there is only the valiant illusion of a permanence that is hardly more substantial than the shadow that touches it. The house is to be torn down. Nicholas has his apartment by the month, no lease, and no assurance that he will still be here a year or even three months from now. Sometimes the furnace breaks down in the dead of winter, and then there is a very cold spell for a few days until the furnace is repaired—the landlord is too sensible to buy a new furnace for a house that may vanish overnight. When anything gets out of order inside the apartment, Nicholas repairs it himself. (He thinks about the low rent he pays and not about the reason for the low rent.) When a wall or a ceiling has to be painted, he paints it. When the books begin to pile up on the floor, he puts up more shelves to join the shelves that now cover most of one long wall from the floor to the ceiling. He builds a cabinet to hide a bad spot in the end wall. The two old rooms, his one room, never had such attention as they are getting in their last days.

The house looks north and Nicholas has the second floor, with windows looking north onto Twelfth Street and south onto backyards and the backs and sides of other houses and buildings. The neighborhood is a kind of no man's land, bleak in the daytime and forbidding at night, very near to the Village but not part of the Village, and not a part, either, of the lower East Side. Twelfth Street at that point is very narrow and noisy. Elderly buildings that are not going to last much longer stand side by side with the enormous, blank façades of nearly new apartment houses, and there is a constant caravan of quarrelsome, cumbersome traffic moving toward the comparative freedom of Fourth Avenue. To his right Nicholas looks across the wide, stunted expanse of Fourth Avenue, where the traffic rolls steadily uptown. Like many exceedingly ugly parts of the city, Fourth Avenue is at its best in the rain, especially in the rain at night, when the whole scene, buildings, cars, and street, streams with such a black and garish intensity that it is beautiful, as long as one is safe from it—very safe, with both feet on the familiar floor of a familiar room filled with books, records, living plants, pictures and drawings, a tiny piano, chairs and tables and mirrors, and a long desk and a bed. All that is familiar is inside, and all the discontent is outside, and Nicholas can stand at his windows and look out on the noise and confusion with the cheerful interest of one who contemplates a puzzle he did not create and is not going to be called upon to solve. From the top of a tall filing cabinet near him, Bianca, his small white cat, also gazes at the street. It is afternoon now, and the sun is shining, and Bianca is there on the cabinet, looking out, only to be near Nicholas and to see what he sees. But she sees nothing.

What is that out there?

That is a view, Bianca.

And what is a view?

A view is where we are not. Where we are is never a view.

Bianca is interested only in where she is, and what she can see and hope to touch with her nose and paws. She looks down at the floor. She knows it well—the polished wood and the small rugs that are arranged here and there. She knows the floor—how safe it is, always there to catch her when she jumps down, and always very solid and familiar under her paws when she is getting ready to jump up. She likes to fly through the air, from a bookcase on one side of the room to a table on the other side, flying across the room without even looking at the floor and without making a sound. But whether she looks at it or not, she knows the floor is always there, the dependable floor, all over the apartment. Even in the bathroom, under the old-fashioned bathtub, and even under the bed, and under the lowest shelf in the kitchen, Bianca finds the well-known floor that has been her ground—her playground and her proving ground—during all of her three years of life.

Nicholas has been standing and staring at rowdy Twelfth Street for a long time now, and Bianca, rising, stretching, and yawning on top of the filing cabinet, looks down at the floor and sees a patch of sunlight there. She jumps down and walks over to the patch of sun and sits in it. Very nice in the sun, and Bianca sinks slowly down until she is lying full length in the warmth. The hot strong light makes her fur whiter and denser. She is drowsy now. The sun that draws the color from her eyes, making them empty and bright, has also drawn all resistance from her bones, and she grows limp and flattens out into sleep. She is very flat there on the shining floor—flat and blurred—a thin cat with soft white fur and a blunt, patient Egyptian head. She sleeps peacefully on her side, with her front paws crossed and her back paws placed neatly one behind the other, and from time to time her tail twitches impatiently in her dream. But the dream is too frail to hold her, and she sinks through it and continues to sink until she lies motionless in the abyss of deepest sleep. There is glittering dust in the broad ray that shines on her, and now Bianca is dust-colored, paler and purer than white, and so weightless that she seems about to vanish, as though she were made of the radiance that pours down on her and must go when it goes.

Bianca is sleeping not far from Nicholas's bed, which is wide and low and stands sidewise against the wall. Behind the wall at that point is a long-lost fireplace, hidden away years before Nicholas took the apartment. But he has a second fireplace in the back part of the long room, and although it stopped working years ago, it was left open, and Nicholas has made a garden in it, a conservatory. The plants stand in tiers in the fireplace and on the floor close around it, and they flourish in the perpetual illumination of an electric bulb hidden in the chimney. Something is always in bloom. There are an ivy geranium, a rose geranium, and plain geraniums in pink and white. Then there are begonias, and feathery ferns, and a white violet, and several unnamed infant plants starting their lives in tiny pots. The jug for watering them all stands on the floor beside them, and it is kept full because Bianca likes to drink from it and occasionally to play with it, dipping in first one paw and then the other. She disturbs the water so that she can peer down into it and see the strange new depths she has created. She taps the leaves of the plants and then sits watching them. Perhaps she hopes they will hit back.

Also in this back half is Nicholas's kitchen, which is complete and well furnished, and separated from the rest of the room by a high counter. The kitchen gets the full light of one of the two windows that give him his back view. When he looks directly across, he sees the blank side wall of an old warehouse and, above, the sky. Looking straight down, he sees a neglected patch, a tiny wasteland that was once the garden of this house. It is a pathetic little spot of ground, hidden and forgotten and closed in and nearly sunless, but there is still enough strength in the earth to receive and nourish a stray ailan-thus tree that sprouted there and grew unnoticed until it reached Nicholas's window. Nobody saw the little tree grow past the basement and the first floor because nobody lives down there, but once it touched the sill of Nicholas's room he welcomed it as though it was home at last after having delayed much too long on the way. He loved the tree and carried on about it as though he had been given the key to his inheritance, or a vision of it. He leaned out of the window and touched the leaves, and then he got out on the fire escape and hung over it, making sure it was healthy. He photographed it, and took a leaf, to make a drawing of it. And the little ailanthus, New York's hardship tree, changed at his touch from an overgrown weed to a giant fern of extraordinary importance. From the kitchen counter, Bianca watched, purring speculatively. Her paws were folded under her chest and her tail was curled around her. She was content. Watching Nicholas at the ailanthus was almost as good as watching him at the stove. When he climbed back into the room she continued to watch the few leaves that were high enough to appear, trembling, at the edge of the sill. Nicholas stood and looked at her, but she ignored him. As she stared toward the light her eyes grew paler, and as they grew paler they grew more definite. She looked very alert, but still she ignored him. He wanted to annoy her. He shouted at her. "Bianca!" he shouted. "I see you!" Bianca narrowed her eyes. "I see you!" Nicholas yelled. "I see you, Bianca. I *see* you, Bianca. I see you. I see you. I SEE you!" Then he was silent, and after a minute Bianca turned her head and looked at him, but only to show there was no contest—her will was stronger, why did he bother?—and then she looked away. She had won. She always did.

In the summer it rains—sudden summer rain that hammers against the windowpanes and causes the ailanthus to stagger and shiver in gratitude for having enough water for once in its life. What a change in the weather, as the heavy breathless summer lifts to reveal a new world of freedom—free air, free movement, clean streets and clean roofs and easy sleep. Bianca stares at the rain as it streams down the glass of the window. One drop survives the battering and rolls, all in one piece, down the pane. Bianca jumps for it, and through the glass she catches it, flattening it with her paw so that she can no longer see it. Then she looks at her chilled paw and, finding it empty, she begins to wash it, chewing irritably at it. But one paw leads to another and she has four of them. She washes industriously. She takes very good care of her only coat. She is never idle, with her grooming to do, and her journeys to take, and then she attends on Nicholas. He is in and out of the apartment a good deal, and she often waits for him at the head of the stairs, so that he will see her first thing when he opens the door from the outside. When he is in the apartment she stays near him. If she happens to be on one of her journeys when he gets home, she appears at the window almost before he has taken off his coat. She goes out a good deal, up and down the fire escape and up and down the inside stairs that lead to the upper apartment and the roof. She wanders. Nicholas knows about it. He likes to think that she is free.

Bianca and the ailanthus provide Nicholas with the extra dimension all apartment dwellers long for. People who have no terraces and no gardens long to escape from their own four walls, but not to wander far. They only want to step outside for a minute. They stand outside their apartment houses on summer nights and during summer days. They stand around in groups or they sit together on the front steps of their buildings, taking the air and looking around at the street. Sometimes they carry a chair out, so that an old person can have a little outing. They lean out of their windows, with their elbows on the sills, and look into the faces of their neighbors at their windows on the other side of the street, all of them escaping from the rooms they live in and that they are glad to have but not to be closed up in. It should not be a problem, to have shelter without being shut away. The window sills are safety hatches into the open, and so are the fire escapes and the roofs and the front stoops. Bianca and the ailanthus make Nicholas's life infinitely spacious. The ailanthus casts its new green light into his room, and Bianca draws a thread of his life all around the outside of the house and all around the inside, up and down the stairs. Where else does she go? Nobody knows. She has never been seen to stray from the walls of the house. Nicholas points out to his friends that it is possible to keep a cat in an apartment and still not make a prisoner of her. He says disaster comes only to those who attract it. He says Bianca is very smart, and that no harm will come to her.

She likes to sit on the window sills of the upper-floor tenants, but she never visits any of them unless they invite her in. She also likes to sit in the ruins of the garden Nicholas once kept on the roof. She watched him make the garden there. It was a real garden and grew well, until the top-floor tenant began to complain bitterly about his leaking ceiling. Even plants hardy enough to thrive in a thin bed of city dust and soot need watering. Nicholas still climbs to the roof, not to mourn his garden—it was an experiment, and he does not regret it —but to look about at the Gulliver world he lives in: the new buildings too tall for the streets they stand in and the older, smaller buildings out of proportion to everything except the past that will soon absorb them. From the street, or from any window, the city often seems like a place thrown up without regard for reason, and haunted by chaos. But from any rooftop the city comes into focus. The roof is in proportion to the building beneath it, and from any roof it can easily be seen that all the other roofs, and their walls, are in proportion to each other and to the city. The buildings are tightly packed together, without regard to size or height, and light and shadow strike across them so that the scene changes every minute. The struggle for space in Manhattan creates an oceanic uproar in the air above the streets, and every roof turns into a magic carpet just as soon as someone is standing on it.

Nicholas climbs to the roof by his fire escape, but when he leaves the roof to go back to his apartment he goes down through the house, down three flights to his own landing, or all the way down to the street floor. He likes the house and he likes to walk around in it. Bianca follows him. She likes to be taken for a walk. She likes to walk around the downstairs hall, where the door is that gives onto the street. It is an old hall, old and cramped, the natural entrance to the family place this house once was. To the left as you enter from the street there are two doors opening into what were once the sitting room and the dining room. The doors are always locked now—there are no tenants there. The hall is narrow, and it is cut in half by the stairs leading up to Nicholas's landing. Under the stairs, beside the door that leads down into the basement, there is a mysterious cubbyhole, big enough for galoshes, or wine bottles, or for a very small suitcase. Nobody knows what the cubbyhole was made for, but Bianca took it for one of her hiding places, and it was there Nicholas first looked for her when he realized he had not seen her all day—which is to say for about ten hours. He was certain she was in the cubbyhole, and that she wanted to be coaxed out. He called her from the landing, and then he went downstairs, calling her, and then he knelt down and peered into the dark little recess. Bianca was not there, and she was not on the roof, or under the bed, or down at the foot of the ailanthus trying to climb up, and she was not anywhere. Bianca was gone. She was nowhere to be found. She was nowhere.

There is no end to Bianca's story because nobody knows what happened to her. She has been gone for several months now. Nicholas has given up putting advertisements in the paper, and he took down all the little cards he put up in the cleaner's and in the grocery store and in the drugstore and the flower shop and the shoeshine parlor. He has stopped watching for her in the street. At first he walked through the street whispering her name, and then one night he found himself yelling for her. He was furious with her. He said to himself that if she turned up at that moment he would kill her. He would certainly not be glad to see her. All he wanted was, one way or another, to know whether she was alive or dead. But there was no word from Bianca, and no word from anyone with actual news of her, although the phone rang constantly with people who thought they had seen her, so that he spent a good many hours running around the neighborhood in answer to false reports. It was no good. She was gone. He reminded himself that he hadn't really wanted a cat. He had only taken Bianca because a friend of his, burdened with too many kittens, pleaded with him. He finds himself wondering what happened to Bianca, but he wonders less and less. Now, he tells himself, she has shrunk so that she is little more than an occasional irritation in his mind. He does not really miss her very much. After all, she brought nothing into the apartment with her except her silence. She was very quiet and not especially playful. She liked to roll and turn and paw the air in the moonlight, but otherwise she was almost sedate. But whatever she was, she is gone now, and Nicholas thinks that if he only knew for sure what happened to her he would have forgotten her completely by this time.

Contributors

ALICE ADAMS has published eleven books. Her seventh novel, *Caroline's Daughters*, was published last year by Alfred A. Knopf. She lives in San Francisco with two cats.

GINA BERRIAULT is the author of several novels, the most recent of which is *The Lights of the Earth*, and the story collection *The Infinite Passion of Expectation*. North Point Press has also released paperback versions of her earlier works.

MAEVE BRENNAN has written two collections of short stories, *Christmas Eve* and *In and Out of Never-Never Land*, and a book of prose, *The Long-Winded Lady Writes: Notes from* The New Yorker, a gathering of her contributions to *The New Yorker*, where she worked for many years.

ROZ CHAST has been a contributor to *Mother Jones*, *National Lampoon*, and particularly *The New Yorker*, where she has published most of her drawings in the last decade. Her cartoons have been collected in several books, including *Unscientific Americans, Last Resorts, Parallel Universes, Mondo Boxo,* and, most recently, *Proof of Life on Earth.*

ROALD DAHL, who died as this book was in production, is the celebrated fiction writer of *Kiss Kiss, Switch Bitch, Selected Stories,* and *My Uncle Oswald,* as well as the beloved children's book author of such classics as *Charlie and the Chocolate Factory* and *James and the Giant Peach.*

MERRILL JOAN GERBER has published three novels, eight young adult novels, and three collections of short stories; Longstreet Press will publish her fourth collection, *The Peaceable Kingdom,* this fall. Her stories have appeared in *The New Yorker, Redbook, The Atlantic,* and *Prize Stories: The O. Henry Awards.* She lives in Sierra Madre, California, and teaches at Caltech and UCLA.

MOLLY GILES is the author of *Rough Translations,* a collection of stories that won the Flannery O'Connor Award for Short Fiction. Her recent stories have appeared in *McCall's, The Greensboro Review,* and *Shenandoah.* She teaches creative writing at San Francisco State University and is at work on a new collection of stories and a novel.

AMY HEMPEL is the author of two collections of stories, *Reasons to Live* and *At the Gates of the Animal Kingdom.* The title story of the latter book appeared in *The Company of Dogs.*

WENDY LESSER, editor of *The Threepenny Review,* is the author of *The Life Below the Ground* and *His Other Half.*

DORIS LESSING is one of the most renowned authors of this century, having published novels, stories, and poems for over forty years, including such classic volumes as *African Stories, The Golden Notebook, Briefing for a Descent into Hell,* and the cycle *Children of Violence.*

PENELOPE LIVELY is the author of many books of fiction, including *Moon Tiger, Going Back, Judgment Day,* and *A Pack of Cards.*

KATINKA LOESER was a former editor of *Poetry Magazine,* as well as a contributor to it. Many of her stories, now collected in three volumes, have appeared in *The New Yorker.* She lived in Westport, Connecticut until her death in 1991.

PHILLIP LOPATE is the author of the essay collections *Bachelorhood* and *Against Joie de Vivre,* and the novel *The Rug Merchant.* He teaches at Columbia University and is a member of the New York Film Festival selection committee. He lives in New York with two cats and a wife.

VALERIE MARTIN is the author of *The Consolation of Nature and Other Stories,* and the novels *A Recent Martyr, Alexandra, Set in Motion,* and, most recently, *Mary Reilly.*

BOBBIE ANN MASON has published two collections of stories, *Shiloh and Other Stories* and *Love Life,* and two novels, *In Country* and *Spence + Lila.* Her short story "Lying Doggo" appeared in *The Company of Dogs.*

TONY MENDOZA is the celebrated photographer of *Ernie* and *Ernie's Postcard Book,* two collections issued by Capra Press, as well *Stories,* a series of photographs and texts centered on his Cuban and American family. The recipient of numerous awards, including fellowships from the NEA and Guggenheim Foundation, he is currently on the faculty at The Ohio State University.

WRIGHT MORRIS is the author of more than thirty books of fiction, memoirs, essays, and photo-texts, including *Collected Stories 1948– 1986,* from which "The Cat in the Picture" is taken. His story "Victrola" appeared in *The Company of Dogs.*

CORNELIA NIXON's novel-in-stories, *Now You See It,* was published by Little, Brown in 1991; "Affection" is part of that book. She loves cats but is allergic to them.

PAMELA PAINTER is the author of an award-winning collection of stories, *Getting to Know the Weather,* and co-author of *What If? Writing Exer-*

cises for Fiction Writers. Her stories have appeared in recent issues of *The Atlantic, Story, Harper's,* and *Ploughshares.* She lives in Boston and has two cats.

SUSAN FROMBERG SCHAEFFER is the author of eight novels, including *Anya, The Madness of a Seduced Woman,* and *Buffalo Afternoon.* She has published many short stories, and five collections of poetry, and has received many awards for her work, including an O'Henry Prize, The Lawrence Award, and a Guggenheim Fellowship.

ARTURO VIVANTE has lived in Italy, England, Canada, and the United States. He has written poems, novels, plays, essays, and mainly short stories, seventy of which appeared in *The New Yorker.* His latest books are *Leopardi; Poems* (a translation), and *The Tales of Arturo Vivante.* His home is in Wellfleet, Cape Cod.

ROBLEY WILSON, JR., is the author of four books of stories, most recently, *Terrible Kisses.* Simon & Schuster published his first novel, *The Victim's Daughter,* in 1991. He is the editor of *The North American Review.*

Permissions

Acknowledgments

This anthology owes a special thanks for the emboldening support of Jeanne Schinto, Lee K. Abbott, and Mark Svede, as well as a note of deep appreciation to the many writers who answered my queries and whose stories this volume could not accommodate.

Sources, Resources, and Further Reading

The following selected books have either been quoted in the Introduction or have provided significant groundwork and perspective for my particular undertaking. Because of the overwhelming number of books continually published on the subject of the cat and because I believe the reader possesses a general familiarity and access to the literature, I have declined the commission to be conclusive or encompassing. Moreover, so many of the most readily available volumes include lists and appendixes providing further readings, organizations, and publications that deal specifically with the cat. Carl Van Vechten's *The Tiger in the House,* while stopping well short of this decade, contains a bibliography substantial enough to satisfy even the most zealous ailurophile.

Sources for quotations excerpted from the stories included in this anthology can be found on the Permissions page.

AISENBERG, NADYA, ed. *We Animals.* San Francisco: Sierra Club Books, 1989.

AYMAR, BRANDT. *The Personality of the Cat.* New York: Crown, 1958.

BECK, ALAN, and AARON KATCHER. *Between Pets and People.* New York: G. P. Putnam, 1983.

BENTHAM, JEREMY. "Introduction to the Principles of Morals and Legislation," quoted in Serpell, James, *The Company of Animals.* Oxford: Basil Blackwell, Inc., 1986.

BRENNAN, MAEVE. *In and Out of Never-Never Land.* New York: Scribners, 1969.

BYRNE, ROBERT and KELTON, TERESSA, eds. *Cat Scan: All the Best from the Literature of Cats.* New York: Atheneum, 1983.

CARAS, ROGER A. *A Cat Is Watching: A Look at the Way Cats See Us.* New York: Simon & Schuster, 1989.

————. *A Celebration of Cats.* New York: Simon & Schuster, 1989.

————. *The Roger Caras Treasury of Great Cat Stories.* New York: Dutton, 1987.

COCTEAU, JEAN. *The Hand of a Stranger.* Translated by Alec Brown. New York: Horizon Press, 1959.

COLETTE. *Creatures Great and Small.* Translated by Enid McLeod. London: Martin Secker & Warburg, Ltd., 1951.

DAY, CLARENCE. *This Simian World.* New York: Alfred A. Knopf. 1920. (See Chapter 6.)

FOX, MICHAEL W. *Inhumane Society: The American Way of Exploiting Animals.* New York: St. Martin's Press, 1990.

————. *Understanding Your Dog and Understanding Your Cat.* New York: Bantam Books, 1977.

KATCHER, AARON H., and ALAN M. BECK, eds. *New Perspectives on our Lives with Animals.* Philadelphia: University of Pennsylvania Press, 1983.

KIRK, MILDRED. *The Everlasting Cat.* Woodstock: The Overlook Press, 1977.

KRITSICK, DVM, Dr. STEVEN M. *Dr. Kritsick's Tender Loving Cat Care.* New York: Linden Press, Simon & Schuster, 1986.

LEGUIN, URSULA. "Schrödinger's Cat," in *The Compass Rose: Short Stories.* New York: Harper & Row, 1982.

LESSING, DORIS. *Particularly Cats.* New York: Simon & Schuster, 1967.

MENDOZA, TONY. *Ernie: A Photographer's Memoir.* Santa Barbara: Capra Press, 1985.

————. *Ernie's Postcard Book.* Santa Barbara: Capra Press, 1989.

MORRIS, DESMOND, *Catwatching.* New York: Crown, 1987.

MORRIS, WRIGHT, "The Cat's Meow," in *Collected Stories 1948–1986.* New York: Harper & Row, 1986.

The New Yorker Book of Cat Cartoons. New York: Alfred A. Knopf, 1990.

RILKE, RAINER MARIA. *Rilke on Love and Other Difficulties.* Edited and translated by John J. L. Mood. New York: Norton, 1975.

SARTON, MAY. *The Fur Person.* New York: Holt, Rinehart & Winston, 1957.

SERPELL, JAMES. *In the Company of Animals.* Oxford: Basil Blackwell, Inc., 1986.

SINGER, PETER. *Animal Liberation.* Revised Edition. New York: New York Review of Books, Inc., Random House, 1990.

STEPHENS, MARTIN L. *Alternatives to Current Uses of Animals in Research, Safety Testing, and Education: A Layman's Guide.* Washington: The Humane Society of the United States, 1986.

VAN VECHTEN, CARL. *The Tiger in the House.* New York: Alfred A. Knopf, 1920.

Likewise, the following organizations have shared a considerable amount of printed materials dealing with various aspects of animal welfare. Each has specific fact sheets, booklets, and newsletters dealing with issues relating to the human alliance with cats. This is a starting point for more information. Readers should not overlook the availability of local resources. Animal shelters, veterinary clinics, local chapters of many national organizations, and hundreds of smaller, region-specific agencies are found in most areas of the country.
(A comprehensive list locating organizations in a particular region can be found in the reliable annual, *Animal Organizations & Services,* compiled by Kathleen A. Reece.)

ASPCA (The American Society for the Prevention of Cruelty to Animals)
441 East 92 Street
New York NY 10128

HSUS (The Humane Society of the United States)
2100 L Street NW
Washington DC 20037

The National Association for the Advancement of Humane Education
P. O. Box 362
East Haddam CT 06423

PETA (People for the Ethical Treatment of Animals)
P. O. Box 42516
Washington DC 20015

The Animals' Agenda
Animal Rights Network
P. O. Box 5234
Westport CT 06881

Delta Society
P. O. Box 1080
Renton WA 98057-1080

The Cat Fanciers' Association, Inc.
1309 Allaire Avenue
Ocean NJ 07712

Culture and Animals Foundation
3509 Eden Croft Drive
Raleigh NC 27612

About the Editor

Michael J. Rosen has edited for Doubleday another book about the animals in our families, *The Company of Dogs*, and is at work on a third in this series of "companion volumes." He has conceived and edited a children's picture book, *No Place Like Home: A Book About the Home to Benefit the Homeless*, on behalf of the organization Share Our Strength, that includes thirty of the country's best-known children's authors and illustrators. He has also edited a volume of Thurber's uncollected work, *Collecting Himself: James Thurber on Writing and Writers, Humor and Himself*. His other books include poetry, *A Drink at the Mirage;* and children's picture books, *50 Odd Jobs, The Kids' Book of Fishing*, and *Elijah's Angel*. His fiction, articles, reviews, poetry, and illustrations appear in magazines and newspapers around the country. He lives in the city of his birth, Columbus, Ohio, where he serves as Literary Director of The Thurber House, the writers' center in the preserved boyhood home of James Thurber.